Sherlock Holmes
and
The Adventure of
The Found Note

By M J H Simmonds

Hardcover ISBN 978-1-80424-300-8
Paperback ISBN 978-1-80424-301-5
ePub ISBN 978-1-80424-302-2
PDF ISBN 978-1-80424-303-9

Published by MX Publishing
335 Princess Park Manor, Royal Drive,
London, N11 3GX
www.mxpublishing.co.uk
Cover design by Brian Belanger

To Henry Hugo Aethelstan,
with all my love.

Introduction

It is exceedingly rare that the inception of an endeavour is as compelling or exhilarating as its conclusion. While I can recall, in fine detail, the resolutions of all the adventures upon which we embarked and the uniqueness of each one, the beginnings of our cases have tended to arrive in a more predictable, even pedestrian, fashion. Most commonly, a message would arrive by letter or telegram, detailing the problem at hand. Similarly, a client – or their agent – might schedule an appointment to visit us at Baker Street in person. Once we had earned a reasonable reputation, certain affairs were even introduced to us directly by the authorities.

Over the years, we welcomed members of all social classes into our rooms, from kings to common criminals, and Sherlock Holmes listened, with equal attention and interest, to every last one of them.

The strange events of autumn, 1884, came to us by, perhaps, the most unique introduction of all.

I
The Unexpected Caller

The rapping on the front door woke me with a start. I stumbled out of bed and quickly lit a candle. I flicked open my hunter to see that it was a little after six. Outside, all remained stygian darkness. The knocking continued as I pulled on a dressing gown and headed towards the living room. Mercifully, it appeared that Mrs. Hudson had not been woken; the cold weather had not been good for my wounds and what little sleep I had managed, recently, had been light and troubled. I passed through the salon, manoeuvring carefully in the darkness, descended the stairs then paused abruptly, upon reaching the front door. Suddenly, I felt wary. Who could possibly be calling at such an hour? However, after a few moments of uncertainty, reason and sanity prevailed. If it truly were an agent of evil, hell-bent upon doing us mischief, why on earth would it announce its arrival beforehand? I shook my head to chase away any lingering remains of the dark night and opened the door.

Standing before me was a short man, darkly dressed in a baggy cap and ill-fitting suit. He had small eager eyes, hair that sprang randomly from beneath his hat, a huge nose and a wide expressive mouth. He rubbed his hands together in automatic supplication. This was plainly a working man, unaccustomed to addressing those of any class other than his own. He also appeared to be waiting for me to instigate the conversation.

"Hello, how can I help you?" I asked, as openly and amicably as I could muster, given the circumstances.

"I am most terrible' sorry to bother you at such an hour, but I have something that I simply must share with you, Mr. Holmes." He spoke so fast that he almost spat out the words.

"I am sorry, sir, but I am not Sherlock Holmes," I began. However, noticing how far and swiftly his face fell upon hearing this news, I quickly added, "But he does reside here, and I am sure that he will be happy to hear your story, in due course."

I had no idea why, but I felt a sympathy for this unusual character and a suspicion that his tale might just be worth hearing.

"Please, come inside." I gestured him into the hallway, where he removed his hat, before obediently following me back up the stairs and into the apartment.

"You may have to wait a little while before Mr. Holmes is ready to see you," I sighed, as I opened the door to the living room.

To my complete surprise, the salon was no longer shrouded in darkness as I had left it. A roaring fire now blazed in the fireplace and the room was bathed in warm candlelight. Holmes stood before us, dressed in his mouse-coloured dressing gown, bright and alert, a whiff of smoke curling from the pipe in his hand.

"Welcome to Baker Street," he announced. "Here you are safe and free to share anything and everything. All that you say will be held in the strictest confidence; we judge nobody. There is but one rule. You must always tell the truth."

"Please, sit down," he asked, gently. "Watson, a brandy for our guest, for he has endured a long, arduous, night of work."

"Why, thank you very much. But how did you know that I had just finished my shift?"

"The time of day, the darkness beneath your eyes, your crumpled suit," I answered quickly, with a smile. "Please don't be alarmed, it is simply a form of logical deduction. Even I can apply it on a basic level."

"Oh, I see. I apologise for my appearance." The diminutive man appeared mortified; I now felt both embarrassed and guilty.

Holmes' sharp and precise voice cut through the awkward silence to come to my rescue.

"Your appearance, perfectly acceptable though it is, I assure you, has no relevance, I believe, to your story. Please ignore my colleague's amateurish, but well-intentioned, attempts at deduction and tell us what has compelled you to visit us at this early hour."

Our guest relaxed, noticeably, took a sip of warming brandy and began his story.

"My name is Mavis. Jonah Mavis. I work in the City as a night watchman. I look after the offices of four small firms, in two adjoining buildings. I spend half an hour in each, before moving on to another. I am careful not to fall into a routine," he emphasised with obvious pride, as his little chest momentarily puffed out, "so as not to fall foul of any observers who might use such information to plot against us."

"Very wise indeed," Holmes commented, with a raised eyebrow and the slightest hint of a smile. "And how do you avoid such repetition creeping in, may I ask?"

Our guest smiled. "I have a trick I learned when serving in India. It is awful simple but works a right treat. I flips a coin, you see? I make a note of how many times I have visited each premises that night and choose the two I have visited the least up to that point. Then the coin chooses the next. By the end of my shift, I have spent pretty much the same time in each and the order cannot be predicted in any way."

Holmes was visibly impressed. "Why, Mr. Mavis, you have come up with a solution to this problem of yours that is worthy of the great mathematicians." He rose, went to a drawer and returned with a small wooden box.

"Cigar?" offered Holmes. "They may only be Sumatran, but certainly the pick of the island."

Mavis eagerly accepted a dark, tapering, cheroot and I offered him a light from a spill that I pulled from the fireplace.

"However, we digress, Mr. Mavis. Now that we are all comfortable, please share with us the reason for your visit this morning," said Holmes, leaning forwards, his dingy clay pipe hanging precariously from his loosely clenched teeth.

"Well, it's like this, gentlemen. I was walking home, looking forward to my dinner and a good sleep, when I noticed that something had attached itself to the bottom of my boot. It was a piece of paper, nothing unusual in that, of course. I stopped and leaned down to remove it. I peeled it off and was about to sling it away when I noticed the writing. It were only two words, but they fair put the wind up me."

"Whatever were these words that shocked you so and led you to seek us out?" I asked, fascinated.

"'Help me,'" replied Mavis, his piggy eyes now wide open.

Holmes straightened instantly and his entire demeanour changed. He leaned forward and stared seriously at our guest.

"You have this note?" he asked.

Mavis nodded. He reached inside his jacket and withdrew a small piece of paper, about four inches by three. He carefully handed this to Holmes.

"I haven't folded or marked it in any way," he stated.

"Before I examine this evidence, please tell me exactly where and how you found it. Every detail, leave nothing out."

"As I told you, I was walking home. I live just off Stoney Street in Southwark. The walk to Cannon Street is not quite a mile, straight over London Bridge. It takes less than half an hour, even in the worst of weathers. I left the offices at the end of my shift this morning and headed towards the river. It was just before I turned right onto the bridge itself that I saw the paper stuck to my boot."

"How long could it have been there?" inquired Holmes. "When did you last see your boot free of encumbrance?"

"Oh, just a few seconds before. I had half-noticed the paper tumbling slowly in the breeze before me. It was pure happenstance that it fell under my footstep and there stuck itself well enough to require removal."

"So, it could have blown in from anywhere," I sighed.

"Please ignore my pessimistic colleague and tell me everything that you remember. Was the note wet, damp or completely dry? Why did it affix itself to your boot? Were your soles wet or had they any substance upon them that might adhere to the note?" Holmes was now in full flow, his eyes bright and focused.

"Well," our guest paused to compose himself. "Let me think. The note was indeed slightly damp, not wet, but perhaps enough to cause it to take to my boot." Here he again puffed out his chest. "My boots are always spotless; I could show you them now if you like." He began to reach down and was almost at his laces before Holmes ordered him to cease.

"Sir, I believe you completely, no need for any undress," he stated. "You say the note was blowing in the wind, did you see from where it had come? Was it travelling towards you?"

"It came right at me. It blew around fair enough but yes it came from straight ahead, I'm sure."

"Well thank you, Mr Mavis, your testimony has been most valuable," Holmes announced, suddenly. He rose swiftly and held out an arm, gesturing that it was time for our visitor to leave.

"Oh, I see. Well, thank you for taking a look," said our guest, with a visible sense of disappointment. He moved towards the door but turned back just before he reached the threshold.

"Do you think you will be able to help this poor soul?" he asked with sad eyes and a fallen face.

"Mr. Mavis, you must not concern yourself. You have played your part in this affair admirably. There is, after all, only a minute chance that this note is a genuine appeal for help. Even if we did believe it to be authentic, the chances of us ever being able to grant this person opitulation are infinitesimal."

"He means helping them," I added, smiling and shaking my head at my friend's archaic tone. "Leave your details with me and if we discover anything, I will be sure to let you know."

Our guest nodded, scribbled down his address on my ever-present notebook, replaced his hat and departed.

"Well, I suppose that's very much that," I declared as I returned to my armchair to refill my briar.

"Whatever are you talking about, Watson? We have work to do," Holmes said with vigour.

"You mean to investigate this matter?" I asked, my mouth open in astonishment. "We have absolutely nothing to work from, just a note which could have come from anywhere at any time. Surely even you cannot divine an answer from what we have here?"

"And what exactly do we have here, Doctor?" Holmes passed me the note and I looked upon it for the first time.

"Very well," I sighed. "Let's see what we have. It is a torn scrap from a larger piece, slightly yellow in colour. It is of good quality, heavier than the average writing paper. Tuppence a page I shouldn't wonder. The writing is well-educated; the curves and loops seem to indicate a female scribe, right-handed. The lines themselves are rather unsteady, this might well have been written under some considerable stress." I looked upwards, hoping for approval.

"Very good, old chap, you have done at least as well as I could have expected from any Scotland Yard detective," replied Holmes.

"I take it that is not exactly a compliment," I replied, through slightly gritted teeth.

"Oh, do not be precious, Doctor, you have done well. All that you say is correct, except that I feel that there is something more to this material. It does not feel quite like writing paper. The surface is rather smooth, see how the ink has spread away from the initial strokes."

I looked closely and saw the tiny veins of ink forking out from the main branches of the intended stroke, just as Holmes had stated. I turned the paper over and examined the reverse.

"It seems to be slightly coarser on the back. I agree, this is not writing paper. Wait a moment, this side seems to still be slightly damp, while the front is dry. No, not damp, it seems to be slightly viscous." I raised the note to my nose. "Can I smell gum?" I speculated.

"Oh, Watson, you have once again shown me to be the fool!" declared Holmes. He slapped either side of his face with his hands, to dramatically show that he was waking up to a revelation.

"Well, thank you, Holmes," I replied, "But be a good chap and share this discovery with me."

"It is paper, Watson, but not writing paper. This is a piece of wallpaper," Holmes revealed, waving his pipe with a flourish.

"Wallpaper, of course. Smooth on one side, coarse and sticky on the reverse. It is almost childishly obvious now. It also explains why it stuck so stubbornly to Mavis's boot."

My elation was swiftly and suddenly ended by a simple realisation. "But how does this help us, Holmes?" I asked, dejectedly.

"It moves us a step further forward. It may not seem significant now, however, it might just be the first step on the road to solving this mystery."

"Do you really believe that there is a case here? Is somebody, somewhere, genuinely begging for help?"

Holmes took a long draw on his pipe before exhaling a cloud of blue-grey smoke. He nodded, slowly. "Yes, someone is in dire trouble, the only question that remains is, can we do anything to help the person or are we already too late?"

"Well, where do we start?" It seemed the most obvious question.

"Once you have had some breakfast, I suggest that you visit the Meteorological Office and obtain as accurate a weather report as you can for the past five days. I doubt they open before eight, so you have ample time."

"Very well," I agreed. "But what will you be doing?"

"I shall examine the location where the note was found. It will be getting light by the time I arrive. I know that the wind usually blows from downstream at this time of year, so I can make some preliminary calculations. Only once you have provided me with accurate data can we begin to speculate whence this missive might have originated."

Holmes still held the sad note in his hand. His steel-grey eyes looked hard upon it.

"One more thing, Watson. This is rather poor-quality paper for a wall covering. Although heavy for notepaper, it is perhaps the thinnest, plainest, wallpaper I have examined. Bear this in mind when we are searching for its origin. I suggest we meet at Fangio's on the Strand for a late lunch at, say, two?"

II
A Weather Eye

Mrs. Hudson served us a fine breakfast and, just after half-past seven, Holmes and I left in a hansom. We shared the cab as far as Whitehall, where I alighted, leaving Holmes to travel onwards to the City alone.

I strolled along the already busy, bustling street until I reached the Meteorological Office, which is a subsidiary of the Board of Trade.

The liveried doorman was exceedingly helpful and led me through various featureless corridors and hallways until we reached the required department. As the door was already open, I entered and knocked as I passed through.

I found myself in a large, well-lit room. Rows of dark wooden desks were covered with all manner of charts and papers. At the far side, I could see telegraph machines spewing thin paper missives in curling rolls. Large maps covered every available inch of wall space, ranging in scale and size from street maps of London to those of the Britain Isles, Europe and, indeed, the World. For a place of such importance, I was surprised to see that there were only three men present. Two young clerks were writing at the desks and an older gentleman was monitoring the telegraphs.

"Ahem," I coughed, the knocking having not been registered.

One of the young clerks looked up.

"Good day, sir, how can we help you?" he asked, politely.

"Good morning," I replied, removing my hat. "I am looking for some weather readings for the past five days. Local, here in London, the City, in fact. Just north of London Bridge, actually."

There was a short pause, broken by a throaty laugh from the far side of the room. The older man at the telegraph machines turned and addressed me. "Please forgive my humour," he said with a wide smile. "We entertain few visitors here."

He was a tall man, of sixty years or more. His face was large and framed with extravagant, long white hair, both beard and head. Small glasses rested upon a large nose.

"I am Trenchant, Doctor Jephsus Trenchant. I am head of the Meteorological Department here at the ministry." He stuck out a long bony hand in greeting which I shook gratefully. His grip was firm and his hand warm, the man was in exceedingly good health for his age.

"You require some very precise and localised weather readings indeed," he smiled, broadly, the direction of the lines on his face suggesting that this was a man more prone to laughing than frowning.

I felt embarrassed as I realised quite how foolish I must have sounded.

"I am sorry, sir, I am really not an expert in such matters," I began, but Trenchant raised a hand to stop me.

"Good sir, I jest. We will, of course, do our best to help you. Wilkinson!" he called to one of the younger men. "Please bring us the City data for the past week."

The young man brought over a sizeable ledger, laid it on an adjacent desk and opened it to the appropriate page.

"This point here is exactly seven days ago," he pointed to a spot on the large facing page. "Simply read on to see the values for the rest of the week."

"Why, thank you." I looked briefly at the page. "I must also admit that I may well need some help in interpreting this," I admitted, once again reddening about the face.

"I am sure young Wilkinson here can aid you. May I inquire after the reason why you might require such very specialised information?"

I have always believed that honesty is indeed the best policy, in most cases anyway. I told Trenchant everything: the note, its discovery and was about to explain my friend's unique profession when Trenchant stopped me.

"Ah, so how is Mr. Holmes?" he grinned. "This means that you must be Doctor Watson. Well, he was quite right, you certainly are both steadfast and dependable."

I wasn't sure which was the stronger feeling, the surprise that this man knew Holmes or the warm feeling of pride that I felt, knowing that my friend had described me in such fine terms.

"Do not worry, I shall get Wilkinson and Saville here to make you a copy of all of the relevant data. It should take no more than half of an hour. In the meantime, would you like me to show you around the department?"

I happily agreed and spent the time engaged in a fascinating discourse with the learned scientist. I discovered that the Meteorological Office was born partly of tragedy. Back in 1859, a passenger ship, the Royal Charter, had sunk due to unforeseen bad weather, with the loss of more than four hundred lives. This led to the first national system of gale warnings. However, the following years had, sadly, seen a steady decline in interest in and funding of the department.

"Mr. Holmes is one of our few friends and champions. I fear that only the outbreak of war might force a revival of interest in our science," he disclosed sadly.

"But let us not end on a sour note," he brightened. "I think your data are ready."

Wilkinson handed me a buff folder containing half a dozen loose sheets of paper covered with tables and notes.

"I cannot begin to thank you enough," I smiled. "Please let me know the fee for your work or arrange for the appropriate invoice to be sent to our rooms."

Trenchant smiled again. It was a wonderful thing to behold, and one I was fortunate enough to experience on several further occasions. With his back to the window, his great crown of hair appeared as a bright halo surrounding his heavily creased but friendly and gentle face.

"We are here to provide information and aid to any who may require it, Doctor. Helping Sherlock Holmes in his work is now, and will always be, our pleasure."

III
By Cold Wind and Water

I left the Meteorological Office in high spirits. On this occasion, Holmes' reputation had been a distinct advantage. I did momentarily wonder why Holmes had not told me in advance of his acquaintance with the head of the department; however, I had long since realised that he preferred me to operate using my abilities, rather than simply relying on his established connections. Although sometimes frustrating and time-consuming, this did prove his genuine faith in me, that I had the wherewithal to succeed by my own means and methods.

I reached the Strand shortly after half-past one, entered Fangio's fine Italian restaurant and prepared myself for a short wait until Holmes arrived. I was surprised to see him already seated, sipping a small, strong coffee.

I joined my friend in a cup of the fine, dark invigorant and handed over the folder of weather data that I had obtained. Holmes took this in his long, thin fingers, opened the light brown cover and studied the information within. His eyes darted across the paper and within two minutes he had examined the entire contents. He tidied the sheets, closed the file and placed it carefully next to his coffee.

"Watson, you have certainly earned your lunch," he declared, a smile almost present on his pale face. "However, sadly, we have no time for such luxuries. Order a quick bite if you must but we shall not be staying long."

I asked for a simple platter of bread, ham and cheese and sat back as the waiter speedily departed.

"So, what next, old man? What did you glean from the weather reports?" I asked, eagerly.

Holmes raised himself upright, reached into his coat pocket and withdrew a map. He spread this upon the table with little thought to the cups and other items present. I barely managed to shepherd these to safety on an adjacent surface before he smoothed down the chart. It was a large-scale map of London, folded to show the area to the east of London Bridge.

"What is the major feature of this area?" Holmes asked, waving a hand randomly over the map.

"Buildings, houses, roads?" I ventured.

"No, Watson," he snapped, abruptly. He waved the same hand up and down along the map.

"The river, of course," I sighed, the familiar feeling of inadequacy running through me.

"But surely the river just complicates things," I added. "We know that it forms the wind into a funnel which blows upstream. It also forms a barrier between each bank, making it far more difficult, and time-consuming, to search properties on either side."

"Not this time, Doctor. Here, for once, the river is our ally. Think about it, Watson, a paper note flying in the breeze, up and down, left and right but generally moving in the direction of the following wind."

"Yes, just as we imagined," I agreed.

"What happens to it if it reaches a body of water, one some three hundred yards across?"

"I suppose it could blow over it, but it would be far more likely to hit the water at some point," I replied.

"Exactly, old chap. The chances of a small note being blown three hundred yards and not touching the surface of the river at any point is remote. The moment it did would be, of course, the end of the note. Once even slightly wet, it would fall and become a prisoner of the river for evermore.

"Therefore, we can use the river as a barrier. The note must have come from north of Old Father Thames. In fact, we can narrow our search even further. If we draw a line from where the note was found, to the next most northerly bend of the river, we can estimate the maximum distance from where the note could have originated. Any further east becomes unlikely due to the presence of the large southward bend of the river, here." Holmes ran his long, bony finger along the map from London Bridge up to the point in question.

"Limehouse. Very impressive, Holmes. However, there remain three miles still to cover."

"And so, we must now introduce the data supplied by Dr Trenchant. I trust you found him well?"

"Yes, indeed. A most impressive and welcoming gentleman. I only wish all of your associates were as accommodating," I added, with a slight grin.

"The wind, yesterday, was from directly due east, fifteen to twenty miles per hour, dropping to ten by early this morning when the note was discovered," Holmes continued, ignoring my response.

"And before that?" I asked.

"The previous twenty-four hours were much calmer. The wind barely reached double figures and came from the northeast."

"So, the note could have come from further north, perhaps?" I speculated.

"Perhaps, but there is more. It rained quite heavily during this period. This could have had two effects on the note. Firstly, and most importantly, it would have become sodden and simply fallen to the ground to be trampled out of existence. And secondly, the rain would have washed away the gum on the reverse, along with the writing on the opposite side. That, or faded it at the very least."

"No, I am certain that the note originated between here and Limehouse, along a narrow corridor and within the last twenty-four hours," declared Holmes, confidently.

"There are still hundreds of buildings we would need to search, between here and Limehouse." I tried to sound optimistic but the reality of the situation, for me, had not changed.

"We can do better than that, Watson. What do we have? A note, torn from a wall. One covered with paper. It may tend towards the less expensive end of the market, but it is still a luxury wallcovering. What lies just a mile east of London Bridge, Doctor?"

"East of London Bridge? Whitechapel, of course," I replied, uncomprehending.

"Exactly. How many houses in Whitechapel would have such wallpaper?" demanded Holmes.

"Very few, I would imagine, practically none. Why, Holmes, this is brilliant! We now have a north, south and eastern boundary to our search."

"I believe we can narrow the search further still." Holmes was studying the map intently, tracing each road and boundary with a long ivory-hued finger. "We can eliminate Billingsgate Market, for two good reasons. It is most unlikely that we should find such a fine wallpaper there and, in any case, it would be a particularly troublesome location in which to hide a captive, far too busy with potential witnesses."

"The Tower presents a rather different proposition," Holmes continued, his lean frame bent over rather in the manner of a feeding stork. "To the layman or uninitiated in deduction, it may appear the perfect place from which a note begging for aid might emanate. However, this is not a fairy tale, nor a penny dreadful; if the note truly originated from one incarcerated in the Tower of London, then that is exactly where they should be and must remain so until the powers responsible deem it no longer necessary."

I was rather taken aback by this last statement. Holmes was always an enigma, never more so than when addressing authority. He was usually the first to cock a snook at the supposed upper classes; however, just occasionally, he would show deep respect for certain offices of state. He generally regarded politics and politicians with utter contempt yet still held a few of their number in great esteem. Similarly, while he endlessly baited and teased the detectives of Scotland Yard, I never witnessed him utter a single negative word against the stout, honest and brave constables that daily risked their lives in this heaving, breathing, living metropolis.

"So, we are looking at somewhere close to the river, before Billingsgate. Somewhere affluent enough to have wallpaper. Perhaps a building connected to the local churches?" I speculated. "The vicarages might well have rooms adorned with a covering something like our note."

"A fine idea, Doctor, one which I investigated this very morning. From St. Magnus the Martyr to St. Dunstan in the East. From St. Margaret Pattens to St. Mary-At-Hill. I spoke to rectors, vergers, secretaries and gardeners. I finally even located an actual vicar, but none of the buildings had a promising aspect. Each was either facing the wrong way entirely or at least two right-angle turns from the riverside – a path highly unlikely to have been taken by a note of paper floating on the breeze."

And then it struck me. Something that had been gnawing away in the back of my mind. I had felt this dull, distant annoyance ever since the beginning of the case, but only now did it manifest itself into reality.

"Holmes, this note," I began, carefully. "It strikes me as being rather heavy to have been simply 'carried along on the breeze.' Do you not think so?"

"I do, indeed, old chap. It raises at least two possibilities, of course. The first, and the one you are alluding to, is that the whole story is a nonsense, designed to fool us or occupy our time, for whatever reasons, almost certainly ones of a nefarious nature."

"And the second?" I asked with keen interest.

"That the high winds, remember, twenty miles an hour was recorded, did indeed blow this missive from somewhere downstream. I agree that the mass of this note makes it unlikely to have travelled far, maybe as little as a few hundred yards."

"Have you genuinely cracked it, Holmes?" I asked, eagerly.

Holmes shot me a serious glance. "I have made a list of possibilities and one emerges as the most likely, given what we have learned so far in this matter."

"So, tell me, where should we be looking? Surely, we must act immediately, without delay, to avoid any further suffering!" I felt my soldierly instincts rising and I gripped my cane as tightly as if it were the stock of a Martini-Henry.

Holmes took a deep breath, composed himself and then pointed dramatically at the chart before him. "Custom House," he declared, tapping his long, bone-white index finger against the map as he spoke. "Everything points to this set of buildings. It is on the right course, less than six hundred yards due east of where the note was discovered. Its rooms range from the austere to the considerably opulent. Most importantly of all, it has cellars, deep, dark and dank, used to store seized contraband, along with an entire facade facing both towards, and away from, the river."

IV
Custom House

By the time Holmes had reached his conclusion, I had long since finished my luncheon and was ready to head directly to Custom House to pursue our lead. Holmes had, as usual, touched little of the food before him; his eyes, however, shone brightly with energy and determination. We left swiftly, caught a hansom and were soon on our way. The two-mile journey along the river was certainly not unpleasant. As we followed the Thames eastwards, the breeze in our faces, a combination of salt, fish and other, less pleasant, industrial and residential odours assailed our senses. I am always astonished by the sheer number and variety of craft plying their trade up and down the river, along with an equal number of vessels moored at almost every available dockside, pier, jetty and wharf.

We reached the landward-facing frontage of Custom House after about twenty minutes. It is a large, long building of solid proportions but little grace or flair. The dun brown brickwork with its white stone cladding, now stained and darkened by smoke and ash, gave the building a cold, austere aspect. We entered, introduced ourselves and were asked to wait on a bench to one side of the large arched and vaulted atrium.

To my considerable surprise, we were joined within a few minutes by an official who appeared both adept and enthusiastic to help us. He guided us along a lengthy hallway and showed us into his office; a plain but comfortable room with myriad maritime charts pinned on one wall while the opposite one was stacked floor to ceiling with heavy, leather-bound volumes.

"As I said outside, my name is Smitherson. I am a manager here, overseeing several departments," he began, waving a hand, almost as if dismissing his position as unimportant.

He offered us seats before his desk before sitting himself down and leaning forward rather eagerly.

"I must now admit that I overheard your conversation at reception and was instantly intrigued by that which you imparted. Do you really believe that someone might have been held here against their will?"

Smitherson was a man of early middle years, above average in height with a fine, almost military, bearing. He had dark hair, greying at the temples and kind, eager brown eyes. Small, wire-framed spectacles sat on the tip of his thin nose. He wore a smart black suit and a white, high-collared shirt. A gold hunter hung upon a heavy double-Albert chain, strung across his waistcoat.

"That is what we hope to ascertain or disprove," replied Holmes. He recounted our story as briefly as possible. "As you can imagine, we are certainly not convinced of the matter, however, we do have a duty to investigate as best we can until we are satisfied that there is nothing in it."

"Well, let me take a look at this note you discovered. Maybe I will recognise this wallpaper. There is a little here but only in offices far grander than my own, I can assure you," replied Smitherson, gesturing to his own plainly painted walls.

Holmes reached into his jacket and removed the scrap of paper from his wallet. He placed it on the flat of his hand and presented it to Smitherson.

The Customs official pushed his glasses up further towards the bridge of his nose and peered at the note. After a few moments, he gave a slight start and looked up.

"I know this paper," he declared. "It covers the walls of a room just off one of the upper corridors. I could easily have overlooked it, the office has not been used for many years, deteriorating recently to such an extent that the paper hangs off the walls in rolling sheets. This part of the building has been uninhabited since the re-build some fifty years back. Even now, it is used only by those of us who enjoy a pipe and stroll up there while enjoying the view of the river."

"Can you show us this corridor?" I asked, hopefully.

"Of course, gentlemen, we should go right away. Please follow me."

Our host rose excitedly and ushered us out of his office and back toward the atrium and its wide staircases. We ascended three floors, turned right and passed along a hallway, for maybe twenty yards, before we reached another staircase. This was smaller than the grand stair that had brought us to this height but still finely worked in dark hardwoods and grey, black-veined marble. As we climbed higher, Smitherson imparted further information.

"You see," he began, "Custom House was rebuilt to a modern, far more efficient design than the previous edifice. However, it was soon discovered to have far more offices than were necessary, so this entire floor was left empty. As I previously stated, some of us still wander up here for a quiet smoke for, as you will soon see, it offers fine views of the river."

We reached the top of the stairs and turned back left into the heart of the building. After only a few yards the plain right-hand wall gave way to long windows, seemingly running the entire length of the building. Each window was four feet tall by three wide, with only a few inches of frame between each pane. This gave the impression of being inside a glasshouse looking out over the Thames from a height of, perhaps, fifty feet. The effect was glorious; light streamed in, making the hallway feel airy, weightless and quite magical. The mighty Thames flowed below, all black and grey and terrifying but also powerful and majestic. Boats of all shapes and sizes wended their way along this central artery of the city. Warehouses, docks, wharfs and all manner of boatyards clung to the opposite bank, rising above the thick black mud of the foreshore.

"Yes, it is all very picturesque, Watson," Holmes whispered, harshly, bringing me back to reality, "but we are not here to enjoy the view. Stay alert, Doctor."

"As you can see," continued Smitherson, "the walls here do have paper, but it is not quite the same as the one you discovered. That, I believe will be found here."

Smitherson stopped and gestured to a door on the left. It was dark and solid but with a slight patina of wear as if it had not been polished or varnished for many years. The brass handle, though, was bright and appeared to have been used recently. I mentioned as much to Holmes, however, he simply nodded and followed Smitherson as he opened the door and entered.

The office was fairly large, perfectly square and, at a first glance, completely empty. Two of the walls were indeed covered in wallpaper, the others simply painted white; for bookshelves or cabinets, I presumed. The paper was just as described by Smitherson, peeling and hanging off the walls in large swirls and folds. Holmes moved forwards to examine the wall to our left as we entered. I followed closely behind, eager to observe Holmes as he investigated the scene.

Holmes began to study the papered areas closely. He picked up the fallen rolls and placed them back upon the wall. I quickly realised his intention; he was looking for an area of paper corresponding to that of our message. It was at this point that I finally believed that this whole episode could actually be genuine; that someone might have been incarcerated here against their will. I began to follow Holmes' lead and lifted the fallen paper, attempting to match what was still in situ and looking for a gap that might correspond to the shape of our mysterious note. After a few failed attempts at finding a match, I hoisted up a particular roll of fallen paper and pushed it up and back onto the wall, holding it in place with my right hand, as high as I could manage. The top of the fallen paper did not quite reach that of the paper still attached to the wall. However, the shape of the gap between the two suddenly looked very familiar.

"Holmes," I called. "Over here, old chap. I think I have it."

Holmes turned and looked at the wall above me. His eyes opened wide and the merest of smiles broke his steely countenance. "Watson, I believe you have," replied Holmes, reaching into his coat for the note to confirm my discovery.

My reply was silenced by a heavy thump as the office door slammed shut behind us. We both turned in perfect unison, to find the sturdy door firmly closed and Smitherson nowhere to be seen. The room was now in almost total darkness, illuminated only by the light that entered through cracks around the door frame. Holmes rushed forwards, pulled at the door, found it locked, and let out a shout of anger and frustration.

"Watson, for goodness' sake, what is wrong with me? I fully suspected that this might happen, yet I still walked into the trap like a greenhorn constable."

Altogether confused, I could only manage to ask asinine questions. "What the devil is going on? Did he just lock us in? What did you mean by you 'suspected that this might happen'?" I spluttered, somewhat incoherently.

"Did you not hear him, Watson?" Holmes asked.

I shook my head, guiltily.

"He said 'might have been held here.' Note the past tense. Not 'being held here'. That raised suspicion, it implies that someone might once have been incarcerated here but is here no longer. How could he know this?"

"However, stupidly, I was distracted by the wallpaper and took my eyes off our guide," Holmes added. He examined the door for a minute or so.

"So, how do we get out of here?" I asked with a sigh.

"Watson, there are three ways to pass through a locked door," replied Holmes, with barely contained anger. "Firstly, you can obtain the key. Secondly, you can pick the lock."

"And the third way?" I asked, tentatively.

"Thirdly, you can break the door down!" exclaimed Holmes, spreading his arms wide with a flourish. He then raised his right foot until he was balanced like a crane. After a second, his foot shot forward with such speed that it could barely be seen. There was a loud crack, and the door flew open, splinters of door frame flew in every direction and daylight flooded back into the room.

"My goodness, Holmes, that was incredible," I managed to stammer.

"The door is worn but still solid. The frame, however, is rotten with the worm, almost to the point of disintegration. I knew a well-placed heel or two would soon see us free," Holmes explained quickly. "However, let us not dally, Smitherson cannot have gone far and will not have expected us to have so swiftly escaped his little trap."

Holmes rushed through the now-open doorway and sped along the corridor. I kept up as best I could, however, by the time I had reached the first staircase, Holmes was already out of sight. I could hear him shouting from below, urging people to clear the way as he moved with exactly the turn of speed that had surprised, and indeed caught, many an unsuspecting villain.

In less than a minute I was back in the entrance hall. Quite out of breath, I was relieved to see Holmes was still in view, talking animatedly to two members of staff. It appeared that Smitherson had eluded us.

"Ah, Watson, there you are," said Holmes, turning towards me as I approached. "It seems that we have been led a merry dance by this 'Smitherson' fellow."

"By your tone, it sounds as if he has escaped us," I replied, trying to catch my breath.

"Not only that but, according to these gentlemen here, there is no Mr. 'Smitherson' employed anywhere in this building. They recognised my description of the man we were chasing but they are adamant that he is not an employee. They did observe him leaving but due to the angle of their position, relative to the entrance, they could not say in which direction he turned as he departed."

"But he had an office, Holmes, and he knew the layout of the building far too well to be just an occasional visitor." I was quickly recovering and felt encouraged that my old wounds appeared not to have been overly agitated by the pursuit.

"I agree. I have recounted our experience to these gentlemen, and they will report it to the security officer, who will join us shortly. In the meantime, I suggest we return to the office upstairs and examine it fully. There may remain other, vital clues; after all, the author of our plea for help had access to a pencil and may well have written more."

We returned to the upper floor and made a full inspection of the empty office. We had searched for half an hour with nothing to show for our efforts, when a tall man knocked, leaned in and introduced himself as the head of security for Custom House.

"I am Captain Broadstairs. It is a pleasure to meet you, gentlemen. I must admit to having read your account of the Jefferson Hope case, Doctor, so I know you to be serious men. I am most troubled by what has occurred today. I have no explanation to offer you, other than this must be a most brazen fellow, indeed, to have acted so blatantly."

Broadstairs was a solid, large-chested man. He must have been a formidable officer when in service. He was perhaps fifty years of age with thick, white hair, piercing blue eyes and a prominent brow. His nose was long but twisted, the man had certainly seen action of one sort or another. He wore a simple uniform; his woollen tunic and trousers were plain black apart from a line of brightly polished brass buttons.

"We are finished here, thank you," announced Holmes. "Other than the note, torn from the paper on the far wall, there are no signs of anyone having been incarcerated here."

"That is unfortunate," replied Broadstairs. "However, I do have some better news. I have inquired upon all of the security staff currently on duty and they confirm that, although no 'Smitherson' is engaged here in any capacity, they do recognise the man whom you encountered today."

"A lead, at last," I declared.

"They could supply no name for this man but have observed him regularly, carrying papers and files through the corridors. They simply assumed that he was a member of staff or a client. Dozens pass through here daily; merchants, ships' captains, accountants and all manner of officials and agents. Our job is mostly to keep order and watch the impounded or bonded goods until they are released. The idea of a bogus official is quite fantastical." The captain looked genuinely puzzled.

"This matter requires some thought," Holmes admitted, after a long pause. "There are aspects to this case that are most troubling."

Holmes straightened and addressed Broadstairs. "Thank you, Captain. Could I ask you to interview as many members of staff as possible over the next few hours? Please keep us informed of any unusual activity or any new information you might receive. You can contact us at 221B Baker Street or via Inspector Lestrade of Scotland Yard if you prefer."

We left Custom House and quickly found a cab on the busy street outside the austere front of the building. Holmes muttered a destination to the driver, and we headed back west along the river. The afternoon air was cooling, and I was glad that the wind was now blowing to our backs, the raised hood of the cab providing shelter from the worst of the chill. The river appeared even darker now, its waters icy cold and unforgiving.

"Whatever shall we do now?" I asked, hanging my head, trying not to sound as disconsolate as I felt.

"Do not be quite so glum, old man, we still have a couple of clues to follow up."

I looked up, surprised. "I thought this was a total dead end, Holmes. Please, I would be more than grateful to hear any words of encouragement right now, for I can think only of some poor woman who was in distress then and is now in utter despair."

"Very well, Watson, think upon this." Holmes placed both hands on the top of his cane and leaned closer towards me. "How did this 'Smitherson' fellow come to be in exactly the right place and at the precise moment that we arrived at Custom House?

"Now I think of it, it is rather a coincidence that he was there to overhear our inquiry, lead us to the exact place we were looking for and there attempt to incarcerate us." I paused a moment to ponder this further. "You believe he was waiting there for us? A set-up?" I exclaimed, suddenly. "Have we been manipulated this entire time? But why and by whom?"

"That is what I intend to discover, Doctor. We shall learn more when we arrive."

"Arrive where? What have you seen that I missed?"

"Come now, Watson," chided Holmes, as we trundled over the grey cobbles. "Did nothing about this 'Smitherson' character strike you as unusual? Any identifying features, perhaps?"

"From your tone, I can only assume that there were. Now I think of it, there was a crest engraved on his gold Hunter. I cannot be certain but to me, it looked like the Royal Coat of Arms, not exactly unusual for a government official."

Once again, I cursed myself for not following Holmes' methodology. This time it particularly rankled, as I still believed that a life may be at real risk.

"'*Domine Dirige Nos*', Watson. Does that ring any bells?"

"Lord lead us? Lord direct us? Sorry, Holmes, my Latin is a little rusty. It does have a familiar ring, though. It isn't a military motto, as far as I can recall." I thought deeply and tried to remember where I had seen this quote.

"Think more locally, Doctor," Holmes teased.

"I have it!" I declared. "Or, at least, in part. It is the motto of one of the livery companies, is it not?"

"Not just of one of the guilds. The crest is, in fact, that of the City of London Corporation itself," Holmes revealed, finally.

"Two dragons, either side of a shield bearing a red cross. I am sure an expert would inform me it is an image steeped in some ancient meaning or other; I merely commit such crests to memory as a means to aid identification."

"The Corporation? Well, that certainly explains our route," I smiled.

"Yes, indeed, Doctor. Our next stop will be Guildhall. Perhaps we will finally find some answers within its ancient halls."

V
Through the City of London

It was late afternoon when we alighted from our cab outside the magnificent front entrance to the venerable old building. Having survived plague, revolution, and trial by fire, I was certain that whatever was being plotted within, however nefarious, would warrant barely a mention in its long and illustrious history.

The low sun sharply picked out the fine details of the warm, cream-coloured stonework. The smooth, modern surface of the gatehouse was in stark contrast to the ancient pitted medieval stone and mortar flanking it to either side. Tall thin towers and turrets reached upwards like long skeletal fingers, grasping for the sky.

"This place is just as large as Custom House," I noted as we entered, "with vastly more incumbents. Where do we start? Did you observe anything that might narrow our search?"

"Watches such as the one worn by Smitherson are worn by aldermen; they are awarded upon election. This I know from previous experience," replied Holmes, with unexpected candour.

"The engraving was new, the lines deep and still sharp, reflecting the light crisply and cleanly," he added. "No matter how much you clean and polish an older watch, you will never replicate the patina of a fresh engraving. Such a bright finish to the etching would dull down permanently in the gold surface after just a few months, so we are looking for an alderman appointed within the last ninety days. As aldermen are usually elected in the spring, I do not expect a long list of candidates."

I was, once again, struck dumb by Holmes' simple but brilliant logic. His esoteric knowledge had, not for the first or last time, proved the difference between progress and abject failure. As we strolled beneath the magnificent, vaulted roof, a thought that had been growing for a while, finally found form.

"Holmes, old man," I began, slightly unsurely. "If this whole business has been a set-up, how on earth did they manufacture the whole 'note on the breeze' incident?"

"Why, Watson, you are asking pertinent questions all of a sudden," Holmes replied, his tone leading me to expect a chiding. However, he simply added, "It is something I have already considered, more so as this case has progressed. We have to remember that we only have this Mr. Mavis' word that he discovered the note in the manner described. He could just as easily have been handed it along with a shilling and instructed to spin us the tale he told."

"Have we travelled the breadth of London chasing the proverbial wild goose? Is it some sort of test? Or, worse, is somebody playing a terrible practical joke on us?" I sighed, as I weighed up the possibilities.

"I must apologise in advance if my amateurish writings are in any way responsible for this debacle, Holmes." My head fell as I spoke. "I must admit that I have wondered whether publicising your successes might, one day, leave you open to abuse or ridicule."

"Your florid scribblings may be sensational, Watson, however, I believe they will always lead those in genuine need to my door in far greater numbers than those bent on wanton mischief." Holmes turned and flashed a brief smile. Its warmth both surprised and reinvigorated me.

Ignoring the main reception, Holmes led me down a small hallway to the left of the entrance. We passed several offices until we stopped outside a large, dark, iron-bound door. Without knocking, Holmes thrust open the heavy wooden portal. He strode inside, removed his hat and bashed his cane loudly on the stone floor. Once the sharp echo had subsided, Holmes addressed the dozen or so men who sat, evenly spaced, around the edge of the whitewashed room. "Gentlemen, good evening," began Holmes. As the sun was already low in the early evening sky, its now diffuse light filled the austere room with a warm subtle hue.

A tall man, dressed smartly, and bearing considerable regalia of office, rose to protest this unexpected interruption but Holmes spoke forcefully over his complaints.

"My name is Sherlock Holmes." He introduced himself with a slight bow. "Forgive me for my brusqueness but time really is of the essence here. I have information that this room contains the brightest and best minds of the companies of the City of London. Many more things are known to me regarding your influence and 'activities' but these are currently of no concern. I am here for information which you will provide voluntarily and without delay." Holmes smiled obsequiously as he addressed his stunned and now visibly angered audience.

"I have heard of you, a paid pawfoot, a detective for hire," growled the tall man, pointing a gnarled finger at Holmes. His thick black hair rose in an unholy halo, his cruel eyes squinted above a long, thin nose. A large handlebar moustache failed to completely cover his mouth and the damp, quivering liver-coloured lips beneath.

"You have no business here. We are," here he paused, "respectable tradesmen. We meet here regularly to discuss how best we can serve the City and its residents, for that is our résumé."

"You will cooperate for the simple reason that when we meet again, and you can be assured that we shall, you will be grateful for the mitigation that the aid you have given me today might grant you."

I was quite surprised to hear such a threat from Holmes, however veiled. The two tall men stared at each other, unblinking, for what seemed an eternity until the liveried man broke off with a humourless laugh.

"Very well. Mr. Hulmes, was it? We will humour you for a moment or two. What is this information that you require so urgently?"

"The identity of the most recently invested alderman," Holmes demanded.

The tall, pinch-faced man chuckled. "Is that what this is about? Information that you could have obtained at the front desk? Or from any passing porter or clerk?" The objectionable man laughed again, removed a handkerchief to wipe his ugly, wet mouth and continued. "The alderman for Bishopsgate died about a month back. This new man calls himself Turkle, Michael Turkle. That is all I know about him, I have never met the man," he sneered, "and neither has anyone else here present," he added, strongly implying that the conversation, along with his patience, had reached its end.

"Gentlemen, you have both my thanks and my apologies for this unwarranted interruption. We bid you a good day," Holmes again bowed. Turning swiftly upon his heels he marched out of the room. I nodded briefly at the row of distinctly unfriendly faces before me and followed as quickly as decorum would allow.

It was not until we were back inside the grand entrance hall that I felt confident enough to speak. "Whatever was all that about, Holmes?" I asked, with feeling. "Why deliberately ruffle so many feathers when our answers were freely available within ten yards of our entry?"

"An investment, Watson. We will be seeing those gentlemen again, maybe not for a few years, but their activities are growing and becoming interesting."

Although the euphemism was not lost on me, I chose to ignore it as I was already struggling with our current case. I remained silent as we left the gloom of Guildhall for the mellow early evening sun.

I fully expected Holmes to hail a hansom and instruct the driver to take us back to Baker Street, however, quite unexpectedly, he set off eastwards on foot. With his long stride, cane swinging in the air beside him, he made swift progress towards Threadneedle Street. I struggled to keep up as he passed the colonnaded frontages of the Bank of England and the Royal Exchange. The latter's once pristine white stone was already dark with soot and dirt, now almost matching the Bank's much older patina, all this after a mere forty years.

Shaking my head at the thought of the damage being done to the people and places of London by its foul air, I stumbled on, a yard behind the racing detective. We turned north onto Bishopsgate, our pace undiminished.

Suddenly, after maybe two hundred yards, Holmes halted and sidled closer to the brick wall to our left. Twenty yards further was a solid, three-storey townhouse. Such a building looked oddly out of place in this ward of business and trades, but there it stood, resolutely unique.

"This is the residence of a man that I know as Michal Turek," Holmes spoke, quietly. "He is a local businessman of

Polish origin and dubious nature. I strongly suspect that he and this 'Michael Turkle' are one and the same."

"It's not a crime to Anglicise your surname, Holmes. It is very common, especially among those of Jewish and East European heritage. Sadly, too many are prepared to judge someone simply on their given family name. If nothing else, it makes their life slightly easier."

Holmes looked at me blankly. It would have never dawned on him that such prejudice was possible, he was simply stating a fact.

"A discussion for another time," I quickly retreated. "What do you know then of this Turek character?"

"He is a trader in unusual, rare and outré items. He has a reputation for being able to obtain anything that the mind can envisage."

"Including things of questionable provenance and those officially proscribed, I suppose?"

"I have had cause to investigate him on more than one occasion. He keeps mostly to the right side of the law but treads a close path. I have observed him stray, but never in a way serious enough to alert Lestrade or his kin. There was talk abroad that he was standing for office, having gained the trust of, or certain leverage over, his more influential customers."

"But wait a minute, Holmes," I replied, as realisation struck. "If you know this man, why did you not recognise him back at Custom House?"

"Because that man was not Michal Turek," Holmes replied, his face cold and expressionless.

VI
Found and Lost

After taking a moment to absorb this new, shocking information and realising what it must imply, I automatically reached towards my pocket. It had never occurred to me that I might have need of my revolver when setting off this morning.

"Do not fret, Watson," said Holmes, seeing my fruitless groping. "We shall meet him head-on. After all, we are two and he will surely not be expecting us."

After Holmes had whispered a quick and simple plan, I approached the front door. I rapped hard upon the jet-black portal and waited. After a short delay, the door began to open. As instructed, I quickly turned to the left to obscure my face.

"What is it, who are you?" came an irritated voice from just inside. I turned back to confront the speaker. It was, indeed, the man who had attempted to incarcerate us at Custom House.

His eyes opened nearly as wide as his mouth and he took a step backwards, reaching into his jacket for what must have been a concealed weapon. Before his hand had even reached his chest, Sherlock Holmes spun round from his hiding place, against the wall to the right of the doorway, and brought his cane crashing down upon the head of our would-be captor. His years of practice in the art of single-stick were shown in his speed and agility; his turn and strike were executed in a single, flowing movement.

"My goodness, Holmes, I hope you haven't killed him," I spluttered.

"Despite that being exactly what he deserves, I can assure you that he is merely stunned, Doctor. We still have need of him; bring him inside and secure him. Do not make him too comfortable, Watson, remember that time may still be critical."

Holmes strode purposely past me and vanished from sight as I struggled to drag the prone figure back inside the house, along a hallway lined with bizarre paintings of what appeared to be obscure, and rather graphic, myths and legends. I pulled him into the front room where I sat the mysterious man on a wooden chair. Holmes reappeared, holding a ball of twine.

"I won't ask you where you found that so quickly," I puffed. Together we secured the "alderman" to the chair. Once he was tightly bound, I sat down heavily in the nearest armchair.

"We have either captured a murderer or just committed a terrible assault upon this man," I ventured, darkly. I reached inside his jacket and was not in the least surprised to find a short-barrelled revolver of American origin, lurking deep within his left side pocket.

"Watson, I need you to find the nearest telegraph office and contact Inspector Lestrade. I believe there is one adjacent to the Royal Exchange."

"Very well," I sighed, pushing myself back to my feet with the aid of my cane. "What will you be doing in the meantime?" I asked, with no attempt to hide the concern in my voice.

"Do not worry, Watson, I will quickly search the house and then, if he wakes, put to him a few simple questions."

Before I departed, I double-checked that the bindings on our prisoner were secure and set off in haste to call for the authorities. Within ten minutes, and less than a hundred yards from the Royal Exchange, I had the good fortune to spot a policeman of City Division out on patrol. Although I did not recognise the smart young man, he seemed to be aware of Holmes by name. Once I had briefed him on the situation, he swiftly and eagerly rushed off to summon help and inform Lestrade.

Buoyed by this stroke of luck, I turned and started off back up towards Bishopsgate. I was, by now, tiring and my injury was making its presence felt, more so with every step. It took me considerably longer to make the return journey, back to the house of Turkle, or Turek, I was still unsure of his identity. As I hobbled onwards, I wondered what further information Holmes might have discovered, as if this case needed any further complications. I was still uncertain, exactly, of what the case entailed. A missing person, a kidnapping? We now had the added possibility of impersonation and even murder.

The front door was unlocked and opened easily with a light push. I called out for Holmes but there was no reply. Unconcerned, for I fully expected him to be deep in study somewhere about the house, I checked on our prisoner. The man had awoken and scowled at me as I entered the room. I was pleased to see that he was still securely trussed up and a large red lump had risen prominently on his brow. He hissed as I again called for Holmes.

"He's gone, you fool," barked the captive. "Best thing for him, as when I get free, I will tear you apart!"

I pride myself on being a man who does not take kindly to threats of violence. I have seen the real thing in far too much detail and quantity to ever be shocked by mere words of menace.

I opened my coat and withdrew the villain's revolver. I pointed it straight between the man's eyes. "I am Doctor John Watson, late of the Northumberland Fusiliers and I have witnessed and dealt more death in a single day than you will see in your entire lifetime."

The man's eyes opened wide in terror as his mouth closed into silence. I have to sadly admit that it took considerable effort not to shoot him dead on the spot. It was only then that I spied the note which had been left upon the table, just behind the bound and now static prisoner. I picked it up and instantly recognised Holmes' handwriting.

"Turek is in the cellar, murdered. Explain all to Lestrade. Return to Baker Street, await me there. Research City Masonic lodges and any offshoot groups or breakaway factions."

I sighed and replaced the note. My captive laughed, mirthlessly.

"Been left alone, your mate scarpered?" he grunted.

"If you must speak then, pray, tell me what is your game? You have maybe ten minutes until the police arrive. After that, you will be interrogated, probably soundly beaten, stuck in a cell for a few weeks, tried for a day and finally hanged. Your only hope of mitigation is that which you can tell me within the very few minutes you have left before you are passed over to those whose singular aim will be to see you dead as soon as possible.

"Shall we start with your name?" I added, coldly.

"I...I, my name is...no, I cannot say. They will find me, find me anywhere," he stuttered, suddenly terrified.

"Who will find you? Speak up, man," I demanded. "You will be held in a cell deep inside Scotland Yard and then inside a secure prison, nobody will be able to get anywhere near you."

"Ha, you know nothing. They are everywhere." The man was now grinning, maniacally. "Hanging, yes, that will do, quick and painless. Much better."

"Whatever do you mean?" I asked, rather taken aback.

The man in front of me leaned forwards and twisted his head to one side, "Don't you see, Doctor Watson? I am already dead."

"What if I swear not to share with the authorities anything that you confide in me? I can give you my word that anything you now impart will stay with just myself and my colleague."

The man sighed deeply, and a look of infinite sadness swept across his face. "I was not a bad man, Doctor. Ambitious? Certainly. Greedy? Perhaps. But a murderer? I would never have thought myself capable until I met him. He told us we could be wealthy and powerful beyond our dreams. We believed him and, for a while, we flourished. However, we only later discovered that his empire was built on threats, violence and much worse. By then it was too late to leave. Betrayal was death, disobedience was death, dissent was death."

"My God, who is this man? What foul organisation does he head?" Shocked, I demanded answers.

"You asked me my name. It is Adam Gold. I..." he began but was halted by the sound of the front door opening. Two large constables entered, brushed past me and lifted Gold from his chair.

"Wait a moment, I just need a few more minutes with the prisoner," I demanded, urgently.

The constable closest to me turned and grunted negatively. It was at that moment that I noticed something was amiss with this burly policeman. In contrast to his pristine white collar, his face was unshaven, darkened by at least two days' growth of stubble.

"I say, what is your name, Constable?" I demanded, slowly raising the pistol still clutched in my hand.

Before he could answer, I heard a loud crack from behind me. The impact of the bullet spun me around and I fell, my head hitting the ground hard, plunging me into absolute darkness.

VII
Recovery

"Doctor Watson? Doctor Watson? Can you hear me, Doctor?"

I heard a familiar voice, far off in the distance.

"Drink this, Doctor." The same voice again, closer this time.

I felt a liquid on my lips and then my tongue. Cold but then warm in an instant. The world rushed in towards me, reconstructed itself and finally burst open, blinding me with its light.

I coughed awake and saw the concerned face of Inspector Lestrade above me, holding a glass of brandy to my lips. He smiled as I regained focus.

"What on Earth happened?" I asked. "I remember... a bang. I was shot! Good grief!" In a panic, I examined my torso for a gaping wound, however, I appeared unhurt. A throbbing in my head reminded me of my fall. I felt, tentatively, for the large lump on my forehead. Fortunately, although it was tender, I felt no sickness or other symptoms of concussion.

"Your coat, Doctor," Lestrade explained gently. "It seems that the bullet passed through on the left-hand side; it missed your torso but caught a button on the way out."

As I had still not quite recovered from the knock on my head, I simply stared back at the Inspector, uncomprehending.

"Your buttons are solid brass, the force of the impact spun you around and you fell, bashing your head on the tiles." Lestrade helped me slowly to my feet.

"How long was I unconscious?" I asked, wearily.

"No more than ten minutes. The constable you alerted by the Royal Exchange was quick off the mark; he and his colleagues wasted no time in getting here. I was right behind them."

"Just too late to catch the miscreants," I sighed. I wanted nothing more than to return home, run a hot bath and take to my bed.

"Come with me, Doctor," asked Lestrade. "We shall take a cab back to Baker Street. On the way, you can relax and perhaps tell me what on Earth this business is all about."

The cab trundled along the darkening streets as I explained all that had happened to an ever-more incredulous Inspector Lestrade. I concluded with the contents of the note left at Turek's house by Holmes.

"Rather ironically, I am now actually following Holmes' instructions to the letter," I managed to smile.

"You have no idea where he has gone?" asked Lestrade, still showing concern for my health.

"Not a clue, he just asked me to wait for him back at 221B," I shrugged.

"This is most extraordinary. The note, the Custom House episode, Guildhall and now murder in Bishopsgate. Are these events really connected, or is it all just a bizarre coincidence?"

"I am not sure that I believe in coincidences, Inspector. The note led us to this Gold character and then to poor Turkle or Turek; this business is complicated enough without the addition of pseudonyms." I watched as, all around us, London faded into darkness, the sound of hooves and bouncing wheel rims becoming hypnotic and leadening my eyelids.

I came back to life with a jolt as I remembered the second part of Holmes' missive.

"There was one more thing," I recalled. "Holmes ordered me to investigate the City's Masonic Lodges and look for any breakaway groups or societies."

"You should leave that to me for now. Get some rest and I will make enquiries back at the Yard. We may not have files on the lodges, for reasons which, I am sure, you are fully aware, but any unauthorised or unofficial offshoots are watched closely, for exactly the same reasons." Lestrade's attempt at a conspiratorial wink was probably visible from the far bank of the Thames, however, the point was well made.

"I think we should also include secret societies and the more sophisticated of the criminal gangs," I added. "Although, I have a feeling, from what Gold managed to impart before he was spirited away, that this is something altogether new. Could this be a middle-class criminal gang?"

"It wouldn't be the first, Doctor. In my time I have dealt with criminals ranging from prince to pauper, the only difference is in the reportage. High society closes ranks around its worst elements."

Lestrade made no attempt to hide his contempt. As a self-made man, he loathed privilege and its immoral powers of self-preservation.

We spoke little more as we left the river and headed north. Alighting on Baker Street, I bade Lestrade farewell and thanked him for his touching concern. I struggled up the stairs to our rooms where I poured myself a glass of brandy, slumped into an armchair before the unlit fireplace and prepared my pipe. I got no further than filling the bowl and tamping down the soft brown Cavendish before my head dropped to one side and I succumbed to my exhaustion. This unaccustomed sleeping position meant that I woke just an hour later and, with considerable effort, forced myself to my bed.

VIII
Narrowing the Field

I awoke to a glare of early morning light, blasting through my wide-open curtains. I had not the energy to pull them closed as I fell into bed the night before and, at first, turned away in an attempt to ignore the intruding brightness. As the events of the previous day slowly filtered themselves back into my consciousness, the lethargy was swept away. I gingerly traced the swelling on my head and reached for my watch; half-past seven, I had slept for nearly ten hours. I panicked; what had I missed? Where was Holmes? I jumped out of bed and within a few minutes, I had shaved, dressed and was rushing, expectantly, into the living room.

I was greatly taken aback to observe Holmes reclining in his armchair, wrapped in his dull brown dressing gown, with Inspector Lestrade seated opposite. Both were smoking slim Sumatran cheroots and neither appeared surprised to see me.

"Ah, Watson," Holmes declared. "Good of you to join us. I hope that you have fully recovered from your injuries. I feel quite dreadful that I left you to deal with such a dangerous situation, alone. I should have foreseen such an eventuality and warned you appropriately, I do hope you will forgive me."

"There's really nothing to forgive, old man. I had a revolver, there was but one way inside, I was careless. However, I was also lucky; I will chalk it up as a lesson learned."

It was only then that I noticed a substantial breakfast had been laid out in the adjacent dining room. I sat down and gestured for Lestrade to join me. I didn't waste my breath inviting Holmes to partake.

I had a ravenous appetite, for I had not eaten since lunch the previous day. I happily gorged upon bacon, eggs and toast, chatting amiably with the inspector between bites and sips of Mrs. Hudson's fine coffee. After a while, Holmes surprisingly joined us; however, as far as I could observe, he consumed only coffee and a meagre half slice of unbuttered toast.

Momentarily, forgetting the events of the previous day, we talked as old friends. Lestrade told of a most singular case in which two opposite front doors were swapped overnight, a puzzle that remains unsolved to this day. I recounted some of my inexplicable encounters with the mysterious fakirs of India. I believe Holmes may even have told a joke. Looking back, I now cherish that hour or so of uninhibited conversation with great affection.

We finished our breakfast with an unexpected treat from Holmes. He handed each of us a small Havana, a gift from a very satisfied former client. Together, we sat by the unlit fire and enjoyed the myriad flavours and scents that emanated from these fine Cuban cigars in virtual silence. The columns, wisps and curls of white smoke rose, merged and mingled to form a light fug just above mantle height.

Holmes broke the spell with his crisp crack of a voice. "Now that you appear to have quite recovered, Watson, it is time to bring you up to speed with events."

It was only then that I fully recalled the details of the previous day's adventure.

"Why are we sitting here wasting valuable time?" I complained. "A woman's life may be in the balance; we must get back to work."

"Calm, old man. The inspector and I have not been idle. We have spent much of the night studying records and cross-referencing underground societies and their known members, searching for any clues which might identify this particular group."

"From your lack of urgency, I have to assume that you have been unsuccessful in your efforts so far," I sighed.

"Far from it, Doctor," countered Lestrade. "We have made considerable progress."

"But how?" I asked. "We had next to nothing to go on, just what little that poor wretch Turek imparted before he was whisked away."

"Guildhall, Watson," declared Holmes. "Those twelve unsavoury gentlemen that we addressed yesterday may well be important officers of the livery companies, but they are also high-ranking members of most of the major secret societies of London. Whether it be the Freemasons, or other groups less well known and far less reputable, at least one of their number appears to be a senior member."

"I am impressed that you seem to know the identities of all those who were present, but how does this help us?"

"When I asked him about Turkle, he was not at all evasive. In fact, he didn't hesitate to admit to knowing the man and indeed happily named him."

"And all in front of a dozen high-standing members of the most powerful secret societies in London," added Lestrade.

"Oh, I see it now," I exclaimed. "He must have been genuinely telling the truth. He really did have no connection to Turkle, and neither did anyone else there. As the first rule of all of these groups is loyalty and the second is secrecy, they would never have named a known fellow member."

"So, we can discount any groups of which these men are members," continued Holmes. "Although any public information on the Freemasons is scarce, I count amongst my contacts and former clients, enough members to decisively rule out any involvement on their part. This is the work of a group far smaller, and one which appears to have been founded fairly recently. Last night, the good inspector, here, allowed me access to the Yard's records of such groups. It took several hours but we managed to exclude the majority of these from suspicion due to the links we found to those dozen men in that chamber."

"Incredible, Holmes, and well done to you too, Inspector. That must have been a mammoth effort indeed. So, who do we have left?" I asked, eagerly, my energy and enthusiasm now returned in full measure.

"Well..." began Lestrade, taking out his leather-bound notebook and flicking through to the appropriate page. "We have the foreign groups, but I think we can safely exclude these. Turek may have originally been from abroad, but he appears to have had little love for the country he left behind, according to his neighbours and associates that were brought in and questioned last night. Anarchists? Political agitators? Not likely. Turkle, or rather Gold, talked of gaining wealth and power through criminal means, hardly the aims of these extremists. Religious groups can also be discounted for much the same reasons."

"We were left with three choices," added Holmes. "There are two small, extremely secret groups, currently meeting and operating in the City, who appear to have no links to anyone we have so far encountered in this affair."

"And the third option?" I asked.

"A society so completely secret that we have no knowledge that it even exists," replied Holmes.

"Is such a secret society a real possibility? One with no links to any previous group? I thought these new societies were generally spawned from the ashes of those that went before them."

"Quite right, Watson," agreed Holmes, ignoring my rather mixed metaphor. "Most such groups are fairly well-established; it is rare for a completely new society to emerge. When they do, in order to attract members, they tend to court publicity rather than avoid it. Most are born from disagreements over the direction another group is taking. That, or personal differences, such as a clash of egos or a disagreement over money."

"So, you have identified two possibilities. We must visit these as soon as possible," I concluded.

"A fine plan, Doctor, but neither society meets during the day so, for now, we must wait," replied Lestrade. "We must also plan carefully. How are we to gain entry and upon what pretext?"

"Can you not just raid these clubs, Inspector? A few dozen burly constables would surely be enough to quell any resistance."

"Would that I could, Doctor," replied the inspector, wistfully. "However, no judge will grant me a warrant based upon what little evidence we have."

"A ruthless secret society, one hell-bent on acquiring wealth through what appears to be any means possible. Even their own members seem to be fair game for abuse or exaction," I pondered aloud.

"And there, I believe you may well have struck gold, Watson!" exclaimed Holmes, loudly.

Inspector Lestrade and I both flinched at Holmes' unexpected exclamation.

"Exaction, gentlemen," Holmes continued, his bright eyes now shining with purpose. "Extortion, blackmail. That is what we are dealing with."

"Very possibly," began Lestrade in agreement. "How can we – ?" However, he was cut off by Holmes, who was now in full gallop.

"Sometimes a case is complicated; sometimes it is as slippery as a silver fen eel. You see flashes, glimpses of reflected light yet you cannot quite get a grip upon it. That is what this affair has appeared to be, vague glimpses and hints at a much larger, unknowable whole. We have s little – few clues, no witnesses and no suspects. If it were not for the body of poor Turkle in his cellar, you could even argue that we have no proof that any other crime has been committed at all."

"What are you saying, Holmes? Are we wasting our time?" I asked, surprised at the direction he appeared to be taking.

Holmes ignored my protests and continued. "However, sometimes a case is exactly as it appears. So much so that we attempt to complicate it by adding unnecessary theories and speculation. Doctor, you were quite right when you mentioned exaction. We know that this group would not baulk at using and abusing its own members and I believe that this is exactly what has happened."

Both Lestrade and I were now leaning forward in anticipation. Holmes took a sip of coffee before continuing.

"In this business, we are suspicious of everything and everyone until we have some corroborative data. This is a fine rule and one which serves us well, the vast majority of the time. On this occasion, however, it has added unwanted fog to our thinking."

"If I am following you correctly, I think that you are implying that everything that we have observed has been exactly what it appeared to be," I replied, slowly, far from confident in my reasoning.

"Yes, Watson, everything. The note was genuine. A lady held captive in Custom House – in the very room in which we were briefly imprisoned – tore a scrap of paper from the wall, scribbled a note of help and, when she was able, threw it from an open window. Did she have just a few seconds to write before her captor returned? Perhaps she was thus interrupted and could write nothing further. Either way, the note flew on the wind and found its way onto the boot of Jonah Mavis who brought it to our attention.

"Through logical deduction, we discovered the likely source of the message. I wish now that we had been more discreet in our inquiries. Our eagerness to help has made us careless. We had already determined that the note could have been sent no more than twenty-four hours before it was presented to us. We still harboured hopes that the captive was there at Custom House, waiting to be rescued. Once we discovered that the room was empty, it should have occurred to us that her captors might well have had a permanent presence in the building or, at the very least, left an agent on the premises to report upon any interested parties who may later investigate."

"So, by announcing our presence we alerted this Gold character who had been stationed there for just such an occasion." I shook my head at the incredulity of it all.

"Are you genuinely suggesting that this society might be deliberately holding the wife of one of its own members hostage?" demanded Lestrade. "What heinous crime could possibly require such an action?"

"One that even a loyal member of a secret society might baulk at," replied Holmes, darkly.

"In that case, I am sure I could find a few volunteers from the ranks who would be willing to help us, unofficially," Lestrade offered.

"Thank you, Inspector. Please prepare as many men in plain clothes as you can spare. Watson and I will be busy for the rest of the day, but we shall be back at Baker Street in good time to greet you upon your successful return this evening."

"I will be there; you can be assured of this. I assume that you will be spending the intervening time attempting to identify which of the two societies is involved. I will continue my enquiries from the Yard." Lestrade stubbed out the scant remains of his cigar and gulped down the last of his coffee.

"Contact me if you uncover anything of interest. Gentlemen." Lestrade stood, we all shook hands, warmly, and he departed.

"So, it's kidnapping and blackmail," I ventured, taking out my pipe. "I take it we shall be visiting the two possibilities that you identified."

"It would appear so, and our opponents are way ahead of us. Not only do they still have their captive, but they might now also be aware that we are investigating." Holmes shuffled towards the fireplace. He reached for his long, dirty clay churchwarden and then sat back heavily upon his chair.

"It gets worse, Watson. By now, they will also know, from the testimony of Gold, that we have no idea of the identity of either the victim or perpetrators of this crime."

Holmes piled unspeakable black dottles of old tobacco into his bowl and brought them back to life with a long cedarwood cigar match.

"So, how can we investigate these two societies? If one of them is indeed the one we seek, then not only will they be expecting such a visit, but they also now know exactly who it is that will come!" I joined Holmes before the fireplace but now had little appetite for a smoke.

"Lestrade and his men can help us here. They are unknown to our villains and should be able to confirm that neither of these two societies, however distasteful and deeply involved in illegal activities they may well be, are the one which we seek."

I was shocked at this announcement, but Holmes' face was as fixed as granite, it was clear that he had come to this conclusion after much deduction and deep thought.

"So, where does this leave us? Do we have any leads left to follow?"

"Just one. Adam Gold. By the time I had left Turek's house in Bishopsgate before I learned of your fate from Lestrade back at Scotland Yard, I had already confirmed both Gold's identity and his home address." Holmes was now shrouded in eye-watering, bitter-smelling smoke.

"He was pretty reticent with me. How did you so quickly learn these details? Was he even conscious?" I asked, filling my pipe. I lit it hurriedly, inhaled deeply and blew out a column of finely scented smoke, hoping to counter Holmes' evil miasmas.

"I simply examined his clothes, Doctor. He had two receipts upon him. One for the purchase of books, the other for the repair of a pair of riding boots. A quick visit to both establishments, along with a brace of sovereigns, provided me with confirmation of both his name and where he lives."

"Why on Earth did you not share this with me and, more importantly, Lestrade?" I thundered.

"Please be calm, Watson. I need Lestrade and his men to eliminate the other possible societies. He would insist on joining us if he knew that we were investigating elsewhere, and I firmly believe that this investigation requires a more subtle approach than that brought by the good inspector."

Holmes could see from my expression that I was a long way from convinced.

"The inspector and his men will be doing a great service, both to this case and to society in general. These two clubs fully deserve to be shut down and their members admonished or incarcerated."

"Very well, but you must inform Lestrade of what you have discovered, once he has eliminated these establishments. I take it that you now intend us to visit the abode of this Gold character?"

"Yes, indeed," Holmes nodded. "And I assure you I shall wire Lestrade as and when we have the opportunity."

We left our unfinished pipes to cool by the fireplace, descended the stairs and hailed a hansom on Baker Street. Holmes ordered the driver to take us to Stoke Newington and we trundled east along the Euston Road. This time, the reassuring weight of my service revolver nestled safely in my coat pocket.

IX
Suburban Secrets

Holmes was in a far from talkative mood, so I contented myself to mull over the case as we passed through the northern suburbs of London. After twenty minutes or so, the density of housing began to noticeably fall, and small fields and undeveloped land become more common.

As we approached Stoke Newington, it felt as though we had left the city altogether and were entering a far more bucolic environment. The air was sweeter and the view far more pleasant to the eye. I could certainly see the attraction of moving to one of these satellite villages which were now springing up in a ring around London's noxious centre.

Gold's house was one of several handsome new red-brick villas that lined a gently curving street on the outskirts of the small town. Once the immature trees and shrubs were fully grown, this would indeed be a most attractive location. We drew to a halt in front of the largest of these houses, right on the apex of the corner. We alighted the cab and walked through the first of two open gates and along the short gravel drive that led from each and met at the front of the house.

Holmes rapped loudly with his cane upon the highly lacquered black front door. After a minute he knocked again, this time with such vigour that he left clear dents on the surface of the otherwise pristine door.

"Steady on, old chap," I admonished. "We can't go around damaging property."

Holmes looked at me with brief anger, followed almost instantaneously with a sigh and a slight smile. "Dear Watson, you shall ever be my conscience," he said softly. "However, in this case, sadly, I am almost certain that the true owner of this property is far beyond the realm of human hearing."

"He may yet have a family or staff," I protested.

"And such would have responded to my initial introduction. My continued vigorous knocking was to establish whether our villains have left any guard or observer, as they did at Custom House."

"I don't understand," I replied, bluntly. "Why announce our arrival so? Surely that hands the advantage to our opponents."

"Far from it, Watson. If they were on the lookout, they would have surely spotted us as soon as our cab pulled up outside. Anyone inside will be unnerved by our continued knocking – it implies that we know they are secreted inside."

I slowly shook my head, not entirely convinced by this twisted logic, reached into my coat and withdrew my revolver. I suddenly remembered that I still had Gold's stocky revolver in my opposite pocket. I pulled it out and offered it to Holmes.

"Thank you, Doctor, perhaps later." Holmes waved away my offer. "I have heard nothing from inside and observed no movement from the windows as we approached. Be on your guard, but I believe we are alone."

Holmes ran his slim fingers around the brass facing of the lock before reaching inside his coat and removing a slim metal instrument. He carefully pushed this into the mechanism, eased it up and down to allow ingress then twisted it clockwise. There was a click and the heavy door moved slightly inwards. Holmes gave it a further push and it swung away from us silently upon its new, well-oiled hinges.

We entered the hallway, cautiously. I kept my pistol raised, scanning from left to right in the half-light of the corridor. We passed through the hallway and examined the rooms on the lower floor. Parlour, living room, kitchen and pantry were all clear. I headed upstairs as Holmes examined what appeared to be Gold's office at the back of the house.

It took no more than five minutes to prove that Holmes was right. The house was quite empty. I relaxed, pocketed my pistol and sauntered back down the stairs to join Holmes in the back office.

I found him standing over a partner's desk, the surface of which was littered with various papers, folders and notebooks. Not content with merely covering Gold's desk with his various private papers, Holmes had also seen fit to discard anything that was not of interest. The floor surrounding the tall, lean figure was thus strewn with the unwanted detritus of Gold's documents.

"What on Earth are you doing, Holmes?" I demanded. "This is a man's private correspondence, surely we should have the police present for such a search."

Holmes turned sharply. "Ah, Watson," he began, completely ignoring my protests, "it seems that Gold had more than a passing interest in the work of Marx and Engels. In fact, he seems to have been in correspondence with at least one of them. Here is a letter from Marx himself, dated just before his death, some two years past."

"An agitator, do you think?" I asked. I had little knowledge of such radical ideas. "Could this be political? Oh, my word," I suddenly thought. "Could this all be a part of a plot, a conspiracy? Revolution?"

"Calm, Watson." Holmes smiled kindly at my panic. "This is a purely criminal act. Any sense of politics or anarchic plotting is merely a blind. Remember what Gold said to you, he was promised wealth and power, hardly the ambitions of an ardent communist."

"I will need a while longer to examine all of Gold's papers; however, I am already formulating a picture of the man. He was an idealist, interested in new ideas, alternative economic and social theories."

"So how did he become involved in this wicked business?" I asked, pulling up the chair that had once sat opposite Gold's desk.

"I know not," Holmes replied, surprisingly. "Greed? Frustration? Boredom? I am not sure that it really matters."

"Well, what does matter then?" I asked, rather harshly.

"Two things, Watson," replied Holmes, again completely ignoring my inference. "Firstly, I can find no record, here, of Mr. Gold's occupation, nothing at all. I have found various financial records and he does appear to have had a regular income. His bank records show the money coming in; however, the source of this funding is not recorded, as all of the payments were deposited in cash. It is inconceivable that such large sums would have been paid to him in such a manner if his occupation were strictly legitimate."

"That is most unusual, and indeed deeply suspicious," I agreed, before adding, "What was the second important point?"

"Look around you, Watson. This is a large house. Did you observe nothing in the rooms you examined?"

"Of course, how stupid of me," I exclaimed. "There were photographs in the living room and the large bedroom upstairs, he did not live here alone…"

Holmes interrupted before I could finish.

"Where is the wife?" he demanded, dramatically.

I paused for a moment while I processed what Holmes was alluding to.

"Gold's wife sent the message?" I managed to blurt out. "It is she who is incarcerated?"

But then a further thought occurred. "Then why on Earth was Gold the one watching over the very place of her incarceration? Surely, he would wish her to be freed. If he is complicit in her imprisonment, then he cannot also be the victim of a blackmail."

"You are quite correct, Watson. He cannot be both captor and blackmail victim, unless..." Holmes left his sentence unfinished, placed both hands on the desk and stared out of the rear window.

"Unless what, Holmes? Is there genuinely some way he could be both?"

"There is one way," Holmes replied, carefully. "If he were playing another part all along and had been discovered for what he truly was. That might explain, maybe not everything, but a great deal of what we have so far witnessed."

"Holmes, you are now talking in riddles about something which was already an enigma," I protested. "Who exactly is Gold, what part is he playing and what about him has been discovered?"

"I must leave you, Watson. For a short while, at least. I need to confirm that which I suspect, and this can only be done alone."

"Oh, for heaven's sake!" I shouted, in desperation. "How can I help you if you refuse to share your theories with me? I am not a dumb constable just here to do your bidding, Holmes. Share with me what you suspect, or I shall return forever to Baker Street and a simpler life of fine tobaccos and warm fires."

For an instant, Holmes' face was completely blank, and then a flash of what almost appeared to be regret was replaced with a warm smile.

"My sincere apologies, dear Watson. Of course, you deserve to hear my hypothesis. Please remember that for many years I worked alone and sometimes I forget that my amanuensis is right beside me." Holmes' reply held more than just a hint of mischief.

"Apology accepted, even if your description of me is not exactly flattering," I replied with a slight grin, acknowledging his subtle put-down of my rather selfish outburst.

"I suspect that Gold may be a government agent," Holmes stated. "His mission was to infiltrate this secret society and report back his findings to the authorities. However, I also believe that someone in this organisation discovered not only that he was a spy but also his true identity. They were then able to force him into working for their interests alone by abducting and threatening his wife. He was to become their puppet, a most dangerous marionette."

"But why did he not reveal his true identity when we captured him?"

"Above all, he feared for the safety of his wife. Which explains why he never broke character, even when those thugs came to take him away."

"Surely, he could have sent some sort of message to his superiors, in code perhaps, to explain what had happened. If nothing else, then his failure to report back must have raised suspicions?" I speculated.

"All good questions, Doctor, for which I will attempt to find answers in due course," replied Holmes, now keen to take his leave.

"Wait a minute, Holmes." I raised my hand to slow his rapid egress. "Could it be that Gold himself sent the note? That this was his coded message? Perhaps we were not the intended recipients?" Holmes' expression did not change. "Or perhaps we were? Nothing, in this case, would now surprise me." I shook my head as Holmes swept past and quickly left the silent and characterless house.

I rushed after my friend and barely managed to climb aboard our waiting cab before the driver flicked at the reins and we moved off at a more than fair pace.

"Where are we going?" I asked, having missed Holmes' instructions to the cabbie.

"Pall Mall. I have an urgent meeting. You should take some lunch, nearby. We will meet at three outside the Athenaeum, from there we can take a cab in whatever direction becomes necessary."

"You are not going to reveal any details of this urgent assignation, are you?" I asked, resignedly.

"Not by choice, old man. This time, I really cannot. In truth, I have no appointment made, but the one whose counsel I seek will certainly be present, one might even say resident.

"But you must take heart, Doctor," continued Holmes, brightening unexpectedly. "It was you who pointed me in this new direction. I have had some minor dealings with the government's more secretive agencies. If this Gold is, as I suspect, an agent, then he may have known who I was, by description or reputation, even if we had never actually met. I should have suspected as much, but I was stupidly blind to this possibility."

"Are you saying, then, that you were indeed the intended recipient of the message?"

"The initial one, perhaps, however, I should also have had the brains to figure out to whom it should have ultimately been delivered!" Holmes declared, both forcefully and enigmatically.

"Well, I have to say, if this Gold is indeed an agent, then he is also the greatest actor I have ever encountered. His terror of the organisation was almost palpable. He spoke convincingly of his descent from decent man to desperate pawn, all the result of his own greed."

Holmes leant forward and placed his hands together in their now familiar arch. "Exactly what he would have said if he feared he was being overheard. What might just help him survive."

"Do you think he may still be alive?" My heart lifted at this possibility. If Holmes were right, this man was brave well beyond my own capacity. And worse still, I had held a loaded pistol to his head. My shame spread across my face in a sea of crimson.

"It is a possibility and one that we must both hope for. However, do not feel guilty, Watson. If an agent he does turn out to be, this man knew very well the risks of his profession."

"These are deep and dark waters, Holmes," I replied, softly. "We must not venture out of our depth."

"No, Watson. If the water deepens, then we must swim," Holmes replied, with a renewed air of brio and confidence.

X
Deeper Waters

A little less than an hour later, we were standing in the busy urban hub that is Trafalgar Square. All around was noise, movement and colour. Holmes strolled off briskly west along Pall Mall and I passed through the columns that form the entrance to the Athenaeum Club. Once inside, all was calm and civility, just like any other of the myriad clubs that line much of Pall Mall.

Although not a member myself, I knew I would have no trouble securing a table for lunch. One mention of the name "Sherlock Holmes" guaranteed the best seats in many a restaurant or club. Holmes had shared with me the tales behind many of these favours; however, I do not recall the exact circumstances in which this particular club had become indebted to him.

After a light luncheon, I retired to the lounge for a pipe and a read of the day's late editions. I found little of interest and nothing that could fully take my mind off our current case. I was drawn back to the fate of the brave but unfortunate Gold. How much could those thugs have possibly heard? The fact that they attempted to dispose of me on the spot, yet took him away with them, alive, gave me some grounds for optimism. They could have simply put a bullet in him and been rid of the problem forever. Unless, of course, he was still vital to their plans. But what were they plotting?

I tried to think logically. They had successfully turned a government agent by means of kidnapping his wife. How they had identified him as a spy and discovered his personal details was a troublesome enough problem; however, the greater question, right now, was why they had done such a thing? For what did they need him? This is where my reasoning stumbled. I did not know in what capacity he was acting for this gang before he was unmasked. Was he impersonating the alderman or plotting some scheme at Custom House? And what of Turek, whom he had replaced? Holmes said that he had discovered his body hidden in the cellar. Who killed him? Surely not Gold, if he were a government agent, at least not of his own free will. I stared ahead blankly as my mind failed to resolve any of these questions. It was several minutes before I noticed a tall, dark figure standing before me.

"Watson, my dear fellow, do not confound yourself with theories that lack both data and facts."

Sherlock Holmes sat down, just to my right, nestling into an identical red, leather-bound and studded Chesterfield armchair. He pulled out his pipe.

"I have acquired a measure of both," he added, helping himself to a pinch of my Latakia and Virginia mixture, pushing this roughly into his dirty black bowl and tamping it down with a long finger.

"How did you know that I was thinking about the case?" I began but held out my hand to stop Holmes before he could reply.

"No, you have no need to explain," I stated. "Sitting here, staring open-mouthed into space. What else could I possibly have been thinking about?" I even managed a half-hearted smile.

"Indeed, Watson. But I do bring information. My meeting has confirmed some of my suspicions and aroused several new ones."

"Well, I have no idea to whom you have been talking but it seems clear that they are highly placed in the murky world of government intrigue. I will press you no further on their identity if you promise now to share with me everything that they have told you."

Holmes lit his pipe with a long cedar cigar match, blew the smoke upwards and leant forwards.

"Gold is, just as I suspected, a government agent. How he was discovered is, as yet, unknown and a cause of great concern to his superiors. His mission was to identify and infiltrate what was suspected to be a particularly unpleasant criminal gang. This group was unusual in that it recruited its members by appearing to be, initially at least, an exciting and enticing secret society. It would then reveal itself, to its most loyal members, to be a guaranteed path to immense riches. Complete secrccy was paramount, and it kept its secrets with ruthless and deadly efficiency."

"Once Gold reached this level, and was accepted into the inner circle, he lost all contact with his controllers. He could not risk sending any messages, but this was expected; agents are used to being out of touch with their superiors for weeks or even months in cases such as these."

"Had he managed to send back any information of use before he was cut off?" I asked.

"A little. I now know the location of this 'club,' but it is of limited help, as there is no discernible connection between the premises and the activities of the hard-core inner group."

"However, we can also infer a little more from what we and the authorities have discovered," Holmes continued. "We now know that Turek was killed between two and four weeks ago. This confirms what we were told at Guildhall; Gold's impersonation of him is relatively recent. I also learned that Gold set out upon his mission some twelve weeks ago. His final report stated that he had taken up a fake position as an official at Custom House. This was six weeks back."

"From what you are saying, Gold must have been turned sometime in the last six weeks, probably soon after he made the breakthrough into the real criminal gang. I still feel that he could have sent a more effective note if he required help. I am sure that spies must have many methods by which they can send and receive messages in secrecy."

"I agree, Doctor. Our investigations have come full circle. I believe that the note that we discovered was completely genuine and dispatched by Gold's wife from her desperate captivity within Custom House, shortly before, or perhaps even while being moved to an unknown location."

I couldn't help but let out a short laugh. "So we are, quite literally, back where we began."

"Not at all, Watson." Holmes raised an eyebrow in admonishment. "The Custom House connection must be important, it is the one thing that connects him, his wife and the criminals."

"But we have little positive to move forwards," I contradicted.

"There are two possibilities here that may well prove decisive. It is still conceivable that our quarry is unaware of our presence. So far, they have only taken a pot-shot at an intruder into Gold's house, probably believing him to be another government agent sent to check on his colleague. If Gold is indeed alive, then it gives us hope that he may eventually find a way to make contact and provide us with the details we require to finish this gang."

"But he has had ample opportunity to do so, surely he is not watched constantly. What is stopping him from making some sort of contact?"

Holmes bolted upright and exclaimed loudly, "Ha! Watson, I am, yet again, in your debt."

Several white-haired club members turned and angrily shushed my companion. Holmes raised a contrite hand to acknowledge the reprimand and continued in a tone more suited to the genteel environment.

"Sometimes the answer to one question is hidden in the asking of another," he explained to my increasing puzzlement.

"Whatever do you mean? Which questions and what answer? Do you mean why he has not made contact? Is it not because of the hold that the villains have over his wife?"

"Partly, of course, but he would still retain the ability to send a coded message without the group being aware, he is a trained government agent after all. So, what prevented him from doing so? Think about it, Watson. What was the other question causing serious concern to the government agency?"

"The manner and method of his discovery, of course," I suddenly realised. "I see it now. The most likely way that the criminals discovered not only that he was an agent but also his true identity. He was betrayed!"

"Yes, it would explain everything," I continued. "How they found him, how they were able to kidnap his wife, how they turned him into working for them and also why he has made no attempt to contact his superiors."

"Because he knows that he was betrayed from within the very government agency for which he was working." I sat back, shocked to my very core.

"This business runs deeper still, my friend. Have you not wondered why the government has taken such an interest in this affair? Why have they not left it to Scotland Yard? They may be a rather blunt instrument, but they are one whose strike is extremely powerful when required. Some basic surveillance and two dozen armed constables would soon put an end to this so-called society."

"If you put it that way then, yes, it does appear strange. Are Government agents not more commonly used in international matters?"

Holmes nodded in agreement. "It would appear that several of the members of this inner circle are foreign nationals, and important ones at that. I was told in strictest confidence that it was, in fact, an agent of one of these foreign powers that first alerted our government to the existence of this group. They were concerned for both the welfare of one of their citizens and also the reputation of their country."

"So, we know the identity of one of the inner members? Surely this is our way to locate and infiltrate the group?" Excitement was growing within me. Finally, a chance for some action.

"We do know his identity, however, sadly, we also know his fate. His name was Clarke Mitchell, and he was found eleven weeks ago, drowned in the Thames. He was an American, a banker. The timing of his death now gains additional significance."

"Secret societies, government agents, betrayal, kidnapping, City Guilds, international intrigue. Somewhere deep inside all of this must be a conspiracy or plot of some sort, one for which this group is more than prepared to kill," I pondered aloud. "Who on earth can we now trust? Are you quite certain of your contact?"

"Completely. I would trust them with my life. However, I can no longer guarantee that the information being fed to them is accurate."

"Then I can see no way forward from here. However, I feel that we should at least attempt to discover the fate of poor Gold. Do we have any clue as to where he may have been taken?"

Holmes did not reply; in fact, he said not a word for the next twenty minutes. Once we had finished our pipes, we left the club and ventured back into the busy London streets to hail a cab and enjoy the pleasant ride back to Baker Street.

"You could well be right, Doctor," said Holmes, breaking the silence as we trotted through the city. "If Gold is still alive and active in the gang, then we must make contact with him. After all, he has already encountered you. Your dramatic confrontation may have actually done us a service. He will be loath to trust anyone, however, following your performance, he must surely believe that you and he are on the same side. Perhaps, if we can find him, you might convince him to share with you all that he knows of this affair."

"But how can we possibly achieve this?" I stressed. "You stated that several members of this cabal were foreign. Do we know the identities of any of these? Or any other of the inner circle members?"

"No, we do not," Holmes replied.

Back at our Baker Street apartment, we settled down and awaited news of Lestrade's activities. It would still be several hours before his men stormed their targets, but it gave us time to think and smoke.

The silence lasted for nearly two hours; the room slowly filled with dancing smoke, scents and echoes of spices from around the Empire. I had finished my first pipe, which was now cooling on the mantel and was neatly rubbing up and packing a bright Virginian broken flake into the bowl of my trusty Lumberman.

"How many members do you think this club has? Overall. A few dozen, perhaps a hundred and fifty, at most?" asked Holmes, suddenly.

"How does this help us?" I yawned in reply.

"And how many are foreign?"

"I have no idea," I sighed.

"Surely few enough to be able to identify and subsequently keep a watch over. With Lestrade's help, ascertaining which are the foreign members should not be difficult. We also know that at least one of these is part of the central circle."

"By Jove, Holmes," I interrupted, excitedly. "You've got it. You have found our way in."

"Let's not get too ahead of ourselves, Watson. Firstly, we have to convince Lestrade to commit the manpower, only then can we begin the surveillance. It may take many weeks. I am not confident at all that we have the time."

"Can your contact in the government not intervene with Lestrade on our behalf?"

"I will not keep anything from Lestrade, but I must swear him to secrecy, Doctor. There is a traitor in the agency, one at a high enough level to know the deepest of its secrets. We can ask no more of my source, nor risk reporting back any further progress we may make."

"Weeks, you say? I suppose you are right. But we need to help Gold now. Damn it all, Holmes, there must be something we can do!"

Holmes raised an eyebrow and frowned in admonishment.

"I am sorry, Holmes, but I cannot just sit here while a brave man and his wife, let's not forget, are in mortal danger." I sat back and sucked hard upon my pipe in frustration.

"Nor shall you, old chap," Holmes smiled. "For tomorrow, you shall join this nefarious society."

Holmes' shocking and unexpected statement left me far too stunned to give voice to all of the questions that sprang instantly to mind, from simple practicality to the probability of discovery.

"Do not worry, my dear fellow," added Holmes. "Your part will be small and fairly brief."

"And why is that?" I spluttered.

"Because I will already be there as a member, to expose you as a spy and to execute you on the spot!"

Once I had recovered from this startling and initially unwelcome revelation, Holmes explained the outline of his plan. Then, after a rapid change of clothes and clutching a large leather bag, he departed by cab. I remained at Baker Street to await Lestrade's return.

As Holmes was out, laying the groundwork for our introductions into the club, I sat back down and tried to absorb all that he had imparted. This case seemed to twist and turn like the very eel that Holmes had earlier broached and was just as slippery. His plan was simple, we would join the club as junior members the very next day. He would attempt to gain instant favour by revealing me to be a government agent. What was to follow was a sketchy and ill-planned scheme at best. I genuinely wondered if I would survive the night. I refilled my pipe and smiled, I had not felt this alive since Jezail bullets were whistling by, mere inches from my head, in the rocky passes and valleys of Afghanistan.

XI
The Chairman of the Club

Lestrade returned late that evening, shortly before midnight. He appeared utterly exhausted and slumped into an armchair, gratefully accepting the large glass of brandy that I proffered. I handed him a decent Sumatran cigar and a long match. He took a long sip, swallowed the amber liquid, replaced the glass with a cigar, struck the match and applied the flame. He seemed to visibly relax, his cheeks regained what little colour they ever possessed, and his eyes brightened.

"Your appearance speaks of a long night of hardship, Inspector," I inquired, finally.

"Hardship and frustration," Lestrade sighed. "On any other night, I would have been proud of our endeavours, Doctor. We have dissolved two most heinous associations and arrested a number of criminals and practitioners of perverted activities. However, I do not need to tell you that we failed to uncover the society behind the kidnapping, do I? I always allow for Mr. Holmes' reluctance to impart upon me all that he knows; however, this time, I feel that I have heard barely a whisper of the whole affair."

There was more than a hint of repressed anger beneath the words of the inspector.

"I am truly sorry, Inspector, your tolerance is admirable, and you are quite right. Although, to be fair, Holmes had

93

explained little more of his plans to me by the time you left this morning," I confirmed, ashamedly.

I spent the next half hour detailing our trip to Gold's house in Stoke Newington, Holmes' enigmatic meeting with his contact in government, our discoveries and deductions and, finally, the two possible plans of action.

Lestrade leaned back and thought for a while, alternately inhaling, then releasing sweet, blue-tinted cigar smoke out into the air.

"I cannot help but feel offended by Holmes' selfish actions in excluding Scotland Yard from his plans, however, in this case, with the real possibility of a foreign agent acting rogue within our own government, I can forgive him. I also agree with his initial plan of action. We can certainly put this club under surveillance; we will soon know which of these foreign members is a part of the inner circle. This more immediate scheme is rather more troublesome. If I thought, for an instant, that there was any chance he would actually listen to me, then I would forbid it completely."

"So, you will support us?" I asked, rather surprised at the swiftness of Lestrade's capitulation.

"I am tired, Doctor. Maybe tomorrow I will be able to muster up a greater outrage." Lestrade stifled a laugh. "I can send a couple of men to keep watch over you, but they won't be able to enter the club. Once you are inside, you are on your own."

"It is late, Inspector, please feel free to stay here for the night. I know that Mrs. Hudson is still awake, she would be happy to send up a late supper."

Lestrade took me up on my offer and we enjoyed a very pleasant couple of hours of conversation, cold cuts, coffee, brandy and a final bowl of tobacco or two, before heading off for bed in the early hours.

I rose at eight, to discover that Lestrade had already departed, leaving a note of thanks and instructing me to keep him informed of our plans. He would be based, primarily, at Scotland Yard for the day, so I needed only to send a wire to alert him of any developments. The presence of a used coffee cup and plates proved, once again, what an irreplaceable housekeeper we had in Mrs. Hudson. Not even a Scotland Yard police inspector could slip through her guard of hospitality, I thought with a smile.

After finishing my breakfast, I filled my pipe and consulted the morning papers. Lestrade's raids had been too late to make the early editions but should feature by midday. Other than the usual European rumblings, German expansion in Africa and the continuing Sino-French War, there was little of interest. A short article about counterfeit currency appearing in London and Birmingham briefly held my attention but it transpired that the amounts involved were insignificant, the work of local gangs, concluded the writer.

I took a stroll in The Regent's Park; not too far, just around the boating lake. Enough to loosen the muscles; I would be needing all my physical strength later in the day. On returning to our rooms, I prepared myself for the mission. I sent Mrs. Hudson out with a message for Lestrade, dressed in my finest suit, attached my gold hunter and Albert and slipped several notes into my wallet. I needed to look the part of a wealthy businessman, with the funds to back it up if challenged.

The notes had been provided by Holmes. I received an almighty shock when he told me to "help myself" from the "petty cash" box under his bed. I had pulled the battered metal container from beneath his unkempt bunk and opened it. Inside was a stack, several inches thick, of banknotes. I took a handful and made a mental note to demand that Holmes explain exactly the provenance of this enormous stash of notes the next time we meet.

I straightened up, checked myself in the mirror and, satisfied that I had prepared as well as I could, set out for Mayfair. I tried to relax in the back of the hansom, but my mind was racing with the uncertainties of my task. I gripped my cane tightly, or rather the cane I had borrowed from Holmes. It was an inch too long for me, but what it lacked in support, it gained in security from within. Holmes had forbidden me from bringing my revolver, quite rightly, as I fully expected to be searched for weapons at least once.

The drive to Berkeley Square took less than fifteen minutes. If I hadn't been sporting such elaborate apparel, I would have happily walked. I disembarked and stood in the leafy street, a light wind blowing through the trees in the gardens beside me. I approached a large villa, all white and rather nondescript among such illustrious company. I climbed the three steps up to the gloss-black front door and knocked three times.

My final strike was still resonating as the door swung inwards. I entered the darkness and offered up a swift, silent prayer, much as I had done so many years earlier and half a world away.

"Doctor Weston, welcome to the Ex Tenebris Club."

Standing before me was a veritable weasel of a man, all sharp features, thin neck and slicked-back hair. I hadn't been comfortable, initially, with Holmes' suggestion of using names so close to our real ones, but it did reduce greatly the chances of us making a mistake and being discovered as interlopers. "Always imbue a falsehood with as much truth as you can," he often advised. As Twain knew well, the truth does not need to be memorised.

I nodded and raised my hat in acknowledgement. Standing next to, and towering over, the weasel was a giant. Well over six and a half feet in height, his suit sleeves barely covered his forearms which were heavily muscled and densely tattooed. His head was bald with a huge protruding forehead. His eyes were bright blue but appeared to be focused on something far distant.

The pinch-faced man sensed my discomfort and gestured inside.

"Please come this way, Doctor. We have just a few formalities to attend to before you can enjoy the full facilities of the club."

"I have been informed that you are sponsored by another recently recruited member," continued the slight man as he walked just ahead of me. "This is somewhat unusual, however, your friend has made quite the impression in the very short time he has been with us here."

The sneer in his voice was matched perfectly by the expression upon his face. I sensed, instinctively, that this fellow was infinitely more dangerous than the huge thug we had left guarding the front door. We passed through an open doorway; I could not help but notice that this door, although painted uniformly black, was ironbound and set upon large steel hinges. Closed and locked it would form a significant barrier to any party attempting ingress, even one both official and well-armed.

The club brightened considerably after this point. Red seemed to be the prominent theme, brightly coloured and patterned paper lined the walls of a short hallway which then opened up into the main entertainment area, on this floor at least. It was about twenty-five yards square and filled with dark mahogany tables surrounded by matching leather-backed chairs. There were perhaps twenty men in the room, less than a quarter of its capacity, I would guess. Half of the tables, those to the right, appeared set for food and drinks. The others, on my left, were gaming tables, topped in brushed green baize. There were two games in progress, the remaining members were eating, drinking or smoking.

My guide led me along one side of the room and opened a door to our left where we entered a dark, wood-lined office. He ushered me into a straight-backed chair, set before a green, leather-topped partner's desk. High on the walls, to the left and right of me, a brace of candles burned atop dark sconces; barely enough to illuminate the surface of the desk. My rodent-featured chaperone then bowed obsequiously and retreated, closing the door as he departed.

I sat for a short while, expecting the door behind me to open at any time. Suddenly, and much to my surprise, a figure lunged forward from the darkness that lay just beyond the desk. Believing that I had been alone, I was momentarily startled; the room must have been considerably larger than it first appeared to have totally concealed this fellow within its depths.

I moved to stand but a gently raised hand and a shake of his head indicated that this was not necessary. The man who stood before me was certainly striking. Tall, lean and impeccably dressed. His jacket may have been of vintage design, but it was also of the finest quality and intricately embroidered throughout. Though he wore no colour other than black, it was still possible to discern shapes, patterns and swirls, all hand-sewn, upon nearly every surface. His silk scarf also appeared, at first glance, to be uniformly dark but as the light moved over its surface it revealed that it too was covered in all manner of strange sigils and designs. His hair was jet black, parted on the right side with arrow-straight precision. A long curl of hair arched its way across his forehead and perfectly framed his left eye, almost as if were a monocle. His nose was straight and his face cleanly shaved. His mouth was rather narrow, although this was offset by his fine, high cheekbones.

I would have described him as exceptionally handsome but for one thing. His eyes were cold and dead. Large black pupils surrounded by a ghostly grey mist, as swirling and lifeless as the smoke from a funeral pyre.

"I am the chairman." The man held out a hand in welcome. It was cold, white, fleshless and appeared considerably older than his face. I struggled to estimate his age, he could have been anything from thirty to fifty years, perhaps even more. His voice was dry and hollow, I imagined that if a reptile could talk, it may well have sounded eerily similar.

"Please call me Mister Chairman," he continued, adding little but deliberately stressing his authority, as he slowly sank back into a deep emerald leather-studded chair.

"Weston, Doctor James Weston," I replied, as nonchalantly as I could manage.

I was asked to sign several papers, the contents of which were not deemed important enough for me to examine. I did so readily and with a flourish that I hoped would exude a sense of confidence. The chairman took the signed papers, examined them briefly and slid the pages into a buff-coloured file. He stretched out a long arm towards a dark filing cabinet lurking in the gloom to his right, pulled it open with his cadaverous fingers and dropped the file inside.

"Welcome to the First Circle." The smile that accompanied these words was so cold and sterile that I struggled to remain seated.

"Please feel free to enjoy all of the amenities on this floor. If your sponsor is to be believed, then it will not be long before you rise to the higher levels," he smiled, before adding, "and lower Circles."

The figure before me rose to his considerable height. We shook hands once again and I turned to leave. I half-expected to find the door locked, however, much to my relief, it opened, and I hurried back out into the lounge.

XII
The Chase

I took a seat at a vacant table and attempted to process all that had just occurred. This "Chairman" certainly had a sense of the dramatic and also a taste for the Gothic. However, there was something more. Those eyes seemed so utterly devoid of life that I felt nothing lay behind them, whatsoever. Good and evil are concepts that we have dealt with many times before, but this was something different – complete ice-cold indifference. This appeared to be a man who would baulk at nothing to achieve his aims.

Dragging my mind away from the appearance of this terrifying man, I realised that he had concisely and conveniently described the structure of the club both physically and hierarchically. One advances through the ranks and, quite literally, rises up in the society. The upper floors, at least two by my reckoning, can only be accessed by those of higher rank. The allusions to Dante had not escaped my notice either. In a none-too-clever, or subtle, inverse relationship, one's elevations through the floors of the building are mirrored, morally, by a fall at each stage, down to the so-called "Lower Circle."

Unsure of the etiquette, I waited to be served. After just a few minutes, a waitress arrived to take my order. I only refer to her thus to provide a technically accurate description of her function. As a gentleman, I will add no more, except to suggest that her attire, such as it was, would not be tolerated anywhere outside the most private of clubs.

Fighting all of my natural instincts, and remembering Holmes' explicit instructions, I tried to engage the girl in conversation. She did not seem surprised that I had taken an interest, which further confirmed my suspicions. I explained that I was a new member and that my questions were all perfectly innocent, but she would reveal nothing other than purely practical information regarding the club. I did not dare offer a financial inducement as I was, by now, convinced that this would be taken as an offer for another type of service altogether.

Feeling flustered and extremely uncomfortable, and also frustrated at my lack of progress, I sent the waitress away and awaited my drink. I knew that I was here, ultimately, as a decoy and whipping boy for Holmes, but I still fully intended to gather as much information as I could while within the building.

My order soon arrived, and I cautiously took a sip. I had chosen a gin and tonic, as its clarity and distinctive taste made it a drink in which it is difficult to successfully conceal a poison or sedative. Looking into the Chairman's eyes had brought out in me an uncommon nervous agitation. I was employing as many of Holmes' teachings as I could recall. I had picked a table closest to a wall, ensuring no one was behind me. I faced outwards with a full view of the room, its exits and all of its occupants. I toyed with the idea of joining a card game, however, experience has taught me that men gambling in clubs tend to take their game far too seriously to wantonly engage in idle conversation.

I still had a while before our plan was due to be enacted, and I was beginning to feel rather self-conscious, sitting alone, quietly deflecting the offers of the hostesses. Much to my surprise, this immediate issue was solved by the arrival at my table of a stranger.

"Mind if I join you, old chap?"

A bald, middle-aged man with a bright red beard sat himself down next to me. His manner, and indeed his breath, indicated that he had already been drinking for quite a while.

"Haven't seen you here before? But that might well be because I am a newcomer also!" He laughed, loudly, as if he had made some hilarious observation. I smiled broadly in reply. Although a recent member, someone in this state should be an ideal candidate for gaining information.

"Weston, James Weston," I replied. "And you are quite right, I joined but today."

"Good to meet you, James." The man stuck out a red and podgy hand, somewhat to my left. I leant across, shook it and raised a questioning eyebrow.

"Oh, me? Of course, so sorry," he guffawed. "Please forgive me, I am Burwin Cosh, importer of affordable fine art from Europe and beyond. If you want an Old Master but don't quite have the budget, then I can get you the next best thing."

Here he tapped his nose before collapsing, once again, into fits of laughter.

I sighed but decided to persevere. In this state he was unpredictable, however, he may still inadvertently share something of interest.

"Have you made much progress yet through the circles?" I asked.

Once again, I was met with a wall of laughter. This time he fell forwards and almost right off his chair. He pulled himself back upright and steadied himself with one arm on the table. After at least two failed attempts, he finally managed to speak.

"Oh, James, dear friend. One such as myself is fortunate enough to be allowed to pass through those doors." He pointed directly at the wall opposite. "But to progress upwards? That is for those far better than the likes of us, I'm afraid."

"And why is that?" I asked.

"Because." Cosh paused and raised a finger.

Perhaps half a minute passed and having received no reply, I repeated the question. However, I quickly realised that he was now too far gone. I saw his glassy eyes closing and head drooping, so I eased him down gently onto the table. That he then began to loudly snore was of no real surprise to me; I simply smiled and finished my drink in one draft. I checked my watch and studied the room for a final time before leaving the table and moving towards the area which most closely resembled the position Holmes had suggested I should take up at this point.

I was now sitting well away from any club patron or member of staff and close to the exit. Looking down the corridor, I could see that the route to the outside door was clear. I adjusted my watch and Albert into the position that we had agreed would be the signal to Holmes that all was well and that the plan should proceed. Exactly how he could arrange to be here at the exact appointed time worried me deeply. I could not remain in this exposed position for long without attracting attention.

After perhaps ten minutes had passed, I began to grow concerned. I lifted my watch slowly, deliberately examining it in minute detail, trying to eat up valuable seconds. I replaced it carefully, returning it, exactingly, to its previous position. Further minutes passed slowly, each second excruciatingly stretched by the tension building up within me.

Just as I was beginning to wonder if something might have gone seriously wrong with our scheme, the double doors directly opposite me burst open. Four men rushed into the room. Leading the way was a tall figure, his open black cape billowing out behind him.

It took me a moment to realise that this was, in fact, Sherlock Holmes. My expression of surprise would certainly have appeared genuine. He seemed to be wearing some sort of disguise. His hair was long and greasy, large lamb chop sideburns covered half his face. Small, tinted, brass-rimmed lenses hid his eyes and his mouth appeared to be full of ugly and crooked false teeth. Following closely behind him were three men that I did not recognise. Two appeared to be well-dressed professional men, the third was a tall, well-built fellow, probably a hired thug of some sort.

Holmes stopped, abruptly raised his right hand and purposefully pointed a long, gloved finger directly towards me. I leapt to my feet and waited for him to speak.

"This is the man!" He announced, with a loud, piercing shriek. "The interloper, the traitor, the saboteur, the *agent provocateur*!"

"Take him, Garnett," ordered one of the well-dressed men. His voice had authority which, along with his bearing, suggested a military background.

"Leave this to me," Holmes bellowed. He spread his arms wide, blocking those behind from advancing while shielding me from their view with his wide, trailing cape.

Then, swiftly as a cat, Holmes reached inside his cape and withdrew a huge, long-barrelled revolver. In one fluid movement, he swung the weapon towards me and squeezed the trigger.

I was already moving when Holmes unleashed his improbable firearm, however, I felt the rush of air as the projectile tore its way through the space just to the left of where I had been sitting. The explosion was deafening. I was vaguely aware of the recoil throwing Holmes, conveniently, backwards, into the path of those standing directly behind him. Almost simultaneously, another huge plume of smoke and flame spurted from his gun, and a huge chunk of the club wall disintegrated in an eruption of plaster, paint and burning wallpaper.

I ran towards the exit as quickly as I could. The noise, smoke and chaos behind me were the greatest possible incentives to get clear of this madness.

As I reached the corridor, Holmes fired again, this time just above my head. The lintel over the door exploded in a shower of wooden splinters and shards of lathe. What on earth had Holmes got hold of? Was it merely a pistol or, having witnessed the destruction it rent, some sort of hand-held cannon?

Reaching the end of the short corridor, my way was suddenly blocked by the enormous doorman I had encountered on my way into the club. He spread himself to block my egress and a grin crossed his simian features. I had no time for any form of one-on-one close combat, so I am utterly ashamed to report that I forced my progression in a most ungentlemanly way.

Holmes' trusty cane was still vibrating from the impact as I skipped over the large figure now lying at my feet, grasping at the area of his injuries. I raised my eyes and offered a swift apology to the Lord, as I passed through the outer door and into the cool air of the London night.

Two more shots whizzed past me as I fled towards the waiting cab. It was a source of not a little concern that these gunshots were now of a far more familiar calibre. The men accompanying Holmes were now opening fire and these bullets really were being aimed at me. I kept my head down and threw myself into the two-seater. The driver gave a short, shrill whistle and his horse took off with such haste that I had to cling on tightly for fear of being thrown clear.

Further shots were fired but we were soon beyond range. The reassuring figure of Bob Watkins turned his head back towards me.

"You all right back there, Doctor? Ready for part two of Mr. Holmes' plan?" asked Watkins with a quite inappropriate grin.

Not for the first, or last, time, the great horseman had saved my life. Watkins was one of Holmes' greatest successes, a man turned from criminal of the highway into a brave, loyal and fearless ally.

"Yes, I am fine," I replied, ignoring the protests issuing from all over my body. "Never felt better, please proceed, good fellow." I settled back as best I could, one hand on the side of the carriage, the other holding onto the special bundle that Holmes had arranged to sit beside me.

Watkins slowed his progress considerably as we headed south along Berkeley Street. The truth was that there was no one alive who could keep up with Bob Watkins through the streets of London. We waited until we caught sight of a pursuing carriage before, once more, increasing our pace. A sharp right turn took us to the borders of Green Park, into which we raced, our pursuers only two hundred yards or so behind.

We continued along the pathway for another hundred yards before taking a sharp left turn into a dense copse of dark evergreens. Here, I jumped from the carriage, quickly thanked Watkins and concealed myself in the thick undergrowth. Watkins tipped his cap, gave another short whistle and sped away towards the centre of the park.

What followed next was the finest display of horsemanship I have ever witnessed. Watkins drove his horse to a full gallop before standing up and climbing forwards towards its flanks. He then jumped, landing perfectly astride his fine mount. Leaning back, he withdrew a large, serrated-edged knife and cut forcefully through the leather straps connecting horse to carriage. Looming before him was a crossroads, at the centre of which was a substantial bandstand. At the last possible moment, he pushed himself free from the carriage and dragged his horse away from the inevitable collision.

The carriage hit the bandstand full-on, with a sickening rending and tearing of wood, steel and fabric. One wheel was launched into the air, only to land some thirty yards distant. Metal twisted and glass shattered as the stand took the full impact of the speeding cab. Two of the supporting columns were seriously damaged, so much so that the bandstand's roof shifted, leaned and dozens of roof tiles rained down, only to smash upon the hard ground below.

The destruction was total. Those sitting in the carriage behind us had been gifted a grandstand view. We hoped that it would be taken to be a terrible accident, a terrified cab driver trying to take a corner far too quickly. At this distance, and in the darkness, it certainly looked convincing from my viewpoint. There was a small chance that they had spotted Watkin's means of escape, but that was a risk that Holmes, surely one of those watching, would certainly have calculated and deemed acceptable.

This would not be the first time that we had relied upon a plan being so grandiose and shocking that no one would ever suspect it to be just that, a premeditated fabrication. The scale of Holmes' plot had at first shocked me, however, once explained in his cold, logical manner, it seemed perfect for our needs. It was only at this point that I began to wonder just how much Holmes had invested, financially, in this dramatic mix of theatre and reality. Once again, he had shown that his thirst for justice would always outstrip any desire for material wealth.

Safely hidden by the surrounding trees and bushes, I had a good view of what followed. Our pursuers' carriage scraped to a halt some twenty yards before the ruins of my cab. A tall figure quickly jumped out, unmistakeably Holmes. He briefly examined the wreckage before turning and holding both arms out wide, a gesture designed to bar the way to the two men who followed him from the car.

"Please, gentlemen," I heard him call. "The scene is terrible; you would be best served by coming no closer. The passenger, and egregious traitor he, is dead. What is left is not something that you should volunteer to look upon."

One of the two men, the fellow with the military bearing, pushed past and bent down to examine the scene. Almost immediately, he jumped back up and stumbled backwards, almost falling over strewn pieces of rent wood and iron. He turned and spoke briefly to the third man in the party. The two men returned to the carriage and gestured to Holmes that he should follow. Once all were on board, the driver cracked his whip and the carriage turned and departed the park at a swift trot.

Once they were out of sight, I left my cover and strolled over to the wrecked cab. I picked my way towards the centre of the destruction and could not suppress a chuckle when I reached the exact spot that had caused such a reaction from the military man. Spread before me was a veritable charnel house; copious blood, broken and twisted body parts and ripped and stained clothing. This so-called military man could not have seen much front-line combat, as what lay before me was not a tragic loss of human life but, rather, a terrible waste of food. Holmes had loaded the cab with a pig carcass, entrails still *in situ*, wrapped in an old black suit. A large glass bottle filled with the poor creature's blood had provided the final touch. The force of the impact and the cloak of darkness had made the scenario laid out upon the pristine parkland appear far more convincing than I had expected.

The sound of approaching hooves alerted me to the return of Watkins. Smiling broadly, he offered me a lift back to Baker Street, but I declined, I had to remain at the scene until Lestrade arrived to clean up and, more importantly, cover up our little escapade.

Less than an hour later, Lestrade arrived with several burly constables in two hansoms and a dray. They swiftly cleared the wreckage and twenty minutes later all that was left to show of the collision was the damage to the bandstand. This seemed to particularly irk the inspector.

"Even though Holmes must have known that it was scheduled for demolition, it still bothers me that he was prepared to damage public property in order to achieve his goals," he moaned as the last of the debris was piled upon the wagon.

I could tell from his demeanour that this was more a complaint against an unwelcome late-night call-out rather than of Holmes' scheming. As the loaded cart pulled away, Lestrade took me aside. "I hope 'His Majesty' knows what he is doing," he sighed. "He does realise that he is now fully embedded in this society, so we can no longer help him."

"We must now trust him. He will contact us when he is ready," I replied confidently.

"Did he perhaps mention how he might do this? I seem to recall that it was this exact issue that so distressed the previous agent."

I had, of course, no answer to the inspector's question, Holmes had not specified a method of communication. In all the excitement surrounding the night's scheme, I had quite overlooked this most basic of provisions. Although I had complete confidence in him, I would simply have to be patient and wait for him to contact us by whatever means he deemed fit.

I joined Lestrade in his carriage and he was happy to take the short diversion back to Baker Street. The inspector commented on the extravagance of Holmes' plan. He was quite right, of course, Holmes must have spent a small fortune on the purchase and destruction of a perfectly serviceable carriage, not to mention all of the other props he had employed. All I could do was agree and attempt to reassure the inspector that Holmes was in full control and knew exactly what he was doing. Our swift arrival at Baker Street, thankfully, spared me from having to provide any further explanation. Wearily, I climbed the stairs to our rooms and eschewing both food and drink, immediately took to my bed.

XIII
The Distraught Client

I rose late the following morning, forcing my aching body upright and out of bed. A hot bath helped to soothe my aching muscles, but I knew that I would not be up to much physical activity for at least another day. Mrs. Hudson provided a fine late breakfast and, having consumed all that was laid before me, I took to my armchair, lit a pipe and picked up the morning's early editions. There was a small mention of Lestrade's raids on the two clubs from the night before last, however, few details were given, and no names were recorded. Whether this was by design, Lestrade not wanting our prey to suspect that we were after them, or through the influence of some of the members, I could not be certain. Either way, I felt that discretion was preferable to publicity at this stage of our investigation.

Other than a story reporting the discovery of yet more counterfeit currency, nothing else held my attention. My thoughts kept returning to our case and from there to Holmes, wherever he might be. I folded the paper, rose and reached for my hat and cane. I forced myself downstairs and along the short walk to The Regent's Park. My aching body protested at each step, but I refused to give in to the physical discomfort. After perhaps a half an hour, I realised that I was no longer obsessing over the case or worrying after Holmes. I smiled and tried to enjoy the weak autumn sun streaming through the darkening leaves of the surrounding trees. At that moment, I resolved to move forwards and do something practical; after all, Holmes was sure to find a way to make contact when our assistance was required.

What warmth there was left in the air, allied with my constant movement, gradually released the tension in my muscles and joints, making the return leg of my walk infinitely more enjoyable than the outbound stroll. I returned to Baker Street in far better spirits than in which I had left.

The day passed without further incident and, feeling far more relaxed than before, I had little trouble falling asleep that evening. The next day followed a similar pattern; I took a walk in the morning and, later that afternoon, caught up with my correspondence, worked on my writing and spent time reading some recent medical journals.

Two further days rolled slowly by in an almost identical fashion, other than for a brief visit from Inspector Lestrade to confirm that our nocturnal activities had been smoothed over. He had planted a small article in a lower-end newspaper, detailing a tragic incident in Green Park involving a carriage and a condemned bandstand. There had been one fatality, the only passenger. The cab driver, an unlicensed rogue, had fled the scene, his identity still unknown. The report would be noted by our quarry, while the lack of any significant coverage in the major papers should help convince them that the authorities were not in active pursuit of any of the parties involved.

As I waited for Holmes to make contact, my attempts to keep busy consisted mainly of managing the regular stream of correspondence from potential clients that continued to arrive daily. I studied the contents of the letters before placing them upon Holmes' desk (I refused to impale them with his hideous dagger, stuck an inch deep into the mantelpiece). Where I felt it necessary, I sent brief replies informing their authors that Holmes was indisposed but would respond as soon as possible. When clients called in person, I found that around half their number left the moment I told them that Holmes was away. Of those that did not immediately turn tail, most simply left their details, however, a few did ask if I would be prepared to listen to their problems. Having little else to do and, admittedly, being more than a little flattered that they believed that I may be able to offer some assistance, I readily agreed to hear what they had to say.

In all, I conducted three interviews in the days that followed our adventure at the Ex Tenebris club. The first two were fairly simple cases, domestic problems involving sensitive issues. Here, my training as a doctor, rather than any deductive ability I had learned from Holmes, was of far greater help in both matters. A referral to Inspector Gregson and one to an old medical colleague, respectively, along with an assurance to the client of their utter discretion, was all that I believed was required to settle the issues at hand. To my great satisfaction, both clients left Baker Street in noticeably better humour than that in which they had arrived.

The third client was anything but straightforward. It was a Friday morning; I had risen early, and when the front bell rang at exactly eight o'clock, I had already breakfasted and was halfway through my first pipe of the day. Mrs. Hudson showed in my guest, a lady wearing a long, hooded cloak of dark indigo, for it was a chilly autumn morning despite the bright sunshine.

She pulled back the hood and removed her outer garment to reveal a young woman of perhaps seven and twenty years. Her hair was dark, held up and back by a selection of pins and short ribbons. She had exquisite features, olive skin, large dark eyes, a slim nose and high cheekbones. Her mouth was small, but her lips were a ripe ruby red. She wore a dress of purple silk and satin; simply cut but of exceedingly high quality. It struck me as a rather unusual outfit to be wearing at such an early hour. However, once I had applied Holmes' methodology, I was able to form my introduction with some confidence.

"Good morning and welcome to Baker Street, home of Sherlock Holmes and myself, Doctor John Watson. I take it that your evening did not end entirely to your satisfaction?"

My guest appeared momentarily unsettled but quickly regained her composure.

"My dress? Why, yes, you are quite correct. I have been in town since yesterday evening and have not yet," here she paused, "been able to return home, to sleep or even to change."

"Please take a seat and tell me everything. Do not spare a single detail, for the smallest, most insignificant sounding of these might just be the key to solving your problems." I gestured to the armchairs before the fire.

My guest took a seat as I called for Mrs. Hudson to bring up coffee and a light breakfast; it was clear that the young lady had not eaten for quite some time. Once we were settled, I gently asked her to begin.

"My name is Catarina Hill. I live in Reddlesham, in Sussex, with my husband. My entire life has been shattered," she began, dramatically.

"I am so sorry to hear that. Please, explain to me exactly what it is that has led to this terrible situation," I replied, as earnestly as I could.

"I live with my husband; in some comfort, if I am honest. He is a solicitor, a junior partner at a firm in Arundel. We have two young boys who board nearby, and we take several holidays each year. I thought our life to be idyllic. Reddlesham is small and peaceful, not much more than a large village, really. Everything was perfect, Doctor, until two weeks ago." Her eyes had now misted over, and it was clear that she was not far from tears.

"Tell me what happened, take your time," I encouraged, gently.

"One Friday, nearly a fortnight ago, my husband, Hugo, did not come home from work." I could hear the struggle in her voice as she stammered out the words.

"I waited all night but still, he did not return. I ventured into Arundel the following day, but being a Saturday, I could find nobody to aid me in my search. The next day, I called upon the village police, but the small local station was closed. When Monday finally came around, I was almost insane with worry. I ran into the office of my husband's firm and demanded to know what had become of him." Mrs. Hill took out a handkerchief and wiped her eyes.

"What did they say? Anything they know could be of vital importance," I urged.

"They told me that they had never heard of him!" she exclaimed, tears now flowing freely down her soft cheeks.

"Good heavens," I spluttered, before gathering my composure. "With whom did you speak? Was it just one individual?" I asked, trying to grasp some sort of understanding of events.

"No. I was horrified by this response, so I demanded to see all of the partners and the clerks."

"And they all said the same?" I asked.

"Yes. Not only did they insist that my husband had never worked there, but they also threatened to call for the police and have me incarcerated as a lunatic!"

"Surely, you have witnesses that you could call upon. Friends, relatives, people that know your husband?"

Mrs. Hill looked down and seemed to slump somewhat in resignation.

"I am not a sociable person, Doctor. I am happy to stay at home during the day and spend my evenings with my husband. When the children are home, I am busy looking after them; when they are away at school, I have my garden, piano and needlework. We have a housekeeper and cook but my husband often jokes that they are probably the least busy servants in all England."

"When it came to providing proof of my husband's profession, I had none. When I realised just how little connection I had to the town and its people, I began to panic. I knew nobody and nobody knew me. More frighteningly, nobody appeared to know my husband."

I was dumbstruck. I could detect no trace of deceit in her account, yet it seemed fantastical, impossible. I attempted to apply my friend's methods, however, I failed to make any logical deductions, let alone a breakthrough that might crack the case.

"Did you, perhaps, have a chance to look into his financial affairs? Did he have a chequebook or any receipts from his bank?"

"Initially, I did not. However, once I had made an official report to the local police, an inspector accompanied me to my husband's bank in town. The manager was very understanding and provided all that the inspector requested. There was a regular income, paid monthly in cash. The deposits were all made by the same man, one whom the staff remembered clearly."

"Your husband?" I asked.

"Yes, it was Hugo. These appear to be the only times he visited the bank. He paid all of our expenses monthly by cheque, the regular deposits more than covered these. According to the bank manager, Hugo had a sizeable balance in his account, along with a portfolio of shares and bonds worth many hundreds of pounds."

"So, he had no financial problems, at least none that we can see." I paused, before adding, "This does appear to rule out two of the most obvious and common scenarios that might explain such a sudden disappearance."

"What are these, Doctor?" implored Mrs. Hill.

"I am going to have to be very direct with you, Mrs. Hill. There is no time and nothing to gain from being reticent," I warned.

"Please go ahead and spare me no detail. I feel I am falling in a downward spiral to an unimagined hell; nothing can shock me now."

I could not help but notice the reference to Dante but brushed it away as mere coincidence.

"The two reasons which are, by far, the most common explanations for abscondment – are money and love. I think that we can reasonably discount the first as your husband had a steady income, whatever its origins may turn out to be, along with substantial savings. His net worth when he disappeared, appears to have been considerable."

"The second possibility also seems unlikely, and for a very similar reason," I continued. "If he had left you for another, then he would surely have required funds with which to start this new life."

I could see immediately that my conclusions had elicited a positive effect on my guest, her breathing slowed, and some colour returned to her cheeks.

"Thank you, Doctor. If you do no more for me than this, then please know that you have provided me with the first words of comfort that I have received since my Hugo vanished."

A smile spread gently across her face. Only a man with a heart dark as coal could fail to be moved by such a beauteous transformation. I felt myself reddening and tried to think of what Holmes might do next. I quickly realised that the only way to make progress would be to visit the scene of this most unusual occurrence.

"I hope to be able to help you further; however, progress will not be made by remaining here in London," I declared. "If it is amenable to you, I should like to visit you tomorrow in

Reddlesham to examine for myself the circumstances under which your husband disappeared."

Mrs. Hill readily agreed and prepared to leave; her spirits much improved. Just before I bade her farewell, a question occurred to me. "May I ask you one more thing? What was it that brought you to London last evening and how did this lead to you staying out the whole night, here in a place so far from the home that you claim to so rarely venture?"

My guest hesitated. A look of confusion crossed her face but was quickly followed by a blink and slow shake of her head.

"I am sorry, Doctor, I should have explained earlier. My husband and I had tickets for a concert this past evening. I was becoming desperate, and I thought that perhaps he might attend. He had booked tickets to be collected at the box office. In my mind, I feared he might be taking someone else, someone new. I just had to know. I took the train into London and made my way to the concert. I asked at the desk for the tickets in my husband's name, secretly both hoping and fearing that they had already been collected. Can you imagine my devastation when two tickets were pressed into my quivering hand?"

"I am sorry to hear that," I replied, quietly.

"What could I do? I was all dressed up, so I continued inside and attended the concert. The music provided a little succour, however, once the performance was over, I again felt empty, scared and alone. I walked around the concert hall until the lights were all finally extinguished. I then took a cab to the station but discovered that I had missed the last train back to Arundel. The stationmaster was a true gentleman and kindly took me in. I passed the time talking to him and his wife over tea and a warm fire. Over the next few hours, I earned their trust and they mine. I finally shared with them my terrible experience and, at that exact moment, the stationmaster, a Mr. Franklyn Flyer, perked up considerably."

"'You must speak to Mr. Holmes, Sherlock Holmes,' he declared."

"He went on to explain how this Sherlock Holmes had solved a terrible mystery on the railway some two years earlier. He claimed he was 'a genius, gifted from above with insights that us mere mortals were not privy to.'"

"That sounds like him," I chuckled.

"So, I pulled myself together, waited until the hour was reasonable, and made my way here. So far, I have not been disappointed," she smiled, weakly. "If you, Doctor, are merely his assistant, then Mr. Holmes, himself, must indeed have formidable powers, almost beyond comprehension."

Unaccustomed to such praise, all I could do was nod and smile warmly. I managed a few more questions before my professional duty of care demanded that I send her home for some much-needed rest. I wished her a safe journey back home, heartened to see that a spark of hope had returned to her eyes.

XIV
Dr Watson Investigates

Once I was alone, I ventured immediately to Holmes' library to conduct some preliminary research. Prior to our latest client's departure, I had requested from her a written list of every detail of her husband's life that she could provide. She had been most cooperative and had furnished me with much data including his full name, date of birth and the names of his last school and university college. She also included the exact years during which he had attended these and even the subjects he studied. It was with these last two institutions that I hoped to make the most progress. However, I thought it prudent to first examine Holmes' records to determine whether they contained anything that might be of help to my nascent investigation.

While Mrs. Hill had revealed that, during their preparations for marriage, she had briefly seen a copy of her husband's birth registration, she admitted that she had not examined it in any detail. However, she added that her husband had made no effort to conceal it from her, it had been available for her to view at any time, in an unlocked drawer in his desk. I had already made a note to examine it when I visited the following day; in a case such as this, confirming his identity was of vital importance. Other than the details she had already provided, Mrs. Hill had little knowledge of her husband's family that she could recount. He was an only child, whose parents had died many years before the couple had first met. She knew of no cousins, and he had never mentioned any other living relatives. This led me to inquire as to whether he was ever evasive when questioned about his family.

Mrs. Hill assured me that he was never agitated by such discussions, in fact, he always replied with the same, slightly wistful, words: "We few Hills have sailed a lonely passage through life." It had been one of his favourite sayings.

Holmes' rather esoteric library contained nothing of obvious relevance. I had remembered to search by Christian name as well as by surname, location as well as subject; Holmes' inconsistencies regarding record-keeping were almost as frustrating as his habit of regularly withholding essential information altogether. I searched by name, date, school and college but nothing appeared to relate to the mysterious Mr. Hill. Satisfied that I had completed my initial due diligence, I retired to the writing desk to compose the first of several letters and telegrams that I hoped might provide some answers.

I wrote two, almost identical, letters; one to Hill's former school, the other to Pemberton, his Cambridge university college. I disguised my true intentions and drafted my missives in the form of requests for character references regarding possible employment. I knew that Holmes had previously employed this method; it allowed for direct and efficient questioning without the risk of raising suspicion.

I then sent two telegrams, firstly to Lestrade, requesting a meeting for lunch to discuss this and our other ongoing case. The second, I addressed to a man whose details Holmes had entrusted to me just before he left to join that infernal club. Although I had no idea as to the true identity of this fellow, or indeed his profession, Holmes had made it clear that he had a great knowledge of the workings of both the government and the underworld. I had little personal experience, and no direct association, with either of these worlds. Without Holmes, I was beginning to realise just how lost and out of my depth I could soon become.

I had summoned one of Holmes' tribe of street urchins to deliver my notes to the telegraph office. As I moved to slip Wiggins a shilling, I paused as a thought struck me. To the boy's initial distress, I took back the silver coin; however, his face lit up when I replaced it with one of a significantly higher denomination.

"What's this for, Doc?" he asked, now smiling eagerly.

"Remember this name – Hugo Hill. Spread it around. If you hear of anything relating to this man, then you must inform me immediately. Any genuine news will be well-rewarded."

Wiggins nodded and left at a pace. I knew it was a long shot, Hill not even being resident in the city, but these youngsters were nothing if not resourceful.

Once Wiggins had departed with my messages, I took to my armchair and filled my pipe. I spent the next couple of hours thinking through the two cases that now occupied my mind. I quickly concluded that I should, for now, focus solely on the Hill affair; a straightforward decision, as our other case was on hiatus until Holmes made contact. I tried to imagine what possible scenarios could have led to the situation in which Mrs. Hill now found herself. To my considerable surprise, several possibilities came swiftly to mind. Although by patient use of logic, alongside Holmes' deductive reasoning, I methodically dismissed these, one by one, I was still encouraged that perhaps I could, after all, unravel the mystery behind this most unusual affair.

At midday, I left for my lunchtime appointment with Lestrade. We had arranged to meet at a small restaurant, close to Scotland Yard. I sat at the front; the large glass window to my right magnifying the weak autumn sun into a pleasant warming glow. The Inspector arrived ten minutes later, looking flustered.

"Many apologies, Doctor. A small problem at the Yard held me up for longer than expected."

"No apologies needed, Inspector," I replied, rising to shake his outstretched hand.

We enjoyed a fine lunch of early-season game bird and finished with strong, dark coffee.

"I managed to make a few enquiries after this Hill character that you say has vanished," revealed Lestrade, unexpectedly, taking a sip of his drink.

"That is wonderful, thank you, Inspector," I replied, leaning forwards in anticipation.

"Don't be so keen to thank me yet, Doctor. I have discovered little, only that the house in which he resides is indeed owned outright by a Mr. Hugo Hill. What might be of some interest is that it was purchased and paid for in cash, some thirty years before the date you gave me for their wedding. Somebody bought the property in his name when he was all but an infant. Other than that, I have yet to discover anything of the man. I have made other inquiries, but it may take a little time before we hear anything."

I, nevertheless, repeated my thanks and urged Lestrade to continue to investigate the affair to the best of his abilities. We spent a further half-hour in idle, but pleasant, conversation before the inspector made his excuses and returned to his duties at the Yard.

I returned to Baker Street and, after spending an hour or so reflecting upon my new case to no avail, decided to completely change tack and refresh my mind by catching up with my diaries and other writings. This had the desired effect, and I was soon tired enough to take a much-needed early night in preparation for the next day's journey.

XV
A House in the Country

I arrived at Arundel's quaint station at just after nine o'clock on a crisp but bright autumn morning. The journey had been pleasant, a relatively short first stage from Victoria to Crawley and then southwest on a branch line of the Brighton and South Coast Railway. As the train left behind the grey and grime of London, I was heartened to be once again in the English countryside. The beauty of the warm gold, russet and bronze leaves on the now swiftly turning trees had raised my spirits and given me confidence that I might just discover something of importance on this expedition.

I climbed aboard one of the handful of cabs waiting at the station and headed off in the direction of the address supplied by Mrs. Hill. The driver seemed to know the place well but upon further questioning admitted that he knew little of its occupants other than the granting of an occasional lift to or from the station.

The Hills' house was located about half a mile outside the village proper. A substantial villa, set back from the road by some twenty yards, it had a slight sense of isolation. The large front garden continued around both sides of the property, giving the whole place the impression of being an island of carefully mown lawn in the sea of uncultivated land that surrounded it. Along the front was a large hedge, over six feet high, which added to the air of privacy that the owners appeared to crave.

Mrs. Hill welcomed me inside, confirming both her independence and the household's paucity of servants. The house was well-kept but simply decorated. My client led me through the hall into the brightly painted front living room. After a few minutes, the housekeeper, a middle-aged lady of fine bearing, brought us some coffee and small sandwiches, for which I was extremely grateful. Mrs. Hill had spent the previous evening collecting together all of her husband's papers and correspondence and had laid these out on a table in several piles, one for each subject matter. I spent the first hour poring over these, hoping to find a clue that might point me toward a reason for his disappearance.

I sighed as I placed the last sheet back upon its pile. I had learned much of Hill's household expenses, and a little of his financial matters, but there was nothing here to indicate that anything was amiss. However, it was what appeared to be missing from these papers that proved to be of the greatest interest.

"Has he no personal correspondence?" I asked, leaning back to address Mrs. Hill, who was waiting patiently, sitting uncomfortably upright upon an armchair, attempting to occupy herself with some sewing.

"I beg your pardon?" she replied, looking up.

"Letters, telegrams, greetings cards? Anything at all from friends, colleagues or family? All that I have here is distinctly impersonal. Did he not have any friends, from his college days, perhaps, with whom he stayed in touch?"

Mrs. Hill paused to consider my question. "Now that you mention it, no. I cannot recall Hugo receiving a single letter or message from anyone other than those that you have before you. He has never spoken of friends and has, as you know, no surviving family."

I reached for a sheet of folded paper from a pile towards the centre of the table. It was a copy of Hill's birth registration. At first glance, all appeared to be in order, yet something about it troubled me. I could not be certain, but I had a distinct impression that it had either been altered or was possibly an entire fabrication. I asked if I could retain the document for a few days. Mrs. Hill readily acceded to my request, adding that I should feel free to take with me anything that may be of help in the search for her husband.

Once I was satisfied that I had missed nothing of value, I asked Mrs. Hill if I could take a look around the house. I concentrated on the areas most often frequented by her husband; his study, and bedroom, along with the garden and outer buildings where he was said to have enjoyed chopping wood and relaxing with a book and pipe. I started at the top of the house and worked downwards. The bedroom was pristine and a thorough search of his drawers and dressing table revealed nothing. Likewise, my examination of his study proved fruitless. In fact, it had the air of a room which was rarely visited. This was confirmed by his wife; it seems that he intensely disliked spending any extended time in the dingy little office.

The garden to the rear of the house was spacious and pleasant, particularly on this bright autumn day. The various sheds and wooden shacks were stocked with nothing more than regular tools and stacks of wood for the winter. After nearly an hour of rooting around the outbuildings and surrounding areas, I took the opportunity to take a seat on a wrought iron-framed wooden bench at the top of the garden, where I rested my legs and filled my pipe. Looking out over the garden and on to the rolling fields opposite, I could not help but feel that this was the very picture of a rural idyll. I lit my briar and attempted to review all that I had learned so far.

After a disconcertingly short time, I realised that the truth was that I had discovered almost nothing. Other than the birth registration, which I was now certain was neither accurate nor genuine, I had to admit that I had failed. Wondering exactly what I would say to Mrs. Hill, I turned back to look at the house where she waited, anxiously hoping for news. It was then that I noticed that the house had a third floor. On this rear aspect, looking right at me, were two gabled dormers, peeping out of the grey slate roof. This meant that there was one final location left to search. I had to momentarily admonish myself. I had not asked Mrs. Hill whether the house had a third floor or an attic; I had simply seen the front of the house and assumed that was all there was to it.

Knocking out the glowing embers of my unfinished pipe, I rushed back inside and asked Mrs. Hill to show me the attic rooms. At first, she seemed surprised; these rooms had not been used since she and her husband had moved in; however, once she realised their possible significance, she quickly located the keys for the upper floor and led me upstairs. At the end of the first-floor corridor, lay a dark wooden door, almost hidden in shadow. My client unlocked the door and gestured for me to climb the narrow, twisting staircase. I climbed carefully up the steep steps and emerged a few moments later into the loft above.

The room in which I found myself was long and low; the pitch of the roof to either side of a central area just high enough to walk through, if I stooped a little. It seemed to stretch the entire length of the house. I could now see to what Mrs. Hill had been alluding; this attic had plainly never been used for anything other than occasional storage. I looked around carefully, the dim light from the pair of dirty windows struggling to penetrate the gloom of the corners of the room.

I almost turned to leave; however, at the very last second, I spotted what appeared to be a dark shape against the far wall. I moved to investigate and found myself looking down at a wooden box, about a foot wide and of a similar height. I carefully lifted it and returned to the landing below.

"Whatever have you found, Doctor?" Mrs. Hill asked, spying the dark shape that I now held before me.

"I am not yet at all certain," I replied.

We returned to the front room, it having the best light at this time of day, and laid the box upon the table by the piles of correspondence. The casket was locked but a combination of my pocket knife, and the memory of an hour's tutelege from Holmes one wet November Sunday afternoon past, were more than enough to gain swift ingress. I opened the lid and peered inside.

The box contained a thick wad of papers, tied with a single purple ribbon, along with some dusty metal artefacts and what appeared to be a selection of children's lead soldiers. I carefully removed the papers, put them to one side and lifted out the small metal figurines. Finally, I withdrew the dust-encrusted metal objects and laid them beside the other contents of the box.

"Well, what have we here?" I inquired. "This little collection certainly appears to be old. Our first and most important task is to ascertain whether it belongs to your husband or is a leftover from a previous owner. It was, after all, hidden away in the depths of shadow. Goodness alone knows how long it has lain there."

This question was answered almost the moment that I carefully removed the ribbon and opened the papers. Amongst the many folded sheets of yellowing paper was a single white envelope. It looked rather out of place amongst the other, much older, documents. Upon the front was a name, carefully written by hand: "Hugo Francis Hill." I turned the envelope over and discovered that it had been sealed with dark red wax. What amazed me was that this seal was intact; the letter had never been opened; its contents never read.

"Oh my!" I spun around to see Mrs. Hill raise her hand to her mouth in surprise. She seemed to momentarily lose her balance and swayed, worryingly. I quickly caught her gently by the arm and guided her into the nearest armchair. I leaned out into the hall and called for a glass of water. The housekeeper appeared in admirably quick time with a full glass and aided Mrs. Hill until some colour had returned to her cheeks.

"Thank you, Janet, you are such a diamond," whispered Mrs. Hill.

"It's nothing, Mrs. Hill." She shot a glance across at the collection laid out upon the table, and I am sure I saw a hint of concern appear fleetingly on her otherwise calm features. Once I was satisfied that my client had quite recovered, I returned to the papers.

"Would you prefer me to take these away with me for now? I would be happy to examine them in private, and report back the moment I have ascertained their full content and meaning."

"Maybe that would be for the best, Doctor. I am quite spent, and another shock right now might push me over the edge," Mrs. Hill smiled, weakly. From what I had already witnessed, Hill would have to be a very rare man indeed to have left this beautiful and charming woman of his own volition. I feared now, more than ever, that foul play must be involved.

I collected up the items and returned them to the box. However, one task still remained, and I had to employ some minor subterfuge in order to achieve my aim. Rather than call for Janet to come and retrieve the glass and plates from earlier, I offered to take them back to the kitchen on my way out, insisting that Mrs. Hill remain seated.

My reasons were as obvious as they indeed appeared. I needed to question the housekeeper away from her mistress. Her reaction to seeing the box and its contents had led me to suspect that she knew something that she had not voluntarily shared with her mistress.

The housekeeper was sitting at the kitchen table, her head in her hands, a disturbed look darkening her face. I decided that this was no time for politeness and, although it went against everything that I believed to be correct when addressing a lady of any class, proceeded in the aggressive style favoured by Holmes.

"Tell me what you know. Now and quickly," I hissed. "If I am satisfied that you have been thorough and honest, I will do everything in my power to ensure that you come to no harm. If you refuse, or I later find out that you have held anything back, I will not be able to protect you from the full force of the law."

The housekeeper froze on the spot, a terrified look flashed upon her face. She began to shake, and I realised that I had made a terrible mistake, poor Janet was far more sensitive than her austere manner would suggest. Mortified, I quickly knelt and attempted to repair the damage my brutal assault had inflicted.

"Please forgive my terrible behaviour," I begged. "This method of forceful interrogation sometimes produces results when used on the intransigent." I rushed to the sink and returned with a glass of water which was readily accepted.

"No, Doctor Watson, you are right," she sniffed. "I do know something more about this affair. I wish I had the courage to tell Mrs. Hill, but I took an oath never to share with her what I know."

"Then share it with me," I replied, as kindly as I could.

Janet paused for a moment, seemingly battling some internal conflict, before finally composing herself.

"I have known Mr. Hill for nearly thirty years. Yes, that is correct, almost his entire life. When I became the housekeeper, here in Reddlesham, Mr. Hill made it clear that I was never to disclose that I had any previous knowledge of him. The truth is that I have barely left his side in those previous three decades."

"So, you knew his family, his parents?" I asked.

Janet's head dropped. She let out a long sigh and suddenly looked terribly old, sad and vulnerable.

"I never met Mr. Hill, senior, nor Hugo's mother." She spoke the words slowly and deliberately. "However, I raised him, all the same, from infant to grown man." There was a glint of defiance in her eyes, or was it the fierce protection of a surrogate mother?

"How did this singular situation arise?" I asked, gently.

"I was young and inexperienced but keen to find work." The housekeeper paused as if to collect and order her thoughts. She dabbed at her eyes with a handkerchief, before continuing. "I answered an advertisement in the evening paper for a full-time nanny and housekeeper. I attended an interview, where I was surprised to be questioned not by parents but by two solicitors. They explained that the child's parents were working abroad and that I would be expected to attend to all of his needs while also running a household. The money that they offered was more than fair, so I accepted."

"After a few weeks, I had established a workable routine but was in need of a few essential items. I wrote to the solicitors, as this was the only contact information that had been provided. Within three days all that I requested had been delivered."

"Fascinating," I remarked.

"Yes, indeed. At first, I simply assumed that this was a regular appointment and the little one's parents would reappear at any moment. However, after six months had passed, I realised that something wasn't quite right. It was small things, at first. I received no correspondence; but who would write to a two-year-old child? Christmas came and went with no contact other than an extra payment, which arrived from the solicitors, to cover 'reasonable decorations to the enhancement of one room and a gift for the child.'"

"My Goodness, I think I see," I replied, the realisation growing inside me. "The poor child."

"I did what I could, but I am not his mother." Janet's face was filled with shame and regret, neither of which I believed was deserved.

"But you did so well, Janet Medcalf," came a quiet voice from behind us. "The boy you raised became a good, decent man."

I turned quickly towards the source. Standing at the kitchen doorway was Mrs. Hill. Her eyes were red with tears, but a wide smile spread across her soft face.

"I am sorry to eavesdrop, Doctor, but I had to hear what you both knew. When it comes to finding Hugo, I will obey no rules nor yield to manners." Her defiance was as impressive as her determination.

"There is one more tale to tell," the housekeeper disclosed, breaking the momentary silence. "On the day Master Hill turned twenty-one, there came a delivery. A man arrived, bearing that box. It was locked up tight. There was no note and not a word of explanation. A few days later he received a letter. There was no address, just Master Hill's name written on the envelope. I was the one who handed it to him. I held it for just a moment, but it was clear that it contained a metal key. He took it and opened it there in front of me. To his surprise, a key was all that was within, no note of explanation. He went straight to the box and opened it.

He looked inside, rummaged around a little and removed some papers and those little toy soldiers. Then, suddenly, he threw the contents back inside and slammed shut the lid. He turned the key in the lock, withdrew it and walked to the front door. He pulled the door open and then flung the key as far as he could, turning back into the house long before the key hit the ground. He had no care to know where it might have landed."

"What happened then?" I asked, genuinely intrigued.

"He took the box upstairs and hid it in the loft. When he returned downstairs, his manner had changed and he was once more his usual self, relaxed and amiable. His final words on the subject were to make me promise that I would never mention this incident or the existence of the box or that sealed letter to anyone."

"And this was the last you heard of the matter?" I asked, carefully.

Janet nodded sadly, struggling to form words.

"I must examine these papers carefully," I declared. "Most appear to be legal documents, regarding property and other related matters. Many look, and feel, extremely old; I feel certain that at least some of the sheets are vellum or parchment. What isn't scribed in Latin appears to be written in a form of English that might be more familiar to Shakespeare or even Chaucer, than to myself. However, I do know people who can make sense of such writings. It may take a few days, but I promise to return with all the knowledge that can be ascertained from these documents."

Feeling assured that Mrs. Hill was in good, supportive company, I left Reddlesham and caught a late afternoon train back to London. Before returning to Baker Street, I took a detour to the British Museum library. There, I dropped off the documents at the office of Professor Gorton Lythlands. Lythlands was a renowned legal historian who had aided us through the course of several investigations. I was confident that he would be of great help in making sense of the enigmatic archaic scribblings.

A thickly bespectacled young secretary guided me to the professor's office, hidden deep among the maze of corridors that snaked through the cavernous library. The way the academic's eyes instantly lit up, and the wide beaming smile that appeared on his face when he saw the rolls of browning papers, proved that my assumptions had been correct. His promise to send a message as soon as he had any conclusions to offer, ensured that I left in good spirits and enthusiastically completed my journey home to Baker Street on foot.

Although the day had been long, I climbed the stairs to our apartment with energy and purpose. The half-hour walk from the museum library had ensured that I was eagerly looking forward to my evening meal and then perhaps a cigar alongside a glass of brandy. I opened the door and strode into the living room, where I was startled to discover Inspector Lestrade slumped motionless in one of our armchairs.

XVI
The Newsagent's Puzzle

At first, I felt a rush of concern for the good inspector, slouched and silent; however, once I observed his chest rising and falling to the rhythm of his muted snoring, I smiled, hung my hat and coat, and prepared two glasses of brandy and cigars. Clutching the drinks, I made a none-too-subtle siren signal by clicking the glasses together. This had the desired effect, and Lestrade's head rose as he awoke with a snort.

"Good evening, Inspector," I smiled, handing him a glass. "I do hope you have not been waiting long."

"A thousand apologies, Doctor, I must have nodded off. It has been a long and busy day." He took the brandy, gratefully.

"First things first, Inspector. Have you eaten? I was about to call down for a light supper, you are more than welcome to join me."

We dined well upon cold cuts and new potatoes, finishing with cheese and water biscuits. Once finished, we retired to the living room with the cigars and fortifying brandy. Lestrade reached inside his jacket, withdrew a letter and handed it to me. I looked at the envelope and frowned. It was addressed to a local newsagent in block capitals, which gave away little information. I opened it and pulled out the letter inside. It was written on cheap halfpenny paper, the sort that could be purchased anywhere in the country. The writing was precise, well-formed and strangely

144

familiar. The ink was, again, cheap and readily available from any stationer. I thought it best to read the letter aloud so that we could both hear its contents.

"'Dear Sirs,

I am writing to request the temporary cancellation of my subscription to the Times newspaper, as of today. I am currently holidaying in the HIghlands and have sourced a local supply, here in Glenthistle. Once I return to London, I will call upon you on the nth to resume my subscription.

Yours in best faith,

Dr. Arthur C. Brownlands
Un Cst'."

"It was delivered to me by the newsagent himself, this afternoon," Lestrade confirmed. "The fellow insisted that it was an important message from Sherlock Holmes. To be honest, at first, I thought it to be a prank, or worse, but the man insisted that Holmes had taken him into his confidence after the shopkeeper had aided him in solving a particularly sensitive problem some years earlier. He claimed that Holmes had made a simple request: should he ever receive a message from an 'Arthur Brownlands,' he must take it immediately to Inspector Lestrade of Scotland Yard."

"Brownlands! Of course, that is the name he gave when he joined that wretched club. I knew I recognised that writing. He has certainly made a concerted effort here, his usual handwriting verges on the illegible."

"Now we just have to decode the meaning of the message," I added, again peering intently at the writing.

"In that case, surely it is simple. He is in the Highlands, at this Glenthistle place. I shall fetch a map from his library." Lestrade rose and began to search for an appropriate chart from the pile of maps that lay upon one of Holmes' cluttered shelves.

"I am not so sure," I hummed, as I re-read the letter several times. "He has taken great care in disguising the nature of the message and even its ultimate intended recipient. He fully expected the letter would be intercepted and read at some point. Moreover, I believe that he probably had to hand the letter over for approval before it was dispatched. The writing on the envelope does not match that of the letter within; see, the capital A, D, G and T, all are different. This letter has been thoroughly examined and only when its contents were approved, was it sealed, addressed and finally posted by an agent of this organisation. If he had included any sensitive information, then his very life would have been at risk. If he simply wanted to cancel his newspaper, he need not mention the location of his holiday and yet he does. This indicates to me that this location is a blind, intended to show the illicit reader that he could be trusted. He purposely lies about where he is to prove that the message is innocent."

"Do you know what, Doctor? I think you could well be right," replied Lestrade, his nose deep in a rather beautiful large-scale map of Scotland. "This is the most comprehensive map of our northern neighbours that I could find and there is not a single town, village, estate, farm or even bothy named 'Glenthistle'."

"So, where is he?" I pondered aloud.

"I did notice one thing unusual about the letter," Lestrade said, folding and returning the map. "That bit about calling on the 'nth'. Sounds like something you would note mentally for clarification later, not something that you would actually write down."

"Quite right. What else could it mean? North, I suppose," I replied, speculatively.

"Wait a minute," I declared. "What about these letters of achievement below his name? They don't look quite right. 'Un' – university? University of where? 'CST', where could that be? It isn't Cambridge or Canterbury."

"Chichester, Cirencester?" suggested Lestrade, hopefully.

"I think it is a clue. This is not the correct way of presenting such things and, in any case, why on Earth would he feel the need to inform his newsagent of his academic position? No, I am certain that it is a code."

"I have to agree with you. One thing that does strike me, though, is that if this is a code and if Holmes intended it to be read by myself..." Lestrade trailed off. He seemed to be embarrassed to complete his statement.

"Whatever is the matter, Inspector?"

"Well, he has a rather, ah, low opinion of my intellectual qualities. So, if he did set a code, intended to be broken by myself, then he would surely not have made it this difficult!"

I smiled and laid a reassuring hand on the inspector's shoulder.

"Do not take it personally, old chap. To Holmes, everybody is intellectually inferior. At least you have an occasional respite from it, whereas I am reminded of my failings on an almost daily basis."

This cheered Lestrade, considerably. We took a break, topped up our glasses, re-filled our pipes and then took a fresh look at the letter.

"'Yours, in best faith'? That is also rather unusual. Not 'yours faithfully' or 'best regards.' Does 'faith' perhaps hint at an ecclesiastical building?" Lestrade pondered, passing the letter back to me.

"Quite possibly," I nodded.

I was concentrating hard on the last two lines when suddenly inspiration hit.

"Wait a minute, this contraction of Doctor is not quite right. Holmes has used the American form with a full stop after the 'r.' He must be deliberately drawing attention to these letters."

"What if it is, just as you thought, deliberately simple?" I wondered aloud. "That would make it, let me see."

"'D', 'R', 'U', 'N'," I spelt the letters one by one. "Or 'Drun' if spoken as one word. What could 'CST' mean? 'Colchester'? No, that doesn't make sense."

"How about 'castle'?" asked Lestrade, excitedly. "I am sure that there is a 'Drun Castle' somewhere!"

We rushed to Holmes' library. Lestrade again searched through maps while I found his volume on the letter 'D.'

Almost instantaneously we both looked up and declared, "Drun Castle!"

"Located on the northeast coast in Druncaster Bay, Northumbria. That's what he meant by 'nth,'" I said, shaking my head in appreciation of Holmes' simple but effective code.

"There is a chapel in the grounds, a church within a hundred yards and a ruined Abbey within half a mile. I would bet a month's wages that he is in one of these," added Lestrade, excitedly pointing to each location on his map.

"Yes, the ecclesiastical building. He was taking a risk by hiding 'Drun Castle' in plain sight. I suppose, if discovered, he could claim it was a simple coincidence and still have some level of deniability as it does not give away their exact location."

"There is one more detail that still troubles me," I added. "'Arthur C Brownlands.' The initial. That part is new, I am certain that he never used it before. What could it mean?"

"The sea?" suggested Lestrade. "All of these features are within half a mile of the coast. Or perhaps it is strictly literal – see, as in 'come and see'?"

"All of the important information regarding his location is hidden in these last three lines, so I suspect that your second theory is the most likely. Then it is settled, we must leave for Northumbria in the morning," I concluded with confidence.

"That might not be quite so simple for myself," replied Lestrade, cautiously. "I am currently engaged in three separate cases, not including this affair. I cannot just up and leave at a moment's notice. I am sorry, Doctor, but you will have to travel without me, and I will follow as soon as I am able. I will aim to take a train up on Thursday noon at the latest."

"I quite understand, I will keep you fully informed until you can join me. At last, we now have a plan of action. However, tomorrow is another day. Another brandy, Inspector?"

XVII
The Trail Leads North

The first post arrived as I was preparing to leave to catch the early train to Newcastle. Of greatest interest was a letter from Professor Lythlands, informing me of the progress that he had made. He gave little detail but promised that he would have significant news in a day or two. If all went well, I hoped to be back in London not long after the delivery of his impending revelations.

I arrived at King's Cross in good time and boarded the eight o'clock train bound for the North-east. I settled down in a first-class carriage with the morning's papers. It was a good five hours before we would reach Newcastle and from there a further hour on the branch line to Alnwick. Once there, a long journey by carriage lay ahead of me. It would be late afternoon or early evening before I arrived in the little town of Druncaster Bay and could begin my search for Sherlock Holmes.

A combination of concern for my friend, coupled with the effects of the previous evening spent in the company of the good inspector, meant that I passed the journey in equal measure of inattentive reading and restive sleep. The aching beauty of the east coast of England was lost on me, as we rushed through the autumn countryside. I woke briefly, as we stopped to take on water and coal, but the final two hours flew by in welcome oblivion. I very nearly missed my stop altogether, only a timely shake of the shoulder from an alert conductor saved me from acute embarrassment and an unexpected trip to Edinburgh.

I had a half-hour wait but then, right on time, the small branch line train steamed into view. Progress was painfully slow, as we stopped at each and every station, but my patience was rewarded after I struck up a friendly conversation with a passenger in an adjacent seat. It transpired that if I remained on the train for a further three stops beyond Alnwick, I could alight at a village just three miles from Druncaster Bay.

I was heartened to reach the quaint fishing village while there was still plenty of light to enjoy the approach. The local inn afforded reasonable accommodation, so I took a room for two nights. I enjoyed a quick supper, before taking an early evening walk to find my bearings. The wan autumn sunlight cast long shadows across the streets, but the hamlet's compact nature made navigation fairly simple. A shingle bay arched around from north to south, the lower end protected by protruding sea walls encompassing a small harbour. The local fleet was preparing for a night of fishing; swinging lamps and laughter filled the air. Whitewashed cottages lined the seafront. A steep road led inland, past the inn, leading up to the long-dissolved abbey. High above, and dark against the evening sky, loomed the cracked and broken crenellations of Drun Castle.

I had just enough daylight left to reach the abbey and walk its circumference. One end still survived almost intact, the high gothic arches and windows now sadly gaping open without their coloured glass. It was a sad sight, made more melancholy by the soft rays of the harvest sun. As the light faded, the warm stone turned cold and skeletal. A chill wind rose from the sea, and I headed back to the warmth of the 'Aad Galloway' Inn.

There were few patrons inside, even in the public bar. I ordered a brandy and sat at the bar, hoping to strike up a conversation with anyone who approached. Those that did shuffle up to the serving counter were either too far gone to impart any coherent information or unwilling to even acknowledge my greetings. I sighed and finished my drink. I was about to leave when the landlord reappeared, offered me the first smile I had encountered in the village and asked if I would care for one more "for the road." As my "road" was simply the stairs to an upper room, this amused me somewhat, so I agreed and asked if he would join me.

The landlord poured two over-large measures and slid one towards me.

"So, what brings you here? You must be looking for something, although you are wasting your time asking these poor sops here."

The landlord, whose name was Moorclough, was a fascinating-looking fellow. One-eyed and heavily scarred, his face was as crinkled as old leather and nearly as dark. It was clear that he had spent many years at sea, his tattooed forearms and the holes in his earlobes spoke of a hard life, one lived across many oceans.

I paused for a moment before replying. Holmes always insisted that a lie should be surrounded by as much truth as possible. This made it both easier to recall and more convincing when spoken.

"I am looking for a friend of mine. He recently took up with some unsavoury types and I fear that he may have been led here against his will."

I gave a brief description of Holmes, deliberately avoiding any mention of his name or the alias he had used. It was always possible that he had introduced himself hereabouts with a different identity, one as yet unknown to ourselves.

"Tall, gaunt, pale fellow you say?" grinned the landlord. "Can't say that I have seen him. Fella like that would stand out, mind you."

Moorclough looked around, aimlessly, and took to a tuneless whistling. It took me a few moments before I suddenly realised the game he was playing. I searched my pocket and took out a shilling. Before I could offer it, Moorclough shook his head dismissively. This riled me, so I returned the coin and replaced it with a sovereign. I held it before me, just out of the old salt's reach.

"This is a one-time-only offer. You tell me all that you know, and I will decide if you have earned this coin. If I feel that you left out anything, or I suspect that you have lied in any way, then you will receive nothing. Agreed?"

The old sailor smiled, then shrugged but nodded his consent. "I have nothing to hide here and nothing to lose. I am but a retired seaman, barely scraping a living here in this, what would you call it? This purgatory? I have seen a hundred countries and lived a hundred lives, yet now I am cursed to spend my final years as a landlocked barkeep."

His laughter at this final remark was sad and hollow, it rather reminded me of the plaintive cries of the animals held captive behind the bars of London's zoological gardens.

"I have seen your man," he whispered, leaning towards me. "He was with that bunch that moved into old Highbay Manor."

"Where can I find this Highbay Manor?" I demanded, excitedly.

"Just follow the bay north and take the last road inland. Keep your eyes open, as it's not much more than a track nowadays. Nobody's been up there for years. Last I heard, the roof was falling in, heaven only knows what they could want with the place."

Further questioning revealed nothing more of interest and once I was convinced that the old seaman had told me all he had to tell, I passed over the coin and retired to my room. For a while, I attempted to plan a course of action for the next day; however, I soon concluded that all I could do was approach my target with caution and be prepared for any eventuality.

I woke before dawn, after a troubled night's sleep. I ventured downstairs and was heartened to see that the landlord had kept his promise of providing an early breakfast. A table was laid with a basic meal of bread, ham and salted fish. Not wishing to waste any time, I gathered up the food in a large napkin and stowed it in my shoulder bag for later. Feeling as prepared as I could possibly be, I headed out into the dark morning air.

XVIII
Highbay Manor

Small veins of navy blue and dark burgundy were beginning to appear in the inky black sky. I estimated that dawn was still an hour away. There was barely enough light by which to navigate, the clear starlit sky was a blessing, but it meant that the air was icy cold, made worse by a chill breeze from the sea. I slapped my gloved hands together in an attempt to generate some warmth, glad that I had packed my warm outdoor clothes and stout boots.

Cautiously, I made my way down the steep hill to the seafront, liberally using my stick as much for testing the lay of the ground ahead as for support. Once opposite the small harbour and out of the shadows of the buildings, visibility improved dramatically. I strode along the road which followed the curve of the bay, some twenty yards up from the beach. In addition to my stick, I also carried a pair of field glasses, their hard, leather box slung around my neck. If spotted, I hoped I might be taken for a simple tourist, a walker out looking to spot the early morning birds, perhaps. The reassuring weight in my right pocket indicated that my last line of defence was present and easily accessible.

I pounded onwards for about twenty minutes, before beginning to seriously investigate the hedgerows, scrub and unkempt fields to my left. Surely any sort of track would be easily spotted along such an unwelcoming stretch of twisted branches and marshy grassland. My hubris was very nearly punished as I came within a footstep of missing the turning entirely.

A further ten minutes had passed, and the sky had lightened enough to allow me to see the whole of the bay and surrounding countryside with relative ease. It was while enjoying this most pleasant vista that I strode past the small and overgrown track. It was only the sound of a rustle in the hedgerow to my left that made my head turn. Out of the black tangle thrust a young gamebird, all brown feathers and madly flapping wings. Momentarily startled, I took a step backwards before laughing aloud at my excitability.

It was only then that I saw the path. It was indeed perilously easy to overlook, just a small gap in a particularly large and undulating thicket. A scattering of broken branches and leaves showed that someone had recently passed, or to be more precise, forced their way through.

Having no time for subtlety, I smashed my way through with my stick, hoping that I was still far enough from the manor to remain unheard. I needn't have worried as, once through the thick tangled barrier, the path opened up and before me lay a clear path stretching several hundred yards upwards towards a small crest. Highbay Manor must lie just beyond sight, I imagined. It was time to proceed with extreme caution.

I moved swiftly, trying to keep as much cover as possible between myself and the ridge ahead. When I found a clump of short, wind-battered trees, I slipped between them and removed my field glasses from their case. The light was improving by the minute, dawn could only be half an hour away, at most. I swept my magnified gaze across the looming outcrop. Although I could see no sign of life, I decided to remain in place for five further minutes as a matter of caution. Still, nothing appeared to move, so I re-joined the path and broke into a quick march, of the type designed to cover large distances at speed. So far, thankfully, my injuries had not made themselves known, and I was determined that they would not undermine me. Thus, I kept my pace steady, refusing to give in to anxiety.

After a surprisingly short time, I found myself cresting the ridge, half-bent to disguise my silhouette against the brightening sky behind me. At the very top, I crouched down and again took stock of my position. I could now see clearly, some two hundred yards ahead, the remains of Highbay Manor. Even at its height, it would have been no more than a grand farmhouse, handsome enough and commanding glorious views across the countryside and out to sea. Now, sadly, it was half gone to ruin. The roof had indeed collapsed in the centre, a black hole in the tiles gaped like the unspeakable maw of a dark, deep-sea creature. The grey stone walls were almost entirely covered with snake-like tendrils as nature fought to take back its territory. Those windows which still held glass were all cracked and broken, the remaining shards stood out from the frames like shattered teeth.

It was clear to me that nobody could possibly be living here, let alone a group of men more used to the comforts of a London club. I raised myself to my knees and began to stand up when a strangely familiar whizzing sound and change of pressure rushed past my ear. Instinct immediately took over and I dropped back towards the ground. An instant after the peculiar noise, I heard the predictable crack of a rifle being discharged.

The memories stormed back into my mind; I was once again under hostile fire. I was surprised to discover that the overwhelming emotion that I felt at this point was not fear but anger. Raw, primordial anger. How dare they open fire on me? Enraged and now almost out of control, I grabbed my revolver and returned fire, at first from a kneeling position. I let off two rounds towards where the rifleman was secreted, the flash and smoke from his gun were now visible in the soft morning light.

A further whiz and crack of a passing round showed that the gunman was still active and beyond the range of my pistol. Rather than retreat, the red mist of anger led me to charge directly at the house, darting left and right, keeping whatever cover I could find between myself and the man intent on killing me. Fortunately for me, it seemed that the man behind the rifle was far from an expert, and evidently not a military man, for I was soon within twenty yards of the house. I ducked behind the upended stump of a tree and loosed off two further rounds into the house. I used the relative safety of my position to take the time to reload. I had two dozen cartridges in my bag; I was prepared for a battle of attrition.

Two rounds thumped into the packed earth in front of me. Using the raised cloud of dust and debris as cover, I unleashed four rounds directly at the source of the shooting. I ducked back down and replaced the spent bullets. I waited for a minute but there was no reply. Had one of my bullets found a target? I waited longer. After five minutes I could wait no more. I fired twice and ran towards the right side of the house. This appeared to offer a safer route inside, a door hung open and I could see enough within to be certain that the room was empty. In a few seconds, I was inside.

I crouched low, pistol held before me. The house was silent. I was beginning to suspect that my tormentor had already fled, but I could not afford to take a single risk. I moved from room to room until I happened upon the position from where my adversary had been shooting. To the satisfaction of a base, primaeval part of my mind, there appeared a small trail of blood leading from just below the window and out towards the back of the house. I had clipped the villain's wings. I rushed towards the rear of the building, out through an open door and saw, in the field beyond, a figure limping and stumbling. He was already a hundred yards away, a difficult shot with a pistol. I raised my arm and took careful aim.

A moment later, my arm dropped. I could not bring myself to shoot a man in the back, however, provoked I had been. Instead, with my adrenaline falling and my breathing slowing, I watched him carefully until he was out of sight. At that exact moment, my knees gave way and I slumped to the ground.

Being both a doctor and military veteran, I immediately recognised the symptoms of shock and took immediate action. I retreated to the house and quickly found enough wood and kindling to start a small fire. As I warmed myself, I forced down the breakfast of bread, ham and salted fish that Moorclough had provided. Within fifteen minutes, I had regained my composure and was ready to continue.

I briefly considered following the gunman, his trail would be simple enough to follow but quickly thought better of it. He must be heading towards his colleagues for aid, and I had no doubt that they would also be armed. I knew neither the lay of the land nor the number of foes I might be facing. There was also the distinct possibility that once the rest of the gang discovered the injured man, they would send men back to the manor to dispose of a possibly troublesome witness to their schemes. The man had been left at the manor to scare off any sightseers who might wander too close. A shot over their heads would deter almost anyone; the fact that I not only failed to run but returned fire and effectively taken the manor from its defender would surely trouble the gunman's colleagues, deeply. I concluded that I should inspect the house as best I could, before retreating to the safer environs of the village.

It took only a brief examination to confirm that Highbay Manor had not been lived in for many a year. The ground floor had, however, been utilised recently, but for what purpose? The floor had been cleared and the rooms showed signs of having contained large items, cases or crates, stored and moved around within the past few weeks. I took out my notebook and made as accurate notes as I could. I even took to drawing what marks were visible upon the floor, in the hope that Holmes might be able to make sense of these once we were reunited.

I returned to my fire and there, once I had poked it back into life, took a moment to take stock of my situation. Despite the leads proffered and the hopes they promised, I was no closer to finding my friend. Feeling rather dispirited, I extinguished the fire and trudged back to Druncaster Bay.

XIX
Mr Moorclough

I reached the Inn just before opening time, fully expecting to be the first customer of the day. To my surprise, several locals were already settled in their seats. If I had not passed through this very room to collect my early breakfast, I would have sworn that these patrons had not moved a single inch since the previous evening. Moorclough held court behind the bar, polishing a glass with a none-too-clean-looking cloth.

"Any luck, Doctor?" he asked, in a hushed, conspiratorial tone as I reached the wooden counter. He then leaned forward and took a sniff of my jacket.

"I know well the smell of firearms, Doctor. What, in the name of heaven, happened up there? What have you done?" Despite his appearance of world-weariness, the old sailor looked genuinely shaken.

I had no option but to offer some sort of explanation. Somehow, I felt that I could trust Moorclough with the truth or, at least, a small part of it.

"I found the manor, just as you directed. However, as I approached, a fellow inside, armed with a rifle, took a shot at me. I took cover and returned fire, just a couple of rounds. He scarpered pretty sharply, once he realised that I was not quite the sitting duck that he believed."

"Looks like you had a lucky escape," replied the landlord.

"But why would a doctor be needing a gun?" he added. "I have half a mind to call on the local constable, something here is very wrong indeed."

The thought of this grizzled old tar being a conscientious citizen almost made me laugh aloud, but, somehow, it endeared him further to me. I was now convinced that my initial instinct, that he could be trusted, was indeed correct.

Sensing that I might be close to feeling able to confide in him, Moorclough decided to take the initiative.

"Doctor Watson, I have been landlord here for nearly three years. Any of these layabouts would testify to this truth if you could get their faces out of their drinks. I work from dawn 'til midnight every day; rain, storm or shine."

Moorclough leaned closer and continued in a lower tone. "The men you seek appeared only in the last few weeks; they are certainly not local. They do not shop, drink, nor stay in the village. They slip through like phantoms, at dusk or dawn, most here have never even seen them in the flesh. People 'round here want no trouble, so they ignore them."

"You are from London as, I believe, are they," he continued. "Whatever schemes they have concocted and in whatever mess your friend has found himself, they were all plotted and planned hundreds of miles away from our little cove."

"I think I have proved that I am not one with your enemies, sir, but I must admit that I offer my assistance for purely selfish reasons," Moorclough grinned.

"Ah, I see," I sighed and reached inside my jacket for my wallet.

Moorclough held up his hands in admonishment. "No, Doctor, not that, not that at all." His smile was as wide as the bay, and just as weather-worn.

"Look around you," he exclaimed, his arms now wide. "This is now my life. The thought of being able to aid you in this adventure, to right wrongs and rescue a kidnapped man? This is what I have dreamed of these many long days. That is my selfish intent."

We retreated to the empty saloon bar, where Moorclough lit a welcome fire beneath the ancient stone inglenook. He returned to the bar to serve another early customer but soon returned clutching a brace of glasses liberally filled with whisky. I briefly explained a simplified version of the case so far, while Moorclough listened in increasingly wide-eyed silence.

Once I had reached the present and recounted my adventure up on the ridge, I sat back and took a large sip of the amber spirit. It was smoky, with a hint of sweetness, much finer than I had been expecting.

"That is quite the tale, Doctor Watson. In fact, I would say that it is so unbelievable, so outrageous and so unlikely that it simply must be the truth." Moorclough grinned, widely.

"I would quite understand if you still felt the need to contact the local constabulary," I admitted. "They should be able to wire Inspector Lestrade in Scotland Yard. He will certainly vouch for me. I am also hopeful that he may be able to join us here at the weekend."

"Ah, Doctor, I think we may already be well past that point. It is still two days before that inspector pal of yours deigns us worthy of his presence; we must do everything in our power to ensure that we have something worthwhile to show him."

Moorclough's enthusiasm should have buoyed me, but I was becoming convinced that I had reached a dead end. Even with an extra man, I did not feel confident enough to return to Highbay Manor, let alone risk a further expedition to trace the route of the injured villain.

"Do you happen to have your missing friend's coded letter with you?" asked Moorclough, breaking the silence that had descended.

"Why, yes I do," I replied, unsure as to his intent. "Would you like me to fetch it?"

Moorclough nodded and took a swig from his glass. I quickly climbed the stairs to my room, located the single sheet and returned to the now comfortably warm lounge. As I re-took my seat, I noticed with a wry smile that our glasses had been refilled. I opened the folded page and passed it to the landlord.

For the next twenty minutes, the grizzled former sailor pored over Holmes' mysterious missive. Occasionally he would grunt an affirmation or ask for clarification, but mostly he would just stare at the paper.

"I would say you have done pretty well here, Doctor. He was certainly taking a risk with 'Drun Castle' hidden in plain sight but for the rest? I think you have interpreted it as well as any could have been asked."

"The truth is," continued my host, with a distinct glint in his eye. "In the past, I may have been involved in the occasional venture which was not entirely, shall we say, 'officially sanctioned.'"

"If I do not ask, you need not explain," I replied with a subtle smile.

"From time to time, we also had need of communicating in a way that would say one thing but mean quite another," explained Moorclough. "Just like your man, here." He pointed at the single sheet of paper lying between us.

"This is the most difficult kind of coded message, one where there has been no previously agreed method to its construction or its solution. The trick here is to hide the secrets in a way that a casual reader would simply fail to notice anything unusual at all in the message. Only one who is really looking with intent will see the clues, the hidden signposts."

I was beginning to wonder exactly what adventures Moorclough had seen to be such an expert at this kind of subterfuge. However, I did welcome his confirmation of the deductions made by Lestrade and myself.

"There is just one thing, though," he added.

"Which is?" I asked a tad abruptly.

"Here, look. This sentence. Do you not see?" He pointed with a gnarled and scarred finger.

"I am currently holidaying in the HIghlands and have located a local supply, here in Glenthistle," I read aloud. "I have been over this statement hundreds of times, I can see no more that might be hidden. There is no Glenthistle and nothing else points to the Highlands."

"Look closely at the letters, man. What do you see?" he growled, impatience growing in his manner.

"Look here," I began, "I have been as open and..." I suddenly stopped. "Wait a moment. I see it now. 'HIghlands'. The second letter, 'i' has been capitalised. That is not a mistake that Sherlock Holmes would make."

My heart raced and the morning's stress and tiredness fell away.

"What could it mean? Stress on the 'i'?" I suggested. "Ighlands? Islands! That must be it!"

"Aye, Doctor, that is what I would also conclude. He is on an Island, somewhere close. We cannot discount the 'H' though. We are, after all, not a huge distance from Holy Island."

"Could that be the answer? Holy Island?" I was now shaking with excitement.

Moorclough considered this for a while, then shook his head.

"No, it's too far. Lindisfarne is over twenty miles north. It is also far too well known, rarely free of pilgrims and can still be reached by foot at low tide. No place to hide a conspiracy. But there are plenty of other small islands that might fit the bill."

I waited in anticipation as Moorclough took a long draught, swallowed and sat back, a large grin spreading across his crisscross-scarred face.

"Four miles east of this town, lies a group of small islands. They are surrounded by low-lying rocks and terrible tides. The local fishermen all give them a wide berth. On the chart, they are called the Isles of St. Mary, but here, locally, we call them the 'Hateful Islands'."

XX
A Way Through

Before the effects of the whisky became too great, I retreated to my room where I wrote a letter to Lestrade, detailing all which I had learned. I passed this to the young lad who helped out around the inn. He promised it would be on the evening carriage to Alnwick. With a bit of luck, it would be in London the following afternoon. I then took a much-needed lunch, followed by a late afternoon nap.

I returned to the saloon bar shortly after five in the early evening. To my surprise and delight, Moorclough had covered our table with a large-scale map of the northeast of England, folded to highlight the region surrounding our very location. Just to the east was, indeed, a group of jagged-edged islands, few of which were more than a hundred yards across. In the centre, almost surrounded by these rocks, was St. Mary Island herself. Five hundred by three hundred yards and the site of a long-abandoned monastery. It was said that a small chapel still stood, defiantly battling the elements, but this had not seen a service in decades. The landward approach was treacherous, so much so that the island was finally abandoned, seemingly forever, more than two hundred years ago.

"The silly fools never saw what was right in front of them," growled Moorclough, appearing suddenly from the hallway.

"Look here," Moorclough pointed to the east side of the island group. "All you need to do is sail around to the far side of the islands and there is a clear way in. Not only that but there is also a small beach here on the east coast of St. Mary Island. A perfect landing spot."

"So why has it had such a terrible reputation for so long?" I asked.

"Seems it has always been a bolthole for smugglers, pirates and other ne'er-do-wells. I expect the locals learned to look the other way; for an appropriate fee, of course."

"I fear you are correct, sir," I replied. "But how do we get to this island? Tonight," I added, with renewed vigour.

"Hold yer horses, Doc!" laughed Moorclough. "I will have a look around tomorrow, ask if there's any a boat free. But don't get your hopes up, this is a working town, the only serviceable boats are out fishing most nights. More likely to find something suitable at the weekend, I reckon."

"And we might also have Inspector Lestrade for company by then," I agreed. "We will need all the strength we can muster; these villains have guns and no qualms about using them."

I leaned in closer to my host. "Do you have a gun I might borrow? Even if the inspector brings his revolver, I would certainly feel more comfortable with a second, loaded firearm in reserve."

"I am sorry, Doctor, I do indeed own one or two guns, purely for defensive purposes, you understand, but I cannot let you take these with you."

"Very well," I grunted. "How much do you want for them?"

"Again, you misunderstand, Doctor. You will not be carrying my guns for the simple reason that they will be carried by me." Moorclough's grin was as welcome as it was quietly disconcerting.

I spent the remainder of the evening studying the charts and conversing with Moorclough. He may have lived a questionable past life; however, I now believed him to be, at heart, a man of honour. He was also a man of action and the prospect of one final great adventure had him running around the inn like a spaniel pup. I smoked my final pipe of the evening at nine and headed upstairs for an early night.

XXI
The Inspector Calls

My sleep was troubled; fear that Holmes might be in distress alternated with images and sounds of battles past and present. I woke early the next morning and resolved to make the best use of the day. Not willing to spend the day waiting idly for news of Moorclough's attempts to find us a vessel, I set forth along the bay, again following the coast path northwards, this time in the hope that it might eventually rise, turn and allow me some sort of view over Highbay Manor. I was desperate to find some viewpoint from where I could observe both the house and the sea, one rather less perilous than the previous day's approach. After less than half of an hour, I passed the turning that I had so nearly missed the previous morning. As a result of my rather extravagant handiwork, the trail was now clear and visible once more. I continued around the headland at the end of the bay and saw that the path did indeed turn inland, but never rose more than twenty yards above the level of the shore. I briefly thought of returning to the inn; however, realising that it would be a waste to spend the entire morning awaiting the return of the local fishing fleet, I decided to ascend the ridge from this side, hoping that the thick foliage might afford me enough cover.

I crawled my way slowly upwards, falling flat whenever I cracked a branch. I inched forwards for perhaps twenty minutes until I reached the top. I emerged into a field of long, yellow grass, inexplicably still uncut, even at this late time of year. Finally, a stroke of luck. Even more fortuitous, two hundred yards ahead of me, and visible just below, was Highbay Manor. I now had a perfect line of sight from the sea and beach below to the old, decrepit farmhouse. I took out my field glasses and notepad, flattened down a circle of grass and settled down for a day of observation.

By noon it was becoming clear that luck had again deserted me. I had seen nothing, no movement in the ruined manor and the beach was as bare and deserted as always. I had intended to remain until the fleet had returned, disembarked their catch and washed down their boats, but it now appeared that the gang had permanently abandoned this particular hideout. No longer worried about any hidden gunmen, I strode across the grassy field, met the path I had followed the previous day, followed it down to the coast road and headed back into town.

As I passed the compact harbour, now filled with activity, I spotted Moorclough, deep in conversation with a local fisherman. I shouted a greeting, which he acknowledged before waving and pointing energetically back up the road towards the inn. I took this to be a signal that a message had arrived, and so stomped enthusiastically back up the hill towards the whitewashed stone building.

Standing at the entrance was the young boy who had, the previous day, carried my letter to Lestrade. He was waving a white envelope. Once I reached him, he handed it over with great ceremony. It was a telegram, something that he had rarely seen, I shouldn't wonder. I slipped him a coin and opened the message.

"Let rcvd am. Tkng train 12 ariv 7 L."

Impressed that my letter had arrived the morning after it was sent, I returned to the dockyard in a positive mood. I arrived to observe Moorclough shaking hands with the fisherman. As I approached, the old sailor greeted me loudly.

"Good day, Doctor Watson," he bellowed. "This is our captain, Malchus Goodstart, he will be taking us to the island. We thought that tomorrow, before dawn, would be ideal."

I shook Goodstart's hand. A firm, rough seaman's grasp. Well over six feet tall and thin as a bean, he was an unlikely-looking captain. However, Moorclough insisted that he had fished these waters for thirty years without losing so much as a boot overboard, and that was a good enough reference for me. As we walked back up the hill, I told Moorclough of Lestrade's arrival and he nodded his approval.

"Whatever these rogues are up to, we are better served by being three men rather than two," he intoned. "Why can't this Scotland Yard friend of yours bring some of his colleagues along with him?"

"As I told you, I have tried my best to persuade Lestrade, but I have struggled even to convince him that a crime has been committed, let alone been able to provide him with any actual evidence. For heaven's sake, I do not even have the name of a single suspect! Sometimes, I fear I am disappearing down into a dark hole with no light ahead and no way back."

"Do not despair, Doctor, we will be three good men and, along with us, we have surprise as our greatest ally." Moorclough patted me enthusiastically, and very firmly, on my back.

I thought that I would spend some of the afternoon writing up my notes regarding this business. I hoped that taking a fresh look at the case from the beginning might help me determine some clue or pattern that we had missed.

The hours passed but all I had created were ashes in the fireplace as I tapped out bowl after bowl. Through this opaque case, I could shine no light. On a more practical note, I did make an account of what information I had so far confided in Moorclough. I meant to share this with Lestrade as soon as he arrived. I had taken a genuine liking to the old sea dog, but I was still far from trusting him completely. As far as he knew, it was a case of kidnap and blackmail. Adding secret societies, impersonation of government officials, secret agents and international intrigue, might well be enough for him to change his mind and wash his hands of the whole affair. To be fair, I would think nothing less of him if he did, this case could drive anyone to mania.

I then turned my attention to my other case, Hugo Hill, the mysterious vanishing man. I cursed my bad luck as to the timing of these affairs. I was torn between the two problems. Professor Lythlands must surely by now have valuable information waiting for me and Hill may very well be in real danger. Despite this guilt nagging at my conscience, I simply could not abandon my search for Holmes.

My decision, though based on Holmes' logic, was still difficult, and it pained me deeply. I had to stay and work on this case until its conclusion. If all went well, I would subsequently have the enormous benefit of Holmes' intellect and experience to help solve the Hill mystery.

Comfortable with my reasoning, I relaxed a little, lit yet another bowl and sat back to contemplate Hill's disappearance. From what I had recognised of the documents that had been secreted in the box, it would appear that Mr. Hill was not quite the poor orphan that his wife had always believed. Along with what I was certain Lythlands would confirm as a fake birth registration document, I had seen what looked like various ancient, legal documents, possibly title deeds. Not all of the papers were quite so old, I now recalled. The sealed envelope, though showing signs of age, could not have lain in the box for more than fifty years, judging by its finish and design.

Was Hill's disappearance connected to the contents of the box? I could not be certain, but every pore of me cried out that this was the link. Ancient deeds and wax-sealed envelopes speak of property and wealth, and not of wealth newly acquired. If one then adds secrecy and mystery, then what usually emerges is a tale of scandal. What hideous acts might have been committed over the years to avoid such indiscretions becoming publicly known? Had Hill seen the documents and somehow understood their meaning? If so, he had rejected them out of hand and disowned any birthright he may have. He had hidden the documents, sworn his guardian to secrecy and literally thrown away the key.

This appeared to have been the end of the matter, until the events which transpired slightly more than two weeks ago. What had changed? If not with the Hills, themselves, then perhaps elsewhere? Something appears to have happened that made Hill and his box of documents a problem, obstacle or enemy. Something serious enough to require the disappearance of Hill, perhaps permanently. I shuddered at the thought.

It was a little after eight in the evening when Inspector Lestrade finally arrived. I am not ashamed to admit to shaking his most welcome outstretched hand with greater enthusiasm than usual. I had abstained until his arrival, so we shared a late supper alone in the saloon bar. This proved ideal, as it allowed me the privacy I required to bring the inspector up to date with all that had happened. Once I had finished, I sat back and awaited the inspector's reaction.

Lestrade slowly shook his head in wonder. "What on Earth have you two found yourselves mixed up in?" he asked. "If you are serious about setting out tomorrow before dawn, then I will have to find a way to get a message to the local constabulary tonight. If we cannot have reinforcements, then at least someone will come looking if we fail to return."

Once I had revealed the unexpected efficiency of the local postal service, the inspector took a moment to arrange with

Moorclough for his young assistant to pick up a note from his room later that evening.

"A wise move, Inspector," I nodded in agreement, as he returned from the bar.

We spent the next two hours going over the plan, what there was of it, in minute detail. We tried to cover every possible eventuality and how we would react in each circumstance. Although we were aware that it was, in reality, a futile exercise, it helped to steady our nerves for the ordeal that we feared was to follow. The last subject that we discussed, before heading off to bed, was that of weapons. I informed the inspector that I would be carrying my service revolver, with a couple of dozen cartridges remaining after my little shootout at the manor. Lestrade tapped the squat, brown leather bag that he had placed on the floor beside him.

"It took a little creative paperwork, but I managed to sign out a decent revolver and a box of four dozen rounds. I also brought my own personal weapon, so that makes three."

"Plus, whatever Moorclough cares to take with him. Lord only knows what manner of hellish contraption it will be," I wondered, taking my final sip of brandy. "A crossbow? Catapult? Greek fire?"

On that less-than-serious note, we parted company for the night. I plodded up the stairs to my little room, nestled amongst the eaves, and prepared myself for a short and difficult night's sleep.

XXII
St. Mary Island

Sleep came easily, as the fatigue of the previous days, and indeed weeks, crept up on me and dragged me down into a deep, dark, dreamless oblivion. I fell through the soundless void, slowly spinning, senseless and timeless. Then, suddenly, a sound tore through my unconscious, ripping at my ears and mind.

The banging on the door continued until my confused brain reconnected with reality and I could call out a response. I rose, shook my head and opened the door. Moorclough's grizzled face appeared more shocking than ever in the half-light of the lamp he held before him.

"Time to get up, Doc. Coffee downstairs in five minutes," he grinned.

I dressed and climbed down the steep stairs into the bar to find Lestrade already waiting, sipping a steaming cup of coffee. He waved me a silent "good morning."

I poured myself a large cup of the inky black beverage and took one of the few biscuits that lay before us upon a cracked white plate.

"Just something light to break your fast, gents," explained Moorclough, as he checked the contents of a large oilskin bag. "The sea may be feisty, so better to not fill your stomachs. There will be plenty of provisions on board for later. I suggest we take a meal once in the lee of the smaller islands, just before we land."

Ten minutes later, we left the inn, walking down the dark, silent lane towards the harbour. What had appeared quaint and picturesque on previous days, was now ominous and forbidding. Ahead, we could just make out the faint glow of an oil lamp, which signalled the location of the Lucky Lass, our optimistically named transport to the island and whatever there awaited us.

We greeted Goodstart and he introduced us to his crew; a man who went by the name of Smith, who had, apparently, uttered not a single word in the twenty years that the captain had known him, and Henry, a fresh-faced young man, keen to learn a trade. The boat was not large, and with six aboard, space was limited. The inspector and I decided to sit at the stern where we hoped to keep out of the way of the crew.

Sails were raised and we eased out of the harbour and past the protective outer wall. Despite Moorclough's warnings, the sea remained calm, and we made steady progress towards the small island group. After an hour or so, Moorclough joined us.

"We have reached the islands. We will now head north for another half an hour or so, just to be safe. Then, the instant we have enough light, we will turn around and pass back through the rocks towards our target, the beach on the north coast of the main island. If Goodstart is half the navigator he claims to be, we should be on that beach in an hour from now, just before the sun comes up."

The tall captain was as good as his word and no more than thirty minutes later, we had turned and were heading south. Huge, jagged rocks on either side loomed over us as we slipped silently through the narrow passage that led to our goal. This would be a difficult journey in daylight; in this virtual blackness, it seemed a miracle to me that we were not smashed to atoms on the dark unforgiving boulders that surrounded our fragile craft. However, up ahead, wheel in hand and pipe in mouth, Goodstart seemed oblivious to any danger, keeping his little boat sailing straight and true.

A rich crimson glow was just appearing in the sky as we reached the beach. A small crescent of surprisingly golden sand lay before us. A low rasping sound from below indicated that we had come as far ashore as we could. The captain turned the boat sideways and dropped anchor to avoid grounding. A small wooden raft was lowered, and upon this, we placed our bags and clothes. We would swim to shore, pushing the raft before us and, once there, dress and take up our equipment.

Moorclough first took the plunge and straight away began to push the laden raft forwards. Lestrade and I took one final look at each other, shrugged and then took to the water. The icy cold of the sea knocked the air from my lungs and for a moment I thought I would drown. I thrashed my arms and legs but soon regained my sensibilities. I then swam after the raft as quickly as I could, sparing a sideways glance to confirm that the inspector was doing the same.

We dressed quickly on the beach and then dragged our equipment up to the top of the shoreline. A low sandbank gave us some cover and time to warm ourselves after the shock of our cold North Sea embrace. For the first time, I could properly observe the weapons that Moorclough had seen fit to bring with him upon this mission. A long hunting rifle was slung over one shoulder and a brace of pistols hung in leather holsters under each arm. As if this were not sufficient to face what was to come, he also had, upon his belt, a naval sword sheathed in its metal scabbard, and a large hunting knife strapped to his left thigh.

Cautiously, I peered around the side of one of the large boulders that peppered the shoreline, just above the high tide line. Lying ahead of us, a dark oblong stood out against the brightening sky – St. Mary's Chapel. Far from being abandoned and derelict, artificial light could be seen issuing from all six of the small windows that faced us.

"So, Doctor, what's your plan?" whispered Moorclough.

"Seeing that you have come so well-prepared, I would suggest a simple covered assault. If you can reach that rise to the left, you can cover the approach of the inspector and myself. With that rifle, it should be a fairly simple task to keep their heads down if they should attempt to take a shot at us."

Moorclough grinned and nodded his agreement.

"My thoughts, exactly, Doctor," Lestrade concurred. "I will take the right flank. Best if we spread out, if they see just the one of us, they may break cover to intercept."

My heart was pounding but my head was clear. It seems a terrible thing to admit, but I felt no fear, only excitement. I was back in action, back in the thick of it. The horror of my injuries and the agony of my extended recovery were now mere distant memories. Full of adrenalin and ambition to rescue my friend, I crawled forward, moving from sand into reedy grass.

Each scrambled yard dragged me closer to the looming chapel but also brought the sun closer to the horizon. I knew that at any moment the small plain before me would be bathed in early morning sunlight, for there was hardly a swirl of cloud in the sky. Even out here, hidden amongst the breakers, I was sure the criminals would have had the foresight to set a lookout.

I was less than ten yards from the chapel wall when I heard a sound from inside. It was a voice engaged in conversation, not raised in alarm. It seems I was mistaken; they had indeed felt invulnerable in their hideaway and had posted no watchman. I smiled inwardly, rose quickly and crept the final few yards to the wall. I waved back towards the shore and saw Lestrade raise an arm in acknowledgement. Moorclough pointed his rifle skywards to indicate his readiness.

I crouched down and moved towards the window closest to the door on the left side of the wall. Trying to control my breathing, I slowly rose to the height of the narrow Gothic stone windows and peered, cautiously, inside.

At first, I feared that we had wasted our time, for the chapel appeared all but lifeless. Then I began to make out several forms lying prone on the floor. We had caught them sleeping, I could not hide the grin that spread across my face. It took mere seconds for it to drop away as I realised that I could not identify who was sleeping in each position. Where was Holmes? Could Gold be among their number? We certainly could not burst in with guns blazing.

I tried to formulate a plan that would allow me to determine who was who, but a movement to my left made me reel backwards. A face loomed into view, directly in front of me. I had been careless; the man must have been standing behind the door to my left and just out of view.

The big, ugly face initially looked perplexed but quickly rearranged its ponderous features into those of anger and hatred. Shouting a foul curse, he raised a pistol to the glassless window and fired.

I ducked down well before the shot of flame passed harmlessly overhead. I momentarily thought of signalling my companions, but instantly realised the redundancy of the idea. I moved a few yards to the right in case the gunman decided to stick his arm out of the window and shoot at where I had been standing. I crouched down and waited for the door to open.

A few seconds later, the wooden door flung back, and three men burst forth. They immediately turned to me and raised their weapons. Three against one, I couldn't hope to get them all, but I had no intention of going down without a fight. Having no choice, I took careful aim and downed the nearest villain with a single shot.

Two shots cracked out in return. Involuntarily, I fell backwards, expecting to see horrific wounds erupt from my chest but, instead, the two men before me stopped in their tracks and fell silently to the ground. I glanced behind and saw wisps of smoke coming from the positions of both Lestrade and Moorclough.

I sprang to my feet and sprinted to the open doorway. A young man in a dirty grey suit and cap emerged, clutching a revolver. This time I was right upon him, so I brought my gun down heavily upon his head; killing must always remain a last resort, even in situations as perilous as these.

I carefully peered inside the chapel. The floor was now strewn with discarded blankets, however, nothing else moved within. With great caution, I slipped into the small hall, but it was already clear that nobody remained inside. It was only then that I saw another door, at the far end of the southern wall, hanging slightly ajar.

I cursed myself and ran towards the far side of the chapel. I kicked open the door, revolver held before me. Two hundred yards ahead, I saw a group of four or five figures running towards a small boat. I squinted hard, hoping that Holmes might be one of their number, but none seemed to have his height or familiar stork-like build. Behind me, I heard a sound and spun around to see Lestrade entering the chapel.

"Secure the man in the cap, he is still alive," I ordered. "The rest of the gang are boarding a boat to the south. Tell Moorclough to follow me, I will need his help."

I sprinted across the open land behind the chapel, desperately hoping that my quarry would not spot me. Before I had covered twenty yards, one of the figures ahead of me turned, raised an arm and fired his weapon. I instinctively dived and heard a round whistle overhead. I rammed myself behind a slight bank as a second volley passed much closer than the first. I was now pinned down, outgunned and helpless.

Just as I thought our goal was lost, a now-familiar blast rent the early morning stillness. I chanced a look up as Moorclough, taking cover inside the chapel and resting its barrel on one of the stone window ledges, launched a second round from his formidable hunting rifle. The poor chap who had fired upon me spun around and fell, broken, to the ground. A third shot shattered the mast of the small wooden boat.

Then a remarkable thing occurred. One of the villains swung viciously at the man closest to him. The assaulted man tumbled forwards, apparently knocked unconscious. Along with this unexpected revolutionary, there were now two remaining villains. One was sat, hunched, and appeared unmoving, the other now aimed his pistol towards this unexpected traitor. The rebel raised his fists to engage him in what appeared to be a most one-sided contest, one he seemed destined to lose.

A fourth and final shot from the old seaman's canon ended the contest, conclusively. What remained of the would-be executioner toppled into the sea. The final, standing, gang member rapidly thrust his arms aloft. The prone figure remained motionless.

I scrambled to my feet and cautiously approached the remaining gang members. As I drew closer, I was shocked to discover that the seated figure was not, as I had expected, some gnarly gangster, but a woman. In the growing light of the early morning, her appearance became clearer. She was perhaps thirty years old with dark brown hair. Her face, though attractive, was deathly pale and her wide-open eyes stared, sightless into the middle distance. She was either in a deep state of shock or had been heavily sedated.

I turned my attention back to the apparent rebel in the group and ordered him to keep his distance as I moved closer to the pair and the boat in which they had attempted to make their escape.

"Please, I am of no threat to you, I swear. My wife, I beg you, I need to help her." The desperation was clear in the man's voice. It was a voice that I had heard before.

"Take off your cap," I barked, wanting a better look at this contradictory character.

The dark-suited man removed his grey cloth cap and looked imploringly at me.

"My goodness!" I exclaimed. "Gold. It's you, Adam Gold."

"Doctor Watson, is that you?" he replied, incredulously. "They told me you were dead."

"We feared the same of you," I replied. "We know who you are, Gold, and what they forced you to do," I quickly added, lowering my revolver.

"What's all this, Doctor?" panted Lestrade as he arrived at a fair pace.

I quickly explained the situation to Lestrade who responded with surprise and concern for both Gold and his ailing wife.

"Wrap her in the warmest coat we have and get her to our boat quickly," I urged. "I have some brandy and a few basic medical supplies stowed in my bag."

"Moorclough and I will look after the two survivors and take them to the beach," replied Lestrade. Before leading away the final gang member, the inspector removed his fine woollen overcoat and placed it around the shoulders of the still-seated figure of Mrs. Gold. Her husband placed his cap gently upon her head and carefully lifted her into his arms.

We walked the short distance back towards the beach in silence. It occurred to me that we now had a slight problem. Including the Golds and our prisoners, we now had ten people to ship back to the mainland. Our boat was sturdy, but it would be a tight squeeze. At worst, I grinned to myself, we could stuff the villains below deck, where they could enjoy the singular atmosphere of a hold that had held countless catches of oily sea fish.

We passed the chapel and were greeted by a most welcome sight. A second vessel now lay at anchor beside the Lucky Lass. Two police constables were helping Moorclough with the prisoners and two more were striding out to meet us, led by a tall man in a long fawn overcoat.

"Inspector Sidebottom," announced the tall man with a wide smile. "Northumberland Police." His shock of blond hair and bright blue eyes, added to his youthful enthusiasm, gave the impression of a man much younger than his forty or more years.

"Lestrade, Scotland Yard," replied the inspector. "Glad to see that someone finally took my concerns seriously."

"I see that your backup has arrived," I noted with a grin. "You should have more faith in your colleagues."

"I hoped that they would, Doctor, but I could not have us relying upon help that may well not have come," Lestrade replied, honestly.

"Well, this makes things a bit easier, I suppose. Inspector Sidebottom, you must get Mrs. Gold ashore as soon as possible. Give her some brandy from my bag and take her to the nearest doctor. Inspector Lestrade and I will need to talk to both her and her husband once we return to the village."

Sidebottom appeared momentarily perturbed by my orders and looked at Lestrade for confirmation. The inspector swiftly nodded his approval.

"You are becoming more like Holmes with each passing day," he whispered, leaning towards me.

"Take the Golds ashore with you, but leave two of your men here," ordered the inspector. "They can help with the bodies. I believe the good doctor would like to take a closer look at the chapel before we depart."

XXIII
A Discovery of Note

As the unfortunate constables attended to the unenviable task of recovering and stowing the bodies of the fallen into the hold of the remaining boat, the inspector and I made a thorough search of the chapel. Other than discarded blankets, some thin metal sheets and the expected detritus of recent habitation, there was little left to indicate what might have led the gang to use this tiny chapel as a base of operations. After an hour of searching, Lestrade had seen enough.

"There is nothing here. They must have taken it, whatever it is, away with them, long before we got here," he sighed, his enthusiasm draining away in front of my eyes.

I looked down at the floor, now free of debris. There were scrapes and scratches, all recently made. It looked almost exactly the same as a floor I had examined only a few days before. Whatever had been stored here, it was the same something that had been kept at Highbay Manor.

Refusing to believe that there was nothing more to discover, I crouched down on my hands and knees and determined to examine the chapel floor once more. Moving east towards the small apse, I noticed that the ground was increasingly marked. I examined the semi-circular recess in detail and just as I was preparing to abandon my search, I spotted something half-hidden between the floor and the first layer of stonework. I pulled at it, tentatively. It unrolled in my hand. It was a roll of paper. I flattened it on the floor in front of me. It was a single sheet of white paper, precisely printed on one side. Suddenly, it was clear exactly what it was. A five-pound note.

I called Lestrade over and handed him the note.

"What do you think, Inspector?" I asked. "This is quite a substantial sum to simply misplace."

Lestrade took the mislaid money out into the bright morning sunshine, and I followed, glad of some fresh air after the musty church atmosphere. He held it at arm's length for a moment before examining it more closely.

"Looks real enough to me," he concluded. "Maybe this points us towards the answer to the question of what was stored here and up at the manor."

"Money?" I replied. "Well, that would explain the presence of the heavy boxes that seem to have been moved around."

"Cases full of cash," Lestrade muttered, quietly. "But if they were filled with five-pound notes," he began to add.

"They would contain tens or perhaps hundreds of thousands of pounds," I exclaimed. "Where on Earth could it have come from? Surely not a robbery, for such a thing could not have been kept secret, could it Inspector?"

"I have heard of no such theft. Amounts of cash as large as this are unheard of outside a bank. No, I cannot countenance such a theory," he then paused. "Unless the money actually is counterfeit, and they were bringing it into the country from abroad," he concluded, excitedly.

Lestrade looked again at the note, then handed it back to me. I looked carefully but could see nothing unusual about the banknote.

"I have to admit that I am no expert on notes, I rarely handle such large denominations. If only Holmes were here, I'd wager he would know in an instant."

"It is something to work from, though," decided Lestrade. "We should re-examine the chapel, this time looking for items that might be associated with the counterfeit money trade."

My mouth almost dropped, and my eyes opened wide as I suddenly remembered what I had come upon, but cast aside, in the dark interior.

"Inspector, I have been a total fool!" I hissed. "Wait here, I will be back in a moment."

I ran back inside the little stone church and rummaged through the blankets that I had thrown into a pile on one side. There they were, right at the bottom. Two sheets of thin steel, about twelve inches square. Although in the darkness, they appeared to be of little interest, I frantically grabbed them and sprinted back outside to find Lestrade waiting with a look of incomprehension on his thin, pinched face.

"Whatever have you got there?" he asked, peering at the metal plates.

I held out one of the sheets and, for the first time, saw it in daylight. The plate was completely smooth apart from a rectangle, about eight inches by five, in the centre. This appeared to be engraved; lines and patterns swirled across its surface. The other plate looked identical.

"Forger's plates!" exclaimed Lestrade. "We were right. That is what this whole business has been about, fake money and lots of it."

"In the quantities that we suspect, it would explain everything. Enough to fuel a huge conspiracy, fund a secret society and enough even to entrap and blackmail a government agent," I added.

"If this note is an example of their wares, it would take a real expert to identify them as forgeries. They could have used the society and its members to introduce the cash into circulation, in return for Lord knows what? The money does appear to have come in from overseas. If it is an international gang, then it could be connected to all manner of operations – opium, gold or, heaven help us, arms. Half a dozen cases of these notes could buy enough weapons to start a small revolution!" Lestrade's face had now turned red with genuine, heartfelt outrage.

"We need to get back to the mainland and talk to Gold," I urged. "Only he can give us the answers we require, and only he can tell us what has happened to Sherlock Holmes."

XXIV
The Secret Agent

The return journey seemed to take forever. Lestrade sat in silence, facing the approaching coast, his face set in dark, determined concentration. I attempted to assemble a list of questions to ask of Gold once we reached shore. As I thought these through, the combination of the unseasonably warm morning sun along with the almost hypnotic beauty of the Northumberland coast, soon had my head lolling forward and sleep became impossible to resist.

I awoke with a start as the fishing boat bumped the cushioned harbour wall. Lestrade smiled and then helped me disembark, still slightly unsure of my footing following my unexpected nap. There was an upside though, as my head felt clearer, and I was now desperate to start questioning Gold.

We quickly found a constable and learned that the captives had been locked in a local storehouse that doubled as the town gaol and the Golds were receiving treatment from the local doctor in the saloon bar of the 'Aad Galloway.' We strode with purpose up the short hill to the white stone inn. The constable on the door saluted Lestrade and we made our way inside.

A camp bed had been set up and upon this lay Mrs. Gold. She appeared to be sleeping. By her side, and holding her hand tenderly, was Adam Gold, concern and fatigue written all over his pale face. A short man dressed in a fine suit stood by Sidebottom, deep in conversation. On the floor, by his side, was an open medical bag. Standing behind the bar, and pouring hot coffee into enamelled metal cups, was Moorclough.

"Doctor! Inspector!" he announced, loudly. "Come in, sit down. I am just preparing something for the constables. Give me a minute and I will find something suitably warming for two more heroes of the hour."

"My dear Moorclough," I replied. "If anyone was a hero today, it was you. You saved both myself and Gold, here, with your remarkable shooting."

For a fraction of a second, Moorclough looked almost bashful, before recovering and roaring with laughter.

"Brandy all round, and strong coffee for the men in blue," he declared.

Lestrade moved towards Sidebottom, and they were soon deeply engaged, discussing the morning's events. I sat down at a nearby table and Gold soon joined me.

"How is your wife?" I asked gently.

Gold smiled, "She is sleeping. Doctor Penrose here has had a good look at her. I saw them giving her sedatives, but the doctor says that the best thing for her is sleep; let the drugs work their way out of her system."

"Quite right," I agreed, quietly impressed with the local doctor's diagnosis.

"I fear that they have been sedating her for some weeks now. I pray that no serious damage has been done." His face was a picture of loving concern.

"I promise you that we will do all we can to ensure that your wife makes a complete recovery," I replied. However, I now had questions that could wait no longer.

"What do you know of the gang's plans and where is Sherlock Holmes?" I asked bluntly. I had determined to not yet disclose that which we had so far discovered.

"Doctor, my story is long and about as far from straightforward as is possible to be. However, you must hear it all before you make any judgement."

"Mr. Gold," I replied, laying a comforting hand upon his shoulder. "I truly believe you to be nothing other than a hero in this affair. You and your wife have suffered dearly in service of your country."

I turned and gestured for Lestrade and Sidebottom to join me.

The two inspectors pulled up chairs close to the Golds, gratefully received their brandies from Moorclough and waited for Gold to recount his tale.

"As you know by now, I am an unofficial agent of Her Majesty's government. My department deals in matters of a sensitive nature. Operations that must remain secret at all costs. We act when the official authorities, for whatever reasons, cannot." The two inspectors nodded, knowingly.

"We were asked by our American counterparts to help with the investigation into the death of one of their countrymen. Mitchell, his name was, Clarke Mitchell. A banker, pretty well-off and found floating face down in the Thames. Usually, we wouldn't have been interested, just another job for Scotland Yard. However, the evening before he died, this banker had attended a fancy do at the American ambassador's residence over on Victoria Street. After consuming copious amounts of fine Bordeaux, he let slip that he was a member of some fancy new secret club and that he had just secured promotion to the highest level."

Gold's words brought a rush of memories flooding back. The mysterious club with its wealthy but louche members. My terrifying encounter with the Chairman, the breathless carriage chase and, finally, my tragic, faked demise in Green Park.

"This was overheard by someone of influence who was concerned enough to report it to an American official," continued Gold. "Once news of Mitchell's death reached the embassy, agents were alerted, and they made contact with us a few days later."

"We are currently cooperating quite constructively with our cousins across the Atlantic," Gold explained. "The government has concluded that there are dangers enough growing in Europe, so we should try to maintain as cordial a relationship with the Americans as we can. In that spirit, I was assigned to liaise with their agents and offer whatever assistance I could."

"At first, I struggled to take the case particularly seriously. I visited this strange little club and quickly gained membership. The United States was paying my expenses, and generous they were with it. After two weeks, I had identified several prominent figures, who were now members. I fully expected that I would simply file my report and await the inevitable police raid and series of arrests that would surely follow. Up to that point, I had not seriously entertained the idea that Mitchell's indiscretion had genuinely cost him his life. The truth was about to hit me with the full force of a hurricane."

Gold paused, his head dropping as he struggled to continue.

"Please, try to continue," I urged, suggesting he take a sip of brandy.

"I too visited this Ex Tenebris club," I said, gently. "I will openly admit that it was one of the most terrifying experiences of my life." I described my meeting with the horrific Chairman and how I had to flee for my life, once exposed as an imposter. I deliberately excluded any mention of Holmes' role for the time being.

"Yes, they told me," replied Gold, invigorated by the warming spirit. "But they also said that you had died in the crash. Hayden Gorge swore that he saw your severed head amongst the wreckage."

I struggled to suppress a chuckle at this suggestion. I then gave a brief account of my escape and how we fooled our pursuers.

Both Gold and Inspector Sidebottom looked incredulous. Lestrade simply shrugged and nodded in confirmation of my account. Gold took another swig of his brandy before continuing. "It was then that my world collapsed around me. I arrived at the club early one evening, some two months ago. I approached the bar to order a drink when I was intercepted by two of the club's hired thugs. They led me to the office of the Chairman. You have seen it; it is so dark you cannot even see to the far wall."

"Yes, a truly intimidating effect," I agreed.

"Well, this time the Chairman was already seated in his chair. He gave me some speech about loyalty and honour, all twisted and perverse. He then made me swear an oath, to obey and be faithful. I agreed to all of it, of course, that was my job. He seemed happy with my responses, he smiled and waved his hand. I had no idea what to expect next." Gold was again stuttering, I felt huge sympathy for him, as a part of me already suspected what was to follow.

"They came from out of the shadows. A huge man holding a limp figure. She looked like a doll, so small and fragile in his monstrous arms. It was a woman. She hung so limply that, at first, I did not recognise her. Then I noticed her dress. Then her hair. Finally, her head lolled upwards, and I saw her face."

"Your wife," gasped Lestrade. "I am so sorry, sir."

"Yes. I do not know how but, somehow, they had discovered my true identity. It should have been impossible. We are protected by the government, even Scotland Yard has no record of our real names, let alone our home addresses. Yet, somehow, they had learned both. I was now lost. How could I contact my superiors? Somebody at the very top level had betrayed me. I could no longer trust anybody. My mission suddenly became singular. I had to save my wife, nothing else mattered."

"So, you went along with their plans? Now would be the time to explain them, fully," demanded Lestrade.

"What would you have done, Inspector?" hissed Gold. "I was now completely at their mercy."

"Now is not the time for recriminations, Inspector," I chided. "Please continue your account, Mr. Gold. It is vitally important that we learn all we can as soon as possible."

"Their demands were simple. I was to continue working for the group, obeying each and every command, without question, while simultaneously reporting back to my superiors that nothing at the club was amiss. I followed their orders to the letter; however, I spent every spare minute attempting to locate where they were holding my wife. I suspected that, initially, she may have been held on one of the upper floors of the Ex Tenebris Club but, despite all my efforts, I could find no way of gaining access."

"What did they have you do, exactly?" asked Sidebottom, scribbling on a notepad with a well-chewed half-pencil.

"Initially, I oversaw deliveries of provisions for the club, food and drinks for the members. It did strike me as very strange, of course. Why go to all of this trouble, kidnap and blackmail, just to have me be a glorified storeman?"

"Well, a few days later I had a visit from one of the senior members," Gold continued. "An ex-officer type, Hayden Gorge was his name. Typical blustering fool of a braggart he was, always claiming to have been the hero of any number of mythical battles. I never believed a word of it. The one time we had some trouble at the club, he was the first to run and hide himself away. Anyway, he told me that I was to take an office over in Custom House. My job would be to allow certain cargos to pass through without inspection."

"I think I am beginning to understand," I said quietly; hardly more than a thought, spoken aloud.

"The money, the fake currency?" added Lestrade. "They were bringing it in through Custom House, right under the noses of the authorities? Well, that certainly takes some nerve." Lestrade sounded almost impressed by the temerity of these criminals.

"Yes, this was the plan. It was also my first inkling that the scheme had more to it than just financial gain. They also seemed to want to humiliate the government and perhaps the entire country."

"I was given an office and told to await further instructions. In the meantime, they ordered me to surreptitiously wander the public areas of the building, listening out for anyone who might be investigating their grand scheme," Gold explained.

"Which is how you came to find Holmes and me," I added, excitedly.

"Yes, you are quite correct, Doctor. I overheard your friend as he questioned the receptionist and guided you away before a genuine official could arrive. But from that moment onwards, I was as intrigued, as were you, with the possibility that my wife might be imprisoned just a few yards from where I stood. Once I was convinced that she was no longer being held in that grim upper office, I had no choice but to make my escape. If we returned together to the atrium, the genuine official that was meant to meet you would immediately identify me as an imposter." Gold's face now appeared even more haggard and fatigued than before, the shame he felt for his actions was now becoming physically manifest.

"You did what you had to, I firmly believe this," I said, encouraging Gold to continue.

"One moment please, gentlemen," interrupted Lestrade. "This is all rather convenient, is it not? You were told to look out for anyone poking around and suddenly Mr. Holmes and the Doctor appear?"

Gold shrugged. "At that point, I was more concerned with escaping and reporting back to my new masters."

"So, if I am correct, Holmes and I unintentionally disrupted the main supply route into the country of the forged currency," I ventured, largely ignoring the Inspector.

"That appears to be the measure of it, Doctor. The gang was most troubled and angered towards me. They made all sorts of threats to myself and my wife, I feared that they might kill her or me at any time. It was only with the arrival of the Chairman that I was spared. He ordered me to return to my residence, the house of an alderman whom I was also impersonating at occasional council meetings."

"Ah, Turek, or Turkle," confirmed Lestrade. "We know that he was murdered, you need to tell us who was responsible, and for heaven's sake, why?"

"They never told me, explicitly, that he was dead, but I suspected that this must be the case," Gold answered, sadly. "By this point, it was already clear that they were intent on bringing something illicit into the country. Turkle was an expert in the distribution of items of dubious provenance. He had been chosen as one of the main outlets for their contraband, but it appears that he had become too greedy and demanded a higher share of the profits. Not for the first or last time, I witnessed the ruthlessness of this gang. I was then ordered to impersonate Turkle as and when it was required."

"So, this was the moment you again encountered him then, Doctor?" asked Lestrade.

"Yes, I suppose it must have been. Holmes had deduced that the man we knew as Smitherson at Custom House was also a recently elected alderman of the City. We learned, from a deeply suspicious-looking cabal within the Corporation, that this alderman was Turkle. However, Holmes knew Turkle personally, and this man was not he. This is why we approached Turkle's house with such trepidation, and why we used force to neutralise him."

"Doctor, I must apologise for my actions. I could not reveal my true identity, the life of my beloved depended on me spinning a tail that you would believe. I knew that those thugs would arrive at any moment, so I just ranted and raved to keep you occupied. I thought that they would just tie you up, maybe knock you out at worst. I never expected that they would shoot you. For the next few hours, I truly believed you to be dead and cursed my damned soul. They interrogated me for hours, going over every detail of our encounter to determine whether I had passed on any information. When they were finally satisfied that I had given away nothing, they released me. I cannot express the joy I felt today when I discovered that you had survived."

"No harm done," I replied with a hint of a grin. "The only injury I sustained was as a result of my own clumsy footwork.

Gold seemed to relax slightly as, for his sake and the needs of the case, I casually shrugged off this attempt on my life.

"So, with their main route of ingress now disrupted, they relocated north?" I asked, attempting to move the narrative forward.

"It was kept quiet, only a few of us were chosen to make the trip. But yes, we were taken by train, then coach at the dead of night, to the abandoned Manor House that overlooks this fine village."

"We spent the first few days sitting around doing next to nothing. We took turns keeping watch, but nothing and nobody came," Gold continued. "Then, one day, a group of men, maybe five or six, approached. They carried a large, iron-clad trunk which they stored in the front room of the old farmhouse; it being the best-preserved covered space. Over the next week or so, several more of these chests arrived and were all stacked, safe from the weather, in the same room."

"Were you not tempted to see what was in these chests?" asked Lestrade.

"Of course, Inspector," replied Gold. "But they were locked and bound with steel rings and in any case, we were promised that anyone attempting to interfere with the cargo would be summarily executed."

"Executed? That is a rather strange word to use, is it not?" I asked.

Gold shrugged but Lestrade hummed and looked deep in thought.

"Perhaps this affair is more political than we thought," he suggested. "One, all of the available evidence suggests that the currency is being brought in from abroad. Two, the aim seems, partly at least, to humiliate the nation. Three, this gang uses words such as 'execute' rather than 'do away with' or simply 'kill.' This is the language of state, not that of the criminal world."

"You may well be onto something there, Inspector," I agreed. "But for now, we must hear the remainder of Mr. Gold's story."

Lestrade nodded and Gold continued his tale. "One night, after we had secreted perhaps a dozen chests, a new, unknown group of men arrived and began to take the chests away, carrying them onto a horse cart and taking them inland. At a rate of two per night, it took about a week."

"As the last cart left, I expected to be ordered to follow along behind. Instead, to my surprise, I was led down to the shore where I was made to board a small fishing boat and transported to that nasty little island. My heart leapt when I saw that they had my wife, even though she had obviously been drugged. Just for a moment, I thought that my job for them was finally done, and they would release us, but it slowly dawned on me that we faced a different fate altogether. We were being reunited as we had served our purpose and were now a loose end that needed trimming."

"Which explains why you attacked your fellow gang members as we advanced on their position," I replied, the image of Gold bravely facing down the armed thugs flashed back through my mind.

"They planned to kill us on that boat and dump our bodies at sea. I believe I have you to thank for saving my life," said Gold, turning to look towards Moorclough who stood at the bar, polishing glasses.

"'Twas an honour helping a man as brave as yourself." As he lifted a glass in salute, it caught the early morning rays of sunlight perfectly and sparkled with a fleeting, bright intensity.

"Mr. Gold, your testimony has been invaluable. I promise you that if you have any difficulties with the authorities, I will do everything in my power to help," I pledged.

"And you can also count on my complete support," Lestrade confirmed.

Gold smiled and was about to respond when a small, weak voice hailed from behind us.

"Adam, Adam, is that you?" It was little more than a whispered, plaintive cry.

Gold immediately rushed to his wife's side. We that remained, sipped upon our drinks in thoughtful silence.

We helped Gold and his wife to more comfortable lodgings at a nearby cottage and then returned to the inn for a much-needed lunch. Moorclough appeared to have endless reserves of energy and, with the help of his lad, swiftly served up a hearty stew of mutton and vegetables. Sidebottom then left us, with the intention of questioning the prisoners. He promised to inform us if he discovered anything of interest.

I suddenly felt the weight of the day's activities descend upon my shoulders. I yawned and apologised to Lestrade for my tiredness.

"Nonsense, it has been a long and difficult morning, Doctor. I suggest we retire for a few hours and later meet for supper. We have much to discuss."

XXV
Interrogations and Revelations

I woke with a start. The sky outside was a bruised purple. For a brief moment, I was unsure of whether it was dusk or dawn. I grasped for my pocket watch; I had slept for three hours. I shook my head, in an attempt to clear the fog and stumbled out of bed. I dressed and descended the stairs to find Lestrade waiting in the saloon bar, relaxing in an easy chair, pipe in hand.

"Good evening, Doctor," he nodded.

"Apologies for keeping you, Inspector. I do hope you haven't been waiting long," I replied, rather guiltily.

"Not at all, I have not long risen myself. Although, I must admit that I am now keen to see what Sidebottom has managed to extract from those two ruffians that we captured."

We walked the short journey down to the waterfront and the storehouse that doubled as the local gaol. It was an ideal building within which to incarcerate our ne'er-do-wells. A low, single-storey block with small, barred windows at the front and back. Built from solid, white-washed stone, a heavy ironbound door was the only way in or out. A constable stood guard and saluted as Lestrade approached. The inspector nodded in reply as the young policeman opened the substantial door for us.

Lamps had already been lit, but the inside was still dim and uninviting. The building had been divided into three parts. The main storage area lay before us and up at the far northern end were two small cells. A brick wall separated these and also formed the front of the small rooms. Each had a thick oak door with a large, barred window.

Sidebottom sat at a table with a constable to each side of him. He was leafing through what appeared to be a wad of handwritten notes, no doubt the testimony of our captives.

He rose and thrust out his hand in greeting. "Gentlemen, good to see you again. Please take a seat." He shooed away the uniformed men and gestured for us to take their place.

"Well, I never expected this," he announced. "Those two back there have been singing like canaries."

I was flabbergasted. After my earlier encounter with Gold, I fully expected these men to hold onto their secrets with a grip of iron. The size of the two constables chosen to aid Sidebottom bore witness to the expected "difficulty" of the process of interrogation. That they were still fully dressed, lacking perspiration and sporting unblemished knuckles, spoke of a rather different story.

"They gave up names, dates, places. Every question we asked, they answered most eagerly. It was all so easy," he said, airily.

"I see," replied Lestrade with a nod and a knowing glance.

"Because, of course," sighed Sidebottom, dropping the pages onto the rough wooden table, "it was all nonsense. Well-drilled, and learned by rote, but all stuff and nonsense. Nearly six hours of questioning wasted. However, we have learned one thing. You were quite right about these men, Doctor Watson, they are serious and loyal to a fault. But loyal to whom and to what? I do now wonder if this is merely a financial crime. Does mere coin earn this level of blind obedience?"

I was impressed by Sidebottom; he was showing himself to be a man of some capability and depth.

"So, you decided that a more 'intense' method of interrogation would be fruitless?" inquired Lestrade sounding somewhat unconvinced.

"Beating these men will achieve nothing. They both seem resigned to the rope, with what else can we scare them?" Sidebottom sat back and shrugged.

"Nevertheless, I would like to see for myself. Would you mind if I borrowed your men?" Lestrade's tone made it clear that it was not a request.

Sidebottom agreed, but added, "I have not the stomach for such things this evening. I shall return to the inn."

I was also none too keen to witness so cruel a beating but volunteered to remain and offer any medical assistance that may be necessary.

Lestrade looked rather taken aback and then leaned closer. "It's mostly for show, I promise," he whispered. "They can hear every word. If we can get them good and frightened, then they might just crack. If not, then these gentlemen will indeed lay hands on them, but they will survive intact, Doctor. No broken bones or stitches, you have my word."

Far from happy but satisfied that no serious harm would befall our prisoners, I nodded my understanding.

"Well, I cannot stay here," I announced loudly. "As a doctor, my oath prevents me from witnessing such terrible carnage. Inspector, what you intend to do to these poor men is illegal, immoral and utterly depraved. I wash my hands of this bloody affair, as you will have to wash the floor of their viscera. May God forgive you."

Lestrade raised his eyes in silent protest at my overblown statement. I simply shrugged. "You did want them to be afraid," I mouthed. Lestrade pointed to the door, a hint I took with no further encouragement required.

Returning to the inn, I re-joined Sidebottom, who was seated, deep in thought. I took the chair opposite him, withdrew my small steel cigar case, pressed the stud and it sprung open. I offered the contents to the Inspector.

"Oh, thank you," he mumbled, plucking out a thin Sumatran. "Sorry, Doctor, I was miles away. However, I look at it, I just cannot get a grip on this case."

"The slippery eel," I replied. "I recall Holmes speaking of such not so long ago."

Sidebottom smiled, lit the cigar, drew deeply and sent a silver-grey cloud of swirling smoke up towards the beamed ceiling of the bar.

"What are we missing, Doctor?" With his hands held wide, he almost appeared to be begging.

"As far as it is possible to be certain, I am convinced that the crates of forged currency are now heading back down south. The favoured port of entry was in London, after all. Other than that, I am bereft of ideas."

"It hardly seems fair," moaned Sidebottom. "You located this gang and their lair, in fact, their two hideaways. We caught them red-handed and unprepared, rescued a government agent along with his wife and gained two prisoners. But what have we to show for it?"

"We have the plot, the conspiracy or whatever it is," I replied, with as much confidence as I could muster. "We have the forger's plates; we know of the cases of fake notes. We know far more now than we did just a day ago. We need more, much more, but I believe we are on the right track. We must persevere."

We sat and smoked in silence for a while. The night had grown chilly, so Moorclough's lad had lit a fire that crackled contentedly before us. I tried to concentrate on how we might proceed but my mind kept drifting back to the makeshift gaol and what violence might be being dished out to our captives. Despite their murderous intentions towards us, I still held onto the ingrained military belief that, once the battle is over, prisoners should be treated with respect and not subject to beatings or torture. Friend or not, I determined to hold Lestrade accountable should any serious harm come to those men. Which made it doubly surprising when the inspector himself burst into the saloon bar just a few moments later.

"Doctor, I have a lead, or an idea, or something," he stammered, almost incoherently.

"Take a seat, Inspector," I suggested. "I will get you a brandy. Compose yourself, old chap, and when I return, I am sure you will be in a better state to share with us that which you have discovered."

Once Lestrade had taken a sip of the reassuring golden spirit and a puff of one of my cigars, he was ready to talk.

"Apologies for my over-excitement gentlemen," he began. "However, a thought struck me as we were preparing to further question the prisoners. I honestly had no appetite this evening for a physical confrontation and, once I had taken a look at the network of scars that line their bodies like a road map of suffered violence, I realised that we were wasting our time. They would tell us nothing, well certainly not anything even vaguely resembling the truth. But then it struck me. We may well learn nothing from their side, but the opposite might also be true."

"What do you mean?" asked Sidebottom. "Surely the opposite is that they learn nothing from us?"

"Exactly," replied Lestrade, a twinkle in his eye. "For the first time, we control the board. We can now influence the whole game. Think about it, Inspector. Everybody that was on the island is now either dead, in custody or an ally. There are no witnesses left to inform the gang of what actually occurred this morning."

"Good Lord!" I exclaimed. "You are quite right, Inspector. When we come to report what has happened here, we are free to say whatever we choose; there is no one to contradict whatever story best suits our needs."

"You have it, Doctor. Now, we have to think carefully. What story should we go with? What would be to our greatest advantage?" Lestrade took out his notebook and laid it before him.

"Firstly, we must protect Gold and his wife," observed Sidebottom.

"Of course," I agreed. "And I think I know exactly how to do just that and at the same time give us the greatest possible advantage."

"Go on, Doctor," urged Lestrade. "Let us see if all that time spent with Holmes has rubbed off."

Despite feeling momentarily saddened by the lack of my friend's presence, I continued with confidence. "Your report should be along the lines of: 'A local fisherman had reported suspicious activity around St. Mary Island. When the authorities went to investigate the sightings, they were attacked by a group of suspected smugglers. Fortunately, the police had the foresight to arrive armed and reluctantly returned fire. In the ensuing gun battle, all of the smugglers were killed, including, sadly, a woman who appeared to be a part of the gang. Their vessel was damaged beyond repair, but no goods were recovered. Several brave police officers were also slightly injured.'"

"That should protect the Golds. It should also make our adversaries believe that their plan is still safe and, most importantly, secret," I suggested. "If they believe Gold and the others are all dead, and that we failed to discover the metal plates, then they will be off their guard. It may be a small advantage, however, I believe that it is the best we can hope for."

"Bravo to you both," declared Sidebottom, raising his glass. "It appears that the stories trickling down to us from London are indeed true. But how can we now make use of this unexpected boon?"

"The first thing that I must do is to have another talk with Gold. He did not mention Holmes by name, which was no surprise as the last time he saw him, Holmes was in disguise. Once I explain to Gold which member of the gang was Holmes, then he might have some idea as to where we might find him."

"Very well, Doctor. I will wire my 'report' down to London and make sure it is released to the press immediately," Lestrade replied, rising to his feet.

"I feel that I should speak to Gold straight away," I replied, as I also took my leave. "I cannot wait any longer, and his wife should by now be soundly asleep. Good evening, Inspectors."

I tipped my hat to the lone policeman now reclining by the fire and left the inn. I made the short walk to the cottage where the Golds had been housed in less than five minutes. A burly sergeant with fine red whiskers opened the door and waved me inside.

Gold sat alone at a small dining room table. In the light of several oil lamps, he was busily writing. Several loose sheets of paper lay in a pile next to him, already filled with his small, neat handwriting.

"Doctor, good to see you again," he said, dipping his pen into a small crystal inkwell. "Have you come to see Catherine? She is sleeping, Doctor Penrose thought it best that she was not disturbed until tomorrow morning at the earliest."

"Quite right, however, it is you that I have come to see. I must ask again, do you have any information as to the whereabouts of Sherlock Holmes? Please think carefully, for any hint or rumour would be worth investigating. Bear in mind that he would have been in disguise and using the name Arthur C. Brownlands."

"I knew that you would come, and I was dreading the moment that you would ask me this question. This is partly the reason behind my current scribblings, I am attempting to make a record of my experiences in as much detail as possible. I felt that the sooner I did this the better, while the memories are still fresh."

I realised that Gold was stalling, and I now also had confirmation that he had deliberately chosen not to answer my earlier request for information regarding Holmes. I steeled myself for the worst, there could be only one reason for Gold to prevaricate so.

"Please, tell me. I must know what has befallen Holmes, however terrible his fate may have been." I ordered, resolutely.

"The final cart, loaded with crates of forged notes, had just arrived. As always, it was attended to by a crew of hired thugs. I overheard two of these talking about a gang member who had been unmasked as a traitor and spy. I later engaged one of these fellows in conversation, over a bottle of cheap whisky. Once the alcohol had suitably loosened his tongue, he recounted what he, himself, had heard from yet another gang member. A recently recruited member of the organisation had risen rapidly through the ranks, due to his unique abilities and some dramatic events back at the Ex Tenebris club. He had become involved in the logistics of moving the crates from the landing site and onto their next destination. Apparently, one morning while dressing, he was disturbed by a minor gang member. This man observed the high-flying newcomer in the process of applying a disguise and he immediately alerted his companions. That was that, really. They discovered a wig, makeup and false teeth, he couldn't talk his way out of this situation. He was trussed up and sent back down to London. It was said that the Chairman, himself, ordered his transportation back to the club so he could confront the imposter face to face. The man to whom I had spoken was, by now, very drunk and could not remember whether a name had been mentioned, but he did say that the conspirator was believed to be some sort of amateur detective from London."

My heart sank as I processed this final revelation. There could be no mistake, they had caught my friend. The idea of him in the hands of that monster at the club made me clench my fists and a hot tide of anger surged through my body. However, I had to remain calm and favour reason over rage.

"When was this, exactly?" I asked, desperately trying to remain calm.

"The evening before last. The way this man spoke, I got the impression that it had all happened very recently, perhaps just a day or two before we talked."

I thought hard for a moment before replying. "So, they have had two days to move him. Travelling by boat would be the obvious choice, safe and quiet but rather slow. I cannot see them putting him on a passenger train, far too risky. They could have travelled in a freight or mail wagon, I suppose. These are less regular and there would still be a chance that he might be detected. No, I believe they must have taken him by sea, which means a journey of more than twenty-four hours, meaning that they could be less than a day ahead of us."

"Then you must leave, immediately. The Chairman likes to play games, so there is a chance that your friend still lives. Do not waste a moment. If you can find a fresh horse, you might yet reach Alnwick before eleven and from there make the midnight train from Newcastle."

Gold was right, I could not stand around while my friend was in mortal danger. I thanked Gold for his candour and timely advice and ran back to the inn where I quickly explained my intentions to Moorclough. He agreed wholeheartedly and swiftly ordered me upstairs to pack while he located a suitable vehicle for the journey.

Quite how he managed it, I will never know, but just twenty minutes later, Moorclough had located a small but serviceable carriage led by two fine black horses. The driver was another local who, like all of his kin in this part of the world, seemed ever eager to help a stranger in need.

As I hauled my bag onto the back of the carriage, it was swiftly joined by another, thrust beside it forcefully.

"You didn't think I would let you return to the hornet's nest alone, did you?" smiled Lestrade.

XXVI
Ex Tenebris

We thundered into Alnwick station with barely ten minutes to spare. By the time we had clambered out of the still-rocking carriage, I was firmly of the belief that our driver, Hawthorn, must have been at least distantly related to Bob Watkins. He had handled the small curricle along narrow lanes and round tight bends in almost total darkness with such ease, it appeared that he had been driving more by instinct than vision.

We boarded the midnight train and settled down for the long journey back to London. As neither of us was much minded to talk, we determined to get as much rest as we could before having to face the unknown perils we would certainly encounter upon reaching our destination.

The Ex Tenebris club. The mere mention of that awful place filled me with a cold dread. Lestrade had, at least, assured me that this time we would not be alone. He had found just enough time, at Alnwick, to wire Scotland Yard. The inspector had been careful not to identify our objective but had ensured that at least half a dozen armed men were to be made ready and waiting for his command upon our arrival.

I no longer feared for my own safety but for that of my friend. I clenched my fists and prayed. Let him be alive. Let the Chairman's vanity and cruelty, for once, work against him. I knew that Holmes could endure the most horrific of tortures and, as perverse as it sounds, hoped that he might still be suffering these as we charged south through the dark night. The alternative was too terrible to contemplate.

The battle between my inner rage and physical exhaustion, after the efforts of the previous few days, could have only one winner. The constant rhythm of the carriage riding on the tracks nudged me gently over the edge and I fell into a fitful sleep. I dimly recall waking when we paused to take on coal and water and again when we stopped briefly at an anonymous-looking station in the Midlands. It was here that I first noticed a change in the weather. A cold front had moved across the southeast, bringing with it mist and a constant drizzle. I pulled my coat tight and was grateful for the blankets that were provided in our first-class carriage. I knew he wouldn't thank me for it, but I also gently placed a tartan-patterned cover across the lap of the inspector, sleeping opposite me.

The inclement weather ensured that there was no real sunrise to observe. The sky lightened slowly from black, through several unpleasant shades of grey, until it settled upon a dull misty white.

The train slowly pulled into King's Cross, just as Lestrade woke from his undisturbed slumber. He stretched, stowed away his Royal Stewart blanket without a word and reached for his luggage. I shrugged and we alighted to the platform.

To our considerable surprise, we were there met by Inspector Tobias Gregson. His bright, grinning face was a complete contrast to the grey and dirty train shed that surrounded us all. Eschewing headwear, his blonde locks blew anarchically as the wind rushed in from the open end of the train shed.

"Good morning, gentlemen," he beamed. "Waiting outside are three hansoms. When I described the dangers that lay ahead, asking only for volunteers, so many men stepped forward that I had the very pick of the Yard. This gave me the luxury of selecting only those I thought were the very best for the job. Eight good men sit in those carriages, sir, each one armed, ready and willing to risk his life on your command."

I was deeply impressed with this show of loyalty and support, while Lestrade smiled, subtly, taking it all in his stride.

"Well done, Inspector," he replied, shaking Gregson warmly by the hand. "Thank you," he added, quietly.

"Doctor," Gregson nodded in greeting, and gestured towards the exit.

We proceeded directly to Mayfair at a fair trot, however, even at this pace, I felt frustrated. Every second could be vital, quite literally in Holmes' case. His very life could right now be hanging in the balance. I tried desperately not to imagine what torments he might be suffering at the hands of that creature.

We came to a halt at the far opposite side of Berkeley Square, hoping that our arrival at the club might pass unobserved. The uniformed men spread out briskly but quietly, keeping close to the sides of the adjoining buildings until six of their number flanked the white-fronted club. The remaining two policemen crouched down directly in the lee of the front wall. The three-foot high, white-painted boundary offered reasonable cover, so the two inspectors and I quickly joined the uniformed men squatting below.

Gregson gave a nod and a wave, and pistols were drawn. For a moment, I wished that I had asked Moorclough to join us, his terrifying rifle would have been a most welcome ally. I chanced a quick glance around the wall and saw two constables sidling along the front of the villa, towards the highly polished black front door. The other men were now out of sight, no doubt moving round the sides of the building to secure the rear of the property.

In a low voice, I explained to Gregson that the door was an impressive obstacle, heavy, iron-bound and steel-hinged.

"It seems to me that the simplest way to gain entry is for our friends, here, to let us in, themselves," grinned Gregson.

Seeing the confusion on our faces, he explained further.

"One of us should simply knock. Once they open the door, even a fraction, we will rush them. They won't be able to hold out against five of us."

I grinned silently at the inspector's plan and how similar it was to the one Holmes himself had used when we first encountered Gold.

"Very well," I replied, adjusting my tie. "I am patently the best man for the task. The way the two of you are attired would not allow you ingress into the shabbiest dive in Soho."

Before the inspectors could react, I rose and strode confidently forward, up the three low stone steps and halted before the dark, forbidding portal. I raised my cane and rapped loudly upon the black monolith. I pulled the brim of my hat low to hide as much of my face as possible. I figured that if they did recognise me, their confusion, believing me to be dead, might actually work in our favour.

The constables, to either side of me, edged ever closer towards the door. After a wait, which seemed to last for an age, we heard the sound of a metal bolt being slid aside. A series of short clicking sounds followed and then, almost imperceptibly, the door began to swing inwards.

I rushed forwards and hit the solid wooden portal with my shoulder in almost perfect synchronisation with the two uniformed men to either side of me. The force of three large men was too much for those inside and the door flung backwards. The three of us fell forwards, unable to halt our forward momentum. We tumbled into a heap, just in front of the two doormen who we had knocked over. The smaller of the two, a weaselly man I recognised from my previous visit, raised his arm. My eyes refocused after my fall, and I saw the grey pistol clasped in his sweaty hand. I reached for my own weapon but knew that I had no chance, all he need do was squeeze his trigger.

The blast was ear-splitting. I fell forwards, expecting to plunge into darkness but instead landed with a jolt upon the thick Persian carpet. I looked up and saw the pinch-faced man convulsing upon his back, a deep crimson stain spreading across his white shirt. The large, dull-faced man beside him was kneeling with his hands held high in the air.

"Take him away," ordered Lestrade, smoke still curling from the barrel of his revolver. The two constables picked themselves up and dragged away the huge doorman. I thanked the inspector and then quickly examined the stricken man, but he had already left this world.

"Damn," swore Gregson. "We are now two men short."

He was quite right. The large doorman would take both of the constables to contain, even when handcuffed. For now, we had to proceed on our own.

I led the way forward, carefully checking each and every room as we passed deeper into the club. It soon became apparent that, at this early hour, there were no members present. Even so, we burst dramatically into the main hall, guns held high. The room was empty. Glasses lay on tables, half full. Cards and tokens were strewn across the green baize gaming tables. The bar was still lit in gaudy colours, but no staff remained.

We moved carefully through the hall, disconcerted by the lack of resistance. I could tell from his demeanour that Lestrade regretted not having questioned the surviving doorman. His natural, methodical approach might have been better utilised here.

Suddenly, a movement on the far side of the room caught my eye. I raised my gun, aimed down the barrel and began to squeeze the trigger.

"Halt, police!"

I heard the words just in time and relaxed my grip. Two darkly clad constables appeared from the gloom on the far side of the hall.

"We have checked the rest of this floor, sirs, it is all clear," declared the closer of the men. "Besides, we still have four men outside, nobody is getting out."

"What is going on here?" asked Gregson. "If they have all scarpered, why leave the doormen?"

"I am not sure," I replied. "But this place is far from straightforward. We need to move upstairs. The club's ethos is to rise upwards through levels, a reversal of Dante's circles of hell. Send for more men, Inspector, we are not yet finished here."

XXVII
London's Finest

It took us several minutes to locate the stairway to the upper levels. A large door was eventually discovered, hidden in the corridor that led to the main hall, by an eager constable inching his way along the walls by the touch of his fingertips. The front face of the portal was completely flat and flush with the surrounding wall. It had been papered and painted so well that it was virtually invisible. The application of brute force via a crowbar soon had it open.

A constable moved carefully into the footwell but jumped back as a sudden volley of gunfire rained down from above.

"Hellfire," swore Lestrade, jumping forwards and returning fire, taking little care to aim his revolver. He helped the second constable pull his colleague back to safety and propped him up against the wall. Gregson peered carefully around the now half-open door, took aim and fired twice. A sharp inhalation of breath, followed by a dull thud, confirmed that the inspector had hit his target.

I checked the stricken constable. Fortunately, the bullet had merely grazed his shoulder. I tried to order him back to safety, however, he merely smiled, offered his appreciation for my attention, and pulled himself back up to resume his duties. Whenever I had occasion to work with them, the character, quality and bravery of the steadfast police constable never ceased to impress me. It was clear to see why Holmes always excluded them from his criticism of the force in general.

Gregson led the way up the stairs. A dark-suited man lay dead, hanging over the last few steps. The tall inspector stepped over the body and stopped before another closed door. The small outer landing was only large enough to accommodate two, so Gregson and the larger of the two constables prepared to break through the substantial door, four hands gripping the crowbar.

This time we were prepared. As the door opened, Lestrade and I pointed our guns through the opening, while keeping our bodies pressed flat against the adjoining wall. The inevitable blasts of gunfire that followed the door screeching and then finally yielding to the pressure of the metal lever were met with an instant response. This time there were two gunmen. I could see one, peering from behind a doorway on the right side of the larger landing that lay behind the splintered door. The other was further back, providing covering fire from the far end of the narrow corridor. This would be a far trickier proposition.

As bullets flashed back and forth, wood and brick shattered and smoke filled the air, I tried to formulate a strategy that would allow us safe progress. Suddenly, I heard Lestrade's voice, booming beside me.

"For heaven's sake, drop your weapons and surrender," he ordered. "We have dozens more armed men behind us, and soldiers are on the way, armed with the kind of weapons that will shoot clean through walls such as these. Think of yourselves. You have killed no one, yet. Why fight and face the rope when you can surrender now and have at least a chance of, one day, seeing freedom again?"

The inspector's words seemed to have worked as the guns of our assailants fell silent. The crack of pistols was replaced by muffled mumbling, rising to the level of shouting as the two gunmen appeared to argue the merits of Lestrade's suggestion.

This acted as a trigger for Gregson and the constable by his side. They pushed the door open and rushed forwards, launching a barrage of rounds at their targets. Leaving Lestrade and I standing idly, the second constable pushed past us and followed his compatriots onto the landing, pistol held high.

I stumbled into the smoke-filled hallway just as the shooting stopped. I crept forwards, as low as my knees would allow. I passed the doorway where the first gang member lay, eyes open, staring eternally heavenwards. I almost fell over Gregson, who was attending to one of the constables, this time seriously injured. I gently urged the inspector aside and examined the fallen policeman. A round had passed through his upper thigh. I panicked for an instant, but the femoral artery had not been hit. I took out a handkerchief and instructed the fellow to keep it pressed tightly to the wound. He looked up at me, imploringly. I placed an arm around his shoulder and assured him that he would be fine, nothing important had been damaged.

I felt an overwhelming sense of relief when the two constables, who had previously been guarding the grounds, shouted to us from below, offering assistance. I replied that we needed their help to remove an injured colleague from the field of battle. It took just a few minutes for them to carry the stricken policeman to safety.

In all the activity and confusion, I had not realised that Gregson had, somehow, captured the second gunman alive. The captured man stood, face to the far wall, hands raised above his head. Gregson stood behind, barking questions and aiming punches towards the kidneys if he disliked the answers.

"The first floor appears to have been completely unused."

I spun around to see Lestrade addressing me, his face dark with dust.

"There is another hidden door, on the small landing," he continued. "I took a quick look inside, but the entire level is empty, just bare floorboards and unpainted walls."

"Are you suggesting that the levels are not real?" I asked.

"Why on earth would they be?" replied the Inspector, gesturing as to encompass the building. "This whole thing is a cover for a forgery racket."

I sighed, inwardly. Of course, Lestrade was right. Everything around us was a sham, an illusion, a mirage created to hide the true purpose of the group. My heart sank as I realised that if everything about this club was fake, then perhaps the

Chairman might also be a fabrication. His order to have Holmes brought here, rather than done away with on the spot, might also be just a fantasy. I feared now for my friend more than I ever had before.

"How many floors? How many more men are there?" barked Gregson.

His captor coughed and muttered under his breath. Gregson slammed a fist into the villain's ribs. I could not help but wince at this mistreatment, but our needs were such that I allowed it to continue.

"Answer him. It is the only chance you have of leaving this building alive," Lestrade added, with menace.

"All right, I'll tell you," wheezed the man. He was short, stocky and dressed in a cheap grey woollen suit. He was, perhaps, thirty years of age, but his eyes looked old and tired. Several scars crossed his face, attesting to a lifetime of violence.

"There's one more floor, then the attic, but that's empty, nothing and no one up there." He coughed and spat on the floor. It was mostly blood.

"How many more men are waiting for us?" repeated Gregson, raising a formidable, clenched fist.

"Two, same as this floor," he spluttered. A second later, his expression appeared to change as a thought seemed to occur to him.

"What is it?" I ordered, impatiently. "What are you keeping from us?"

The man appeared to have entered a state of some confusion. Gregson pulled his fist back and tensed to strike.

"No, wait!" he pleaded. "The other fellow is there too, the prisoner. But now I think about it, I don't really understand our orders at all."

"Prisoner?" My heart leapt. Could it be Holmes? Could he be still alive?

"Who is this prisoner?" demanded Gregson. "Explain yourself."

"I don't rightly know. They told us he was some sort of traitor, but they said he must not be harmed, not under any circumstances."

"Your orders seem straightforward enough, what about them do you not now understand?" asked Lestrade, irritably.

"If he was so important, why did they leave him here? They had plenty of time to empty all those crates, after all."

"Enough of this idle banter!" I shouted. "Holmes could well be just a few yards from us right now, and the Lord only knows in what state he may be."

"You," I pointed to the stocky gangster. "You will precede us. Tell your accomplices what awaits them should they attempt to resist us." I pointed towards his compatriot who still lay behind us, staring sightlessly into the void.

In single file, stalking behind the stout criminal, we passed along the corridor until we spied, just ahead, a narrow flight of steps.

"Call up to your friends. Make it convincing," ordered Gregson, his revolver only inches from the gang member's head.

"The game's up lads" he called. "There's loads of coppers here and the militia is on the way. They got Willy and, I guess, the others too. If we give it up now, I reckon we'll all be out in a few years, we ain't killed nobody."

A single shot cracked out in response. Our captive spun around clutching at his shoulder. Gregson stepped forwards and fired a volley of shots upwards, then retreated, helping me pull the injured man out of range.

We pulled off the man's jacket and tore up his shirt. I located the bullet's entry point. It was an ugly, messy wound, but not fatal.

"You'll live," I snapped, tying one of his shirt sleeves around his shoulder. I took out my revolver and got back on my feet.

The two inspectors, the remaining constable and I steeled ourselves and prepared to move forwards. We were halted by another crackle of gunfire, however, this time it sounded different. There was no sound of impact or ricochet before or behind us, the shot had been aimed somewhere else.

"Wait, please don't shoot, I surrender!" a voice shouted from above. "I told him not to, but he fired anyway. It's all right now, though, I fixed him. He won't be shooting anyone."

"Drop your weapon and come down with your hands held high," ordered Lestrade, slowly enunciating each word.

A clatter of metal on wood was closely followed by a succession of dull footsteps until a man appeared before us, his hands raised.

"Cuff him and take him downstairs," ordered Lestrade.

The burly constable fixed the irons and none too gently pushed the miscreant down the corridor.

Pistols still held high, we moved forwards and cautiously climbed the stairs. The silence boded well, but we refused to let down our guard until we saw the body of the final gang member.

He lay, face down, a few feet from the top of the stairs. A sad, dark red shroud already surrounded him, spreading slowly outwards. Two dull grey pistols lay upon the floor.

Gregson gestured towards the body, he meant for me to confirm his death. It took but a moment. Gregson and Lestrade carefully examined the room, collected the discarded firearms, and, satisfied that there were no further threats, relaxed to the point of lighting and sharing a cigarette.

I, however, had not forgotten the talk of the first prisoner. The room within which we stood was far too small to cover an entire floor of the building. I ran to the far wall and began searching for yet another hidden door. Brushing my hands over the plastered surface it took just moments to find a narrow seam. I followed this until I found a gap large enough to accommodate the business end of the crowbar that Gregson still carried.

A hard wrench upon the metal bar was enough for the door to burst open. I peered inside. In the dull gloom, I spied a horrific sight. A wooden cross has been constructed, in an "x" shape. Upon this was tied, with straps of leather, a man. He was tall, almost naked and thin almost to the point of emaciation. His skin was as white as marble with blue veins crossing his body like a sick railway map. His hair was black, his face sunken, his eye sockets hollow. A large, noble nose rose from a sallow face. The man was completely still, his chest neither rose nor fell.

It was Holmes.

I moved closer, fearing that I had arrived too late. His skin appeared waxy and cadaverous.

"Watson, for goodness' sake, don't just stand there gawping, release me!" he commanded, hoarsely. "We have work to do."

XXVIII
Nota Bene

"Stop tugging on your bonds or I will not be able to cut them," I complained, as Holmes writhed impatiently on his obscene crucifix.

The second he was free, he ran into the next room, still half-naked. He stared at the dead criminal and frowned. "Are there others? Show me the dead!" he demanded, almost stumbling as he rushed down the stairs.

On each level, he stopped and examined the bodies of the fallen. I finally caught up with him as he left the building and approached the covered wagons in which the prisoners had been safely ensconced. He peered inside for a moment and then turned to me, his eyes burning fiercely, in stark contrast to his frail frame.

"It is just as I thought, Watson. I know none of these men and they know nothing of me or the real purpose of this establishment. Don't you see?"

I had no answer and neither, at that time, did Holmes. He stumbled, and I was fortunate to catch him before he collapsed. I guided him to the low front wall where he could sit and rest. I covered him with a blanket and sent a constable back into the club to search for his clothes. My order for him to immediately return with me to Baker Street was summarily ignored. A swig of brandy, procured from a dusty but unharmed constable, was all that he deemed necessary.

The remainder of the day passed in a blur of activity. The surviving gang members were taken by armoured carriage to Scotland Yard, to be interrogated further by the two inspectors. A full search of the building revealed no further concealed criminals. In fact, the examination discovered surprisingly little. The club was, as Lestrade had suggested, a facade. Only the lower floor had been decorated to resemble a gentleman's club. There was little of substance behind the gaudy walls. Only the bar's stock, made up of many hundreds of bottles of wines, beers and spirits, appeared genuine.

What we did find were twenty large crates. These were identified, by both Holmes and the captives, as the very vessels which had held the forged currency on its journey from the far north. They were now, of course, empty but we did come upon two further five-pound notes. Holmes insisted on taking one of these back to Baker Street with him for further examination.

My examination of Holmes was another matter entirely. He had steadfastly refused to let me treat him until we returned to our rooms. Although I was alarmed at his physical condition, I was also fully aware that any argument would be futile.

Finally, we left Mayfair in one of Scotland Yard's carriages and, soon after, arrived back at Baker Street. The familiarity of the handsome brick and stone building made the events of the previous few days seem rather distant and feel slightly unreal.

I called upon Mrs. Hudson, asked for a hot broth to be sent up and sped up the stairs to our rooms. I quickly lit a fire, for I could see that Holmes had begun to shiver. I sat him in his armchair with a large brandy, wrapped in his awful brown dressing gown.

I refused to discuss the case until he had eaten at last one bowl of Mrs. Hudson's warming broth. In the event, he wolfed down three.

"Steady now, you should not eat too much after so long a starvation," I warned.

Holmes nodded and waved towards the fireplace. I smiled and brought him one of his hideous black pipes and the Persian slipper in which he kept his unholy blends of tobacco. He carefully filled the bowl and lit it with a spill that I had plucked for him from the fire. He took a deep pull and sent out a cloud of blue-grey smoke.

"Now, Watson," he began. "Tell me everything that has happened since we were last together."

Over the following two hours, I recounted my adventures, from the moment we had faked my death, escaping from the Ex Tenebris club, until I returned, full circle, to that same accursed place that very morning. Holmes raised an eyebrow on several occasions, most significantly when I recited the strange tale of Hugo Hill. I would swear that he appeared to be genuinely surprised by at least one revelation. I explained how I had deciphered his note and followed the trail northwards, describing all of the ensuing dramas in as much detail as I could remember. I concluded with our assault on St. Mary Island and the liberation of Gold and his wife. This last success appeared to please him greatly.

"So, after hearing the tale of the unmasked traitor, we rushed back south and planned our attack on the club. The rest you already know."

Holmes paused for a minute or so.

"Doctor, in essence, you have been following me around the country, discovering little of any importance along the way. You appear to have learned nothing more about this business than I," he sighed.

Anger rose in me, and I was momentarily unable to respond.

"You did, however, save Gold and his wife. I had not believed that to be a likely outcome, considering all of the variables. The man is brave and honourable, his salvation alone justifies all of your efforts."

Holmes seemed oblivious to the offence he had caused, but his faint praise was just enough to remind me of his singular disposition and keep me from erupting.

"This entire business is wrong, and it has been wrong from the start," Holmes continued, completely unaware of my quiet fuming. "I was left, deliberately, when they could have easily taken me with them, why? Apart from the doormen, none of those left to defend the club was a regular gang member; I believe them to have been hired for this specific purpose. Once again, I must ask, why?"

I sighed and let the anger within me subside. "The answer to your second question seems fairly obvious," I replied. "They expected that one or more might be captured alive, so they deliberately used men who knew nothing of the operation."

Holmes nodded in agreement. "The answer to the first is similarly clear. They wanted me to be found."

"But you are far from ignorant of the affair," I replied, unconvinced.

"This is yet another clue, another inkling that we might have this case all wrong. They are controlling what we know, Doctor. Whoever is behind this affair has a mind of the highest quality. I fear that we have been controlled and manipulated since the very beginnings of this case."

"In that case, what on earth is going on?" I asked.

Holmes leaned forward. "What do we know for certain? At least, what do we think we know for certain, Watson?"

I quickly described the case, the club as a facade and the plot to flood the country with fake currency.

"Forged currency, so perfect that it can fool even me?" Holmes pulled out the note that he had taken earlier. "Do you still have the note that you found on the island?" he asked.

"No, it was taken to Scotland Yard for examination."

"Never mind. Was it as good a replica as this?" He handed me the note.

"Yes, just as convincing. I would certainly be fooled by a note such as this," I admitted, turning the paper in my hand.

"As would I, Watson. Or anyone else for that matter."

I was genuinely surprised at such an admission from Holmes.

"How can this be?" I asked.

"Because it is real, Watson. This note is no forgery, I would stake my reputation upon it."

XXIX
Uncertain Knowledge

Holmes' declaration left me stunned. I could not comprehend the implications of this revelation. I sat in silence for a while, unable to speak, watching Holmes puff upon his filthy briar.

"Are you absolutely certain?" I finally managed to splutter.

"Both this and its companion that we discovered in the club amongst the empty crates, are perfectly genuine five-pound notes. I would also wager double the value of all three notes combined, that the one you found on the island is also perfectly bona fide."

"But what can this possibly mean? How can they have printed genuine notes?"

"Watson, think man! They have done no such thing," chided Holmes. "There is a deliberate purpose behind their actions. I can almost feel the solution, somewhere in front of me; however, I cannot yet grasp it."

"You have yet to tell me of your travails, what on earth have you been doing for the past few weeks?" I asked.

Holmes looked momentarily surprised.

"There is really very little more to add, Watson. I infiltrated the gang and, from them, learned of the great forgery operation.

Initially working and sleeping at the club, I quickly earned the trust of the lowest denizens of the gang through my generous attitude towards alcohol. That I could keep them regularly in their cups while ensuring that I always produced the expected profit from the bar, earned for myself a level of respect that went far beyond my expectations. It simply never occurred to them that I might be paying for their drinks from my own pocket."

"The esteem in which I was now held was noticed by the higher echelon of the group and I was duly promoted, firstly to a position where I oversaw all of the club's purchases and eventually sent up to Highbay Manor to supervise the arrival and departure of the mysterious crates. However, as a result of my complacency, I made an unforgivable error and was unmasked as an imposter. I was then trussed up, brought back to London in a goods wagon and taken to the club where I was hoisted upon that ridiculous wooden stand. And there I remained with no food and precious little water until your most timely arrival."

"Is that it?" I asked, incredulously. "Were you not interrogated by that awful Chairman character?"

Holmes shook his head.

"I could tell you more, and in finer detail, but the truth is that we have independently unearthed much the same information."

"There were some additional points of interest," he then added, nonchalantly. "The first occurred while I was acting for the group as something between an accountant and shipping agent. I happened to overhear a conversation between two senior gang members. These were not your usual low-level thugs, the kind that I had dominion over, but educated men, one of whom I believe to have been a solicitor by trade."

"They were bemoaning the necessity of having had to shift their operations northwards. The initial scheme had been to deliver the currency directly into the heart of London. They had secured safe passage through Custom House, and agents had been planted to ensure that the cargo passed through unmolested and uninspected."

"Good Lord, Holmes!" I exclaimed. "Could it really have been us that forced such a change of plans?" I gasped. I was both pleased and surprised in equal measure at such an unexpected outcome so early in our investigation.

"It appears so," nodded Holmes, dryly, also appreciating the irony of having been so close to those whom we had so inconvenienced. "Their description of us was far from flattering, as were the threats they made against our persons. Despite the inconvenience caused and their clear desire for revenge, they appeared to have been ordered not to pursue the matter, ostensibly due to a lack of available time. However, I cannot now help but connect this detail to the apparent ease of my escape."

"How so?" I yawned. Fatigue was beginning to make its heavy presence felt.

"Both events appear to have been predicted or at least anticipated. However, the more I think upon the matter, the more I believe it is possible, and this would be far more ominous, that these outcomes might have been planned in advance."

"Are you suggesting that we have been led from the start? It was, after all, a possibility that we raised almost as soon as we had received that damp note all those weeks ago."

"If not the start, then soon after. We need meat on the bones old chap," smiled Holmes, gently. "But I do believe that if we can determine the answers to these most singular inconsistencies, we will begin to unravel this entire sordid affair."

"And the other points of interest?" I asked, eager to hear any new evidence for myself.

"Here, we must make a brief foray into the realm of conjecture," replied Holmes, tapping out his dingy briar. "This criminal enterprise is built upon foundations of complete secrecy, as we know. They have shown that they are prepared to kill anyone who reveals even the slightest slither of information about their affairs, whatever their position or status in society."

I nodded, remembering the fate of the poor American banker.

"However, once within the belly of the beast, things became a little different. Of course, some knowledge of the scheme would have to be shared to allow the affair to proceed but

I was rather taken aback at how openly they discussed certain aspects of the plan. Or to be more precise, one aspect. Every man I encountered, from twopenny thug to professional gentleman, seemed perfectly aware that the plan involved counterfeit currency. The talk was of crates of forged notes, dozens of them at least."

"That does seem strange, considering how vicious and mercilessly they appeared to protect their secrets," I agreed. "It is almost as if..." An idea began to form, however, like Holmes' smoke, swirling and dissipating into the agitated air, it gradually escaped me. Tiredness was slowly overtaking my ability to reason.

"And here lies my final observation, Watson. Despite all the talk of chests filled to the brim with fake money, I saw not a single note. The heavy chests passed through and were dispatched south but, without exception, every single one was locked tightly shut. I made enquiries with as many of my fellow workers as I could, without raising suspicion, but the answer was always the same: all knew of the existence of the forged notes, most believed that they originated from across the Channel, many had seen, and indeed carried, the crates in which the bounty was contained."

"However, none had actually seen any of the forged money?" I posited.

Holmes nodded and pointed at the note that I still held between my fingers.

"Apart from that one, and the three others just like it," he concluded.

"Well, I am exhausted and in dire need of sleep." Although it was still early, fatigue was making concentration increasingly difficult. "I seriously recommend that you also get some sleep, this conversation can surely wait until morning."

For once, Holmes agreed, and I was heartened to see him rise from his chair and retire to his bedroom just as I headed towards my own.

XXX
The Commissioner's Statement

My sleep was long and deep; I passed a dreamless night in what seemed but a moment. Despite having taken to my bed at such an early hour, fatigue ensured that it was late into the following morning before I woke. Outside, all appeared murky and grey as I pulled open my curtains. Light spots of autumn rain spattered the misty window pane. I dressed and made my way to the living room, hoping that Mrs. Hudson might still be willing to prepare a late breakfast. I pushed open the door and was immediately heartened by the combination of warmth and scents that enveloped me.

"Do sit down, Watson," snapped Holmes, as I stood and took in the delightful aroma of grilled bacon and fresh coffee. A most welcome fire crackled contentedly in the hearth.

"I predicted that you would not rise early, so I had Mrs. Hudson delay and prepare a later breakfast. Go ahead, Doctor, I know how even moderate physical exertion affects your constitution."

I laughed inwardly; it was too long since I had been the butt of Holmes' barbed truths. In all honesty, it would have been difficult for me to argue the case, as I then proceeded to devour everything that was set before me.

"I have been in touch with Scotland Yard," continued Holmes, as I drained my second cup of coffee. He pointed to a telegram sitting beside him on the tablecloth. "Lestrade will be calling shortly, he says he brings news from the Metropolitan Police Commissioner himself."

"Well, I never," I replied, setting my cup down and dabbing my lips with a serviette. "I cannot see what he might have to communicate with us. The gang is long gone, the best we can do now is to warn the public to be vigilant and be on the lookout for the forged notes."

"I believe that to be exactly what the Commissioner will recommend, which is why we must do all that we can to stop him from making a public statement to this effect."

"Why should we do such a thing? Surely, the public has the right to know of the influx of fake notes," I complained.

"Because every nerve, every cell, every instinct that I have is screaming, Watson. This is exactly what we would be expected to do and, therefore, what they want us to do. I am convinced that we have been manipulated, possibly from the very start. For a reason still alien to me, this is the outcome that was desired right from the moment we entered their conspiracy. As is almost always the case, we must not yield to the obvious. Our foe is operating at the very highest level, perhaps above any we have faced before."

"Very well. I think I understand your reasoning," I replied, with more conviction than I genuinely felt inside. "So, we must ask ourselves the following question," I spoke slowly as the idea formed in my mind.

"What would happen if the authorities made public the knowledge that many hundreds of thousands of pounds worth of fake currency, indistinguishable from the real thing, even by expert eyes, is about to be released into circulation?"

Holmes remained silent, deep in thought.

"On one level, of course, it would alert the public to be vigilant to the presence of the forgeries," I replied, in answer to my own question. "However, if one cannot tell real notes from fake, then no one will be able to trust the validity of any five-pound note."

I thought for a while. Holmes sat impassively.

"I suppose they could simply print a new note, one of a different design," I suggested. "The suspect notes could then all be sent to the Bank of England, where they would, surely, be able to sort the real from the counterfeit. It might take weeks or even months, but the bad eggs would eventually all be weeded out."

"Your suggestion is rather a good one, Watson, but only practical in the long term. I fear that it is the short-term effect which most interests this gang."

"And what would this be?"

"Panic, Doctor. Panic in the banks. Panic in the financial markets. Panic in the houses of anyone with money, whether it be in a deposit account or simply stuffed under a bed. Perhaps we were too quick to dismiss the political motive. Could this be an attempt to destabilise the economy and foment anarchy? Are extremists or foreign agents at work here?"

"Very well, we must try to convince the Commissioner that the affair is best kept secret, for now at least," I agreed.

Lestrade arrived barely ten minutes later. We welcomed him in warmly, served him coffee and soon he was settled in an armchair before the fire, a freshly lit Sumatran cigar in one hand, a note from the Commissioner in the other.

"Spare us the contents." Holmes waved dismissively at the correspondence held by the inspector. "Under no circumstances can the public know of the counterfeit currency conspiracy."

Lestrade frowned and stared intently at our friend. It seemed to me that he was silently questioning Holmes' capacity for reason, concerned, following his brutal incarceration.

Holmes explained, as best he could, his fears that we had all been manipulated and guided to this precise point and that the contents of the Commissioner's statement were exactly what the gang wished to be announced. Lestrade struggled with Holmes's hypothesis but eventually shook his head.

"I understand that you have been through a terrible ordeal and that you have done your country a great service, however, I fear that this is one conspiracy too far, Mr. Holmes. The Doctor and I have investigated this case from one end of the country to the other; no one has more knowledge of the facts than myself. We employed your own methods, followed the clues and we have unearthed the truth. I admit that we failed to catch all of the villains, but now that they know we are close on their trail, they will be far more likely to trip up and then we shall have them."

"Then all is lost." Holmes sighed. "If we only had a few days, I am certain that we could solve this business."

Lestrade laughed. Holmes and I both shot him the coldest of glances.

"Apologies, gentlemen, I meant no offence. The truth is that the Commissioner is currently holidaying in Scotland. He will not be back in London until Monday, which is when he will read his statement."

I jumped to my feet in excitement. The slightest smile formed on Holmes' lips.

"Today is Friday! We have three days to solve the case, Holmes. Do you think we can do it?"

"Yes, old man, I believe we can," he replied, filling his ghastly briar with broken flakes of tobacco, "And I might also have just enough time left to sort out the mystery of this missing solicitor of yours."

XXXI
The Banker

The minute that Lestrade had passed from our rooms, Holmes announced that we were to visit the City and there call on an old colleague of his from his time at Cambridge. The cab ride seemed to take an age; our desire for haste only made the four-mile journey seem longer. Holmes sat forward, ever urging the driver onwards whenever he showed even the slightest sign of slowing. It was not until we were already halfway into our journey, that I realised quite why Holmes was so impatient. It was already close to eleven on a Friday morning – most banks would only be open for a few more hours. If we were to learn anything from those in the financial centre of London, we had to enquire immediately, as all would soon be closed to us until Monday morning.

We alighted on Threadneedle Street, about two hundred yards east of the Bank of England, herself. Our destination was a far humbler affair; a stone and brick building of fine proportions and little unnecessary decoration. The brightness of the stone, and the austerity of its design, marked it out as a relatively recent addition to the City. We climbed six shallow but broad steps and passed through the open front door. "Bringley and Greenford Bank" was engraved onto a highly polished brass plaque, just to the right of the entrance.

Holmes approached the front desk and introduced himself. He apologised most profusely for not having made an appointment but hoped that his dear old friend might find a few moments to indulge an old university colleague. Even after having known Holmes for several years by this time, I was still amazed at quite how charming and persuasive he could be if it aided him in his investigations.

We were shown, presently, to a side office and asked to wait. After just a few minutes, there was a light knock on the door and in walked Holmes' friend. He was slightly shorter than average, with dark hair, heavily slicked with pomade. He wore a nondescript black suit, a white high-collared shirt and a thin black tie. A small Hunter with the finest gold chain I think I have ever seen, hung across his waist. His face was pinched and clean-shaven. He wore thin-rimmed glasses, perched upon the end of his narrow nose.

"Why, Holmes, it is you!" he exclaimed. "When they said that you were here, I could hardly believe it."

Holmes rose and shook him warmly by the hand. "Groves, this is Watson. Apologies, Doctor John Watson, late of the military and the East. Watson, this is Mr. Nathaniel Highstone Groves, the eminent banker. We studied together at Cambridge, for a while."

"Pleasure to meet you," I said, shaking his rather small hand.

"Groves, here, was one of the few who believed in my abilities from the start," Holmes stated, with more bonhomie than I had heard from him in a long while.

"Sadly, he did not stay long. I suppose a gift as wild as his was impossible to tame," smiled Groves, gesturing that we should return to our chairs. He then took a seat behind a dark, leather-covered partner's desk.

"So, what brings such esteemed company to my trifling little bank?" he asked.

"Hardly trifling, old man," corrected Holmes, with a long slim finger held up in admonishment. "When you left for Bringley, they were a one-branch, provincial outfit. Now you sit here on Threadneedle Street. Rumour has it that you have the best banking brain in Europe."

Groves appeared to blush, momentarily. "That is the greatest compliment, coming from you, Holmes." He spoke so quietly that I struggled to make out his words. He then clapped his hands, as if to wake himself from his discomfort.

Holmes then proceeded to outline the case in as simple terms as possible. Groves listened silently until Holmes had finished. He then asked a series of such extremely pertinent questions, that within twenty minutes he knew the case as well as any man in the room. It was a most unusual experience, almost as if there were two of Holmes in the room. Their discussion seemed almost mathematical in construction, such was its sparse efficiency.

"You see, Watson, it was Groves who encouraged me and together we developed a system of pure deductive logic which we applied to our research and then to our careers. We had our differences, of course, but I believe that we have both achieved a degree of success, despite the different paths that we have taken."

He then turned back to Groves.

"What is your conclusion? Have we missed something?"

Groves sat in silence, staring forward with unseeing eyes. Occasionally, he would look one way, raise an eyebrow or breath in, seemingly about to speak. However, he would then simply exhale and return to his original position. This continued for some minutes. It was slightly disconcerting, but I accepted it as the behaviour of a genuine genius. It was, after all, no more eccentric than much of Holmes' own behaviour.

"Has Holmes ever introduced you to a Doctor Trenchant?" he asked, suddenly, turning to address me.

"Why, yes." I rather stumbled out my reply. "I met him just a few weeks back. A most accomplished and charming fellow, I recall."

"He advocates a theory even more simple and logical than that favoured by myself and Holmes. He says that he was inspired by the weather, by the wind and the waves. He believes that everything that has ever happened or will ever happen, can be stripped down to a series of individual events or equations. Each minute action affects the next and so on. From a gentle breeze can grow a devastating hurricane."

"Cause and effect, I suppose, taken from microscopic to macroscopic levels?" I ventured.

"Exactly, Doctor. I should not, of course, be surprised at your perspicacity, being both a scientist and a colleague of Holmes."

"We understand the cause well enough," added Holmes. "The effects we have predicted as best we can. However, you are the expert in such matters."

Holmes reached inside his jacket and withdrew the five-pound note. He handed this to Groves, who pushed his lenses closer to his eyes and proceeded to examine it in great detail.

After a minute or so he began to chuckle and handed back the note.

"Well, it certainly looks real to me, but I am no expert." He spread his arms wide. "The money here, with which I deal, is almost all ephemeral, simply numbers, figures in columns. That may well be the first five-pound note I have held in five years."

"However," he then added, with far more gravity. "You are quite right. Something here is greatly amiss. I agree with your belief that you have been led to this position and that the Commissioner must not make his planned announcement."

"The notion of a conspiracy, plotted by a foreign power, has some weight, what with the importation of the fake notes but, other than being the source of the fake currency, our neighbours appear to have no deeper role in the affair. From what you say, at no point have you uncovered or witnessed a single political statement, written or spoken, by anyone connected with the case. No foreign agents have been encountered, no links to the involvement of another state, whatsoever.

"Revolutionaries and anarchists, on the other hand, tend to make a great deal of noise. They need others to know exactly who they are and what are their aims; otherwise, their cause would remain hidden." Groves rubbed his chin and bit his lip absentmindedly.

"What remains must therefore be a purely economic crime. Yes, money is at the heart of this affair, Sherlock," he concluded.

I was so surprised at Groves' use of Holmes' Christian name that I almost missed his reply.

"Agreed, Highstone." Sherlock's familiarity with Groves was quite touching.

"Let me write down the possible effects of such an event."

Groves dipped his pen and began to compile a list of probable outcomes.

"None are particularly positive in the short term," he read. "The irony here is that the best thing to do might well be to do nothing at all. Let the money filter through the system. It may sound like a large amount but, in an economy the size of ours, it would scarcely be noticed."

Holmes leaned forwards, dramatically. "Could this have been their plan all along? To commit a crime so inconvenient to the country that it would be better to simply let the perpetrators get away with it?"

"If so, it does have a certain genius about it," I commented.

"It would, indeed, be fiendishly clever, except for one thing," smiled Groves. "It will have failed, entirely. If this really is their scheme, then they have lost. The Commissioner will make his statement on Monday and all five-pound notes will become pariah overnight, utterly worthless."

We sat in quiet reflection for a while. I could almost feel the energy as the two learned men worked through their ideas and speculations.

"Whatever theory I begin with, I am always brought back to the same place." Groves broke the silence after several long minutes. "The Commissioner's statement. This appears, to me, to be the logical conclusion of the case as you have described it. If all roads appear to lead to Rome, then Rome is where we will discover our answers," said Groves, but with rather less conviction than before.

"Wait a moment," began Holmes. Although he was beginning to sound more animated, his tone remained measured.

"Could we be looking in completely the wrong direction? We have been concentrating on how such a plan might affect ourselves or the government. But what if the plan had a much wider scope? What effect would the Commissioner's statement have on a larger scale? On a global scale. What effect would it have on the markets, for instance?"

"Holmes, my dear friend," replied Groves, excitedly. "I believe that you might be on the right track here. A sudden influx of fake currency could seriously affect every one of the markets, at least in the short term."

"The stock market is the most volatile and subject to the greatest of swings. The value of government bonds might also be adversely affected, and the value of the pound would probably fall; the currency markets may be in their infancy, you see," he explained, "however, some movement is allowed, to reflect changes in supply and demand. If this gang could effect a swing in the value of any one of these, they could position themselves in a way in which they would profit greatly from such a movement."

"You see, gentlemen, the markets which operate in this City are all based on one thing – confidence," Groves continued." How many times have you opened a newspaper to hear of the demise of a previously successful company due to an unexpected piece of bad news, or even just a rumour of difficult times ahead? Shares begin to be sold off and this alarms others into following suit. Confidence is everything. Once lost, it is almost impossible to recover."

"This is awful, could there be a run on the banks?" I asked.

"I think not," Groves replied. "Once sterling begins to fall too far, trading would be suspended. The government would then almost certainly purchase a large quantity of our currency from private banks and from abroad, to help restore confidence. This should reverse the downward trend and see the pound and gilts return to acceptable levels. Their trick will be to buy when the markets reach their nadir and then to sell when their value recovers."

"This must be the final part of the plan," added Holmes. "The villains realise their profits, which could be even higher than the estimates that you are, I am quite certain, calculating at this very moment."

Groves let out a small laugh. "You are right, once again. At a rough guess, if it is panicked enough, the stock market alone might fall in value by twenty per cent, overnight. That may not sound like a great return for all of this risk but if they had, say, a million of this fake currency available to trade, they could pocket…"

"Two hundred thousand pounds! And humiliate the government, to boot," I exclaimed. "My apologies for the interruption, Mr. Groves." I blushed as much in rage as I did in embarrassment.

"One million, two hundred thousand pounds, actually," corrected Groves. "This affords the gang the added benefit of effectively legitimising their fake notes, as their returns will be paid in undeniably genuine currency."

"Ha! And there it is!" barked Holmes. "Our way back into the game. To enact this plan, their fake currency has to be paid into a bank account. This organisation is nothing if not careful, it would surely leave the depositing of such a noticeable sum of cash until the last possible moment to guard its intentions. I believe, at some point today, a large amount of money will be paid into a bank here in London. If we can identify this deposit, we might be able to discover who is behind it."

"Brilliant, Holmes. I shall make enquiries to that end straight away, for the deposit may already have taken place." Groves rose, excused himself, and left the room, to set in motion a hunt for the suspicious transaction. He promised to return as soon as he had assembled a team and briefed them on the search.

"By the way, tell me more about the final part of the plan that you mentioned, how the gang would extract their ill-gotten gains? How can they be certain that the markets will recover?" I asked, initially to help pass the time as we awaited Groves' return.

"If I am not mistaken, it is the final part of the puzzle," Holmes smiled, as enigmatically as the Sphinx of legend, whose face slowly wears away in the sands of the Egyptian desert.

Holmes watched me sigh, as I grudgingly accepted that he was not yet ready to share his theory.

"Fret not, Doctor, all will be revealed in good time. What I am now certain of, I will happily disseminate."

"We have been guided, maybe not from the very start, but certainly from early on in the affair. While our presence within the case appears to have been convenient for this criminal gang on several occasions, it is only recently that I have begun to speculate as to whether we might have been pawns in the game, used as a means of giving credibility and publicity to the whole affair. Remember that, uniquely, this scheme relies on the authorities discovering and believing the conspiracy. Who better to investigate their scheme than a famed consulting detective and his ally? Have our previous adventures not already appeared in lurid form in the popular press?"

"At what point do you believe we were purposely drawn into the affair? I have to admit that I never suspected Jonah Mavis of having lied to us and, in any case, how on earth could they have faked that business with the note and your incredible deductions that followed?" I asked, with undisguised scepticism.

"An excellent observation, old friend, and one that fixes the earliest possible point at which we could have fallen under the influence of an outside agency. I have expended a significant amount of time and energy attempting to replicate a predictable passage of such a note, but I must conclude that it is impossible. There is no feasible way that anyone could have known that we would trace the missive back to Custom House. We also now know that Mrs. Hill did, indeed, fashion that appeal and so we must conclude that this part of the story is exactly as we witnessed; a random occurrence which led us blindly into this deep, dark conspiracy.

"We were, therefore, at some stage, been effectively engaged by a client without even realising it, Watson. The most likely candidate for the point at which we came under their influence was when we, unwittingly, thwarted the original plan to import the faked currency through Custom House."

"This also appears to be the point at which the gang started to lose interest in Adam Gold and began subtly encouraging us to further our investigations. While the idea of having a government agent as their mouthpiece had originally seemed ideal, is it possible that, once we entered the scene, they changed their focus onto what they believed to be an even better outlet for their propaganda?"

"From this point onwards, it becomes less clear. When I believed I had infiltrated the gang, were they aware of my true identity all along? Even if that were the case, is it really possible that your adventure in the north could in any way have been contrived or premeditated? I cannot be certain, but I believe that we may have both escaped the puppeteer's strings, for a time at least. This is where I do owe you an apology, Doctor."

I raised an eyebrow, for this was almost unique.

"I dismissed your heroic northern activities too readily. The assault upon St. Mary Island was a superlative operation, as was your brave rescue of the Golds. I do hope, one day, to meet this Moorclough character, for I believe him to be a man of substance who, I suspect, holds many more secrets. However, just as at Custom House, the plans of the gang were upset, allowing you to gain an advantage. You used this to uncover my own fate, speed back down to London, fearlessly attack the Ex Tenebris club and free me from captivity."

"Yes, I see that, but it was also quite clear that they were expecting us when we arrived. Wait a moment," a light of illumination filled my head. "They needed us to rescue you. They needed you to reinforce our belief in what they were doing. However you look at this case, it works better for them if we are aware of what they intend to do! The Commissioner's announcement is the ultimate proof of this!"

"One thing does occur to me, though," I added, quietly. "What if we had died; either one of us could easily have been killed at any time?"

"Then the gang would have their headline: 'Famous Consulting Detective, Sherlock Holmes, Murdered in Great Forgery Affair.' Along with his assistant Dr Watson of Baker

Street, etcetera, etcetera," declared Holmes with a twinkle in his eye.

"Very droll," I grumbled. "However, this does make sense, I suppose."

"And they would still have Gold to continue their original plan. Their hold over him would remain, unaltered, absolute," I almost spat out the words, such was my distaste. "He would continue to feed the authorities with whatever information the gang wanted them to believe."

"We have been marionettes, Watson, dancing to another's tune. The strings may not have always been attached, but they were there when it was most important."

"How on Earth have they done this?" I demanded, my anger growing as quickly as my confusion. "Was it all fake from the moment that we identified ourselves to Gold, or Smitherson as he then called himself?"

"It may be less complicated than it first appears. Perhaps they had simply expected us to follow their trail and never dreamt you might storm the island, or that I would attempt to infiltrate the gang itself. Either way, we would have eventually arrived at, or more accurately been led to, the same conclusion. However, harken, for I believe Groves' return is imminent."

I strained to listen but heard nothing. A few seconds later, however, the door swung open, and a breathless Groves wafted in and sat back down, heavily, waving his arms as if to apologise for his inability to speak.

"Calm yourself, Groves," I said, gently. "Do you have any brandy or other spirit in this office?"

Groves pointed towards the desk before him and, within an unlocked drawer, I quickly discovered a bottle of rather questionable-looking whisky alongside an old glass. Despite its ill-provenance, the spirit worked its magic and Groves was soon in a better state to communicate.

"We have them, gentlemen." Groves looked triumphant. "One of the larger private banks received a huge deposit of cash, first thing this morning. My contact at the Coldskill Atlantic Bank assures me that the move was as secretive as it was unexpected."

"What do we do, Holmes?" I asked. "Call Scotland Yard, hand it over to them?"

"Can you imagine a less qualified group to deal with such a situation?" Holmes snorted, dismissively. "No, we must identify those who made this transaction. This is the City of London, remember, not Smithfield Market. Records will have been kept, there will be a trail to follow. Somewhere, there will be something – a name, an address, a company title – that will lead us to those who are ultimately behind this Gordian Knot of a conspiracy."

"Groves, have your men examine this deposit and those behind it," ordered Holmes. "We need to know who made the deposit, who owns the account into which it was paid and what we can find out about the bank, its employees and directors."

"Already being taken care of, old man," smiled Groves.

Holmes nodded in acknowledgement and, once again, Groves left us to set his most efficient employees upon the task of dissecting the details of the suspicious deposit. Not wishing to spend any more time waiting in Groves' rather dull office, Holmes and I left the bank and quickly retreated to a small restaurant, where we ordered some much-needed coffee.

"So, now we just wait?" I asked as a wonderfully scented, steaming pot of coffee was set between us.

"Wait and think," Holmes answered.

I poured myself a cup of the dark brown liquid, expecting an explanation, but he spoke no further.

Nearly an hour passed and still we sat in silence. I had long since finished my coffee, while Holmes' cup sat cold and untouched before him. I had tried to think through all that had occurred that day, but each fact and theory simply added weight to my already heavy head, and I found myself slowly drifting off. Suddenly, the door burst open and a young man rushed towards us.

"Mr. Holmes, Doctor Watson?" he asked, his face flushed from exertion. Holmes nodded without reply. "Please come, Mr. Groves has news of vital importance."

We wasted no time and were back in Groves' office within minutes. He stood behind his desk, deep in conversation with another banker. After a few minutes, the other man left in a hurry, acknowledging us with an apologetic nod.

Groves also began to excuse himself but Holmes stopped him dead.

"This is no time for niceties, old friend. What have you discovered?"

"The people behind this are, as we believed, extremely intelligent and fiendishly cunning. They have covered their tracks well; if it had been anyone but my personal staff examining this deposit, then I truly believe that they would have succeeded and remained safely anonymous.

"Fortunately, for us, they left one clue. Everything appears normal on the paperwork, except for one name. The incoming payments, including today's, were deposited under random names, no two are the same – we can safely assume that these are bogus identities. Until today, the deposits were all confirmed, on behalf of the bank, by the same director. However, the final deposit is different. It is signed by a director whose name appears solely on this one document. My staff contacted the Coldskill Atlantic who confirmed that this gentleman had recently become a director and that all was in order. Our research confirmed the same. On any other occasion, we would have been satisfied with this answer and looked no further. However, my staff is trained to be as fastidious as they are efficient. They showed me the details, here, take a look yourselves."

Groves handed Holmes a sheet of paper.

"Ha! Of course. Excellent work, my dear Groves. Well, that is at least one problem solved; look, Watson."

I took the sheet from Holmes. It showed the deposits by date, alongside the directors who had signed for each. Further down was a list of directors and the dates of their appointments. The most recent entry was unfamiliar, however, the name that appeared opposite the previous three payments rang loudly in my memory.

"Clarke Mitchell! Good heavens, the American banker!" I exclaimed. "So that is what they needed from him; a man on the inside, a respected name to ensure that the money moved smoothly."

"Look at the dates, Doctor, the last one, in particular." Groves gestured back at the paper.

"He last signed on Monday, the twenty-fifth of August. My word, is that not just a few days before his body was found in the Thames?"

"Indeed," confirmed Holmes, darkly. "Two days before. He had performed his function, signed the appropriate documents and the loose end had to be cut."

"How ghastly," I gasped. "But why kill him before the final deposit? Surely his presence would be essential to deal with such a huge amount of cash."

"If I remember correctly," explained Groves, "around this time, the two of you foiled the original scheme, which was to smuggle the fake money in through Custom House. The change of plans meant that everything was put back by several weeks. It appears that poor Mr. Mitchell's dip in the Thames might have been rather premature."

Ignoring Groves' rather dark humour, I felt frustration rising once more.

"As far as I can see, the forged notes are now in the system. I can see no way of stopping them from entering into circulation," I sighed. "To make matters even worse, we do not actually have any proof that anything illegal has occurred or is even being planned."

"Sadly, you are quite correct. Coldskill Atlantic will not act without solid evidence. Banking is based as much on secrecy as it is on trust," Groves agreed, apologetically.

"What are you saying? Are you simply going to give in? Do nothing?" I almost shouted in dismay.

"Calm, Watson. The game is not quite lost. We now have a powerful ally here in Groves. His people will do their best to discover all they can about these transactions. We may yet uncover the miscreants, the only enemy we have now is time. We have until the moment that the gang cashes in on their profits by selling off their holdings. After this, they will disappear like ghosts in the wind."

"There is one more avenue of investigation, of course," Groves stated. "Clarke Mitchell. I do not believe he was chosen at random. Yes, he was a member of the Ex Tenebris club, but so were many others. I posit that he was chosen because of his experience, and standing, in the banking community. He was perfectly qualified to act as a director of their chosen bank and, once there, could act without fear of suspicion. I feel further examination of his affairs is warranted."

"We already have a record of his residence from Lestrade," replied Holmes, before becoming suddenly invigorated.

"His residence! Of course. Groves, where would any correspondence, records or any other communication regarding this trade be sent?"

"Primarily, the bank," Groves answered. "However, if he wanted to show his co-conspirators proof that he had executed their instructions, he may well have had copies sent to a private address."

"There may well be clues to be found in his mail," I agreed. "Or, if we are really lucky, unopened correspondence that arrived after he was so brutally done away with."

"We shall examine the Mitchell residence first thing tomorrow," announced Holmes, unexpectedly. I had fully expected us to head off towards the unfortunate banker's house that very moment.

Holmes had noticed my surprise. "We will need Lestrade and a warrant, Watson. It must be done properly if we hope to snare these villains. I shall wire Scotland Yard on the way back to Baker Street."

"In any case, Doctor, we have a visitor this evening. I hope that, together, we may be able to solve this other little problem of yours. The whereabouts of the mysterious Mr. Hugo Hill."

XXXII
The Strange History of Mr Hugo Hill

It was past six o'clock and the sky was darkening when we finally left Groves' bank. We arrived back at Baker Street just over an hour later, having spent the journey wrapped up tightly against the cold wind within the blankets we were pleased to discover in the back of the cab. The hot supper that the incomparable Mrs. Hudson produced within a half-hour of our return, revived us and greatly improved our spirits.

Holmes had refused to elaborate upon his statement regarding our visitor but the fact that his mood had lightened was proof enough to me that he had somehow solved the case that had, thus far, thwarted my feeble efforts. After we had eaten, Holmes checked his watch and suggested that we take a brandy, warm up by the fire and prepare for the arrival of our guest.

"I have a small confession to make, Watson. This morning, before you woke, I paid a visit to an old friend at the British Museum.

"Professor Lythlands?" I asked, "I am expecting to hear from him any day now."

"In all the excitement to recount our respective tales last night, we both neglected to observe the telegram that Mrs. Hudson had placed upon the mantelpiece. Lythlands had wired that he had information of an urgent nature regarding your case and requested that we visit him as soon as possible. It was early when I discovered the message and, not wishing to wake you from your much-needed rest, I took the opportunity to set off immediately and visit the Professor. Knowing that he was religiously at his desk before seven, I left before dawn and arrived just as he was unlocking the door to his office."

I sat forward, excitedly, my concern for the safety of Hill outweighing any annoyance I might have felt at Holmes' failure to wake me or for usurping my case.

"Tell me all, Holmes, what did you learn?" I demanded.

"Firstly, Lythlands confirmed much of what you suspected. The birth registration certificate was indeed a fake, but the remaining documents are genuine, and almost entirely legal in nature."

I couldn't help but release a sigh, I had expected rather more from Holmes' expert.

"Do not fret, Watson, for this is only the beginning, not the conclusion," scolded Holmes. "It is the nature of these documents, and the order in which Hill discovered them, that is of the greatest interest."

"The order in which he discovered them? What difference could that possibly have made?"

"Remember what you were told by the maid, Medcalf. Hill took one look at the papers, thrust them back inside the box, hid this in the attic and literally threw away the key." Holmes paused to fill and light his mud-coloured Zulu briar.

"Imagine, Doctor, that you were Hill. Placed into the care of strangers, well-looked after and wanting for nothing but a family. Of what would such a young boy dream? What fantasy might he create to explain his most singular circumstance?"

I shrugged, silently, and let Holmes continue.

"An epistolary acquaintance of mine has recently suggested that it is not uncommon for orphans to construct a belief or fantasy in which their parents are not just alive but also wealthy, perhaps even ennobled, and will one day return to reclaim their lost offspring. I would be surprised if Hill had not felt this at some point while growing up. However, such fancies rarely last much past adolescence.

"What else develops, though, at this stage? Self-awareness of course, but also knowledge of the world and how it functions. Just as he is outgrowing such childish notions, he suddenly discovers that somebody, somewhere, has been secretly providing for all of his needs. Who could this be other than a benefactor of some ways and means, perhaps even someone of public standing?"

"Very well," I nodded, "I will concede that this is possible, perhaps even likely. Now, please explain how the order in which he examined the documents could have led to him hiding them away for the next ten years?"

"Do you believe in fate, Watson? I know that in your logical mind, as in my own, you will deny any possibility of its existence. However, in this case, I wonder." Holmes looked unusually pensive.

"I believe that fate is a crude way of explaining, or justifying, the past. How many times have we heard 'It was meant to be' or 'I had no choice, it was fate', to excuse the most terrible behaviour?" I replied, for once taking the cold logical position.

"Hill received the box on his twenty-first birthday," Holmes stated. "Somehow, he found the patience to wait the few days until the key arrived. He opened the box and picked out the first document that came to hand. What if this had been the birth certificate? It would instantly shatter all of his dreams. It would show him that, far from being a forgotten noble, he was just another abandoned child, parents lost or unknown. The origins of the house and money would cease to be of interest; a generous charitable benefactor or a darker pay-off to avoid an unknowable scandal, would probably now be his best guesses."

"Which would explain why he stuffed the documents back into the box and locked it up in the attic," I added, breathlessly.

"I have one problem with this theory though, Holmes," I added. "He was a student of law, how did he not see the birth document for the fake that it was?"

"The answer to that question was delivered by the second post, again placed upon the mantel by the ever-reliable Mrs. Hudson." Holmes passed across an envelope, stamped with a Cambridge postmark.

It was a reply from Hill's college. It confirmed the dates during which he attended Pemberton, along with a few extra details regarding some minor sporting achievements and a glowing character reference.

"Hill did not start at Pemberton until he had reached his twentieth year. He had barely completed his first tripos when the box arrived. While he may have gained enough experience to recognise a birth certificate, he had not quite enough yet to realise that this particular one was a forgery."

"My word, Holmes. That is incredible, I am at a loss for words. I can now see why you mentioned fate. For want of a little more experience, he refused to delve any further into the documents. What would he have found?" I speculated, with not a little dread.

"His answers, Watson. However, you must wait a few minutes longer, for, I believe I hear our guest arriving." Holmes rose, walked to the door, waited a short while, and then flung the door open.

Standing on the landing, right arm raised, ready to knock, was a man, his face the very picture of surprise.

"Lord Sunderton, welcome. Please come in. I am Sherlock Holmes; this is my esteemed colleague Doctor John Watson. Take a seat. Can I offer you a brandy? I also have some rather fine Havanas if you would care to indulge?"

Our visitor nodded and rather grunted his acceptance. He was a fine-looking man of perhaps fifty years, dark-haired and finely featured. He was slim and straight-backed, more athletic than military. He wore a black suit of simple but perfectly tailored design. His shirt was bright white and high-collared, a dark, silk cravat was pinned with a bar of rose-coloured gold. I poured three brandies while Holmes chose cigars from his ebony humidor, carefully snipping these with an ornate gold cutter, a gift from one of many grateful clients.

We took seats before the crackling fire, Holmes passed around a box of long cedar matches. Once three consecutive plumes of smoke signalled that the cigars were all lit, Holmes began.

"I will not waste your time, so please do not waste mine," he began, bluntly. "Where are you holding your brother?"

I was utterly shocked, what could have possessed Holmes? My mouth fell open, but I could form no words. To my utter incredulity, instead of becoming angry, Sunderton's shoulders sagged and his face took on the most pitiable look. He then managed to rally, slightly, and the merest of smiles appeared.

"You genuinely are as remarkable as I have heard. Yes, I did have Hugo; however, he is no longer my captive. I have been a fool, as you know, but now I see that I have been a double fool." Sunderton appeared a man utterly defeated.

"Where is Hill?" I demanded, rising to my feet, fists clenched.

"I expect he is on a train back to his family. You see, I have made the most terrible mistake."

"Indeed, you have, but will you please confirm some details for us?" asked Holmes, taking a more conciliatory tone.

Sunderton nodded. "Of course. Even though it appears that you know almost everything, I will answer any other questions you may have."

"You are the current Lord Sunderton of Hantley and Denster. Your father, the first Lord, made a fortune for himself, and the nation, in the far east. Shortly after his investiture, he married Countess Zabak of Thorn."

"Two years later, you were born. The three of you resided together at Hantley Hall for twenty unremarkable years. Then, unexpectedly, your poor mother died. Less than a year later, much to your surprise, your father remarried and, along with a second wife, there followed a second son."

"There then followed further tragedy. Your stepmother suffered terribly from the effects of childbirth and died, just a few days later. Finally, before the infant was even six months old, his father was lost at sea, attempting a risky early winter crossing of the North Sea. The child was orphaned into the care of his older brother."

"Yes, this is all true and widely known."

"Not at all!" exclaimed Holmes. "The disaster at sea is indeed well known. However, your father was an intensely private man and had not yet announced the birth of his second son. He was still grieving for his wife and, as he already had an heir, saw no reason to make public the news until he had returned from his trip to northern Europe."

"So, now, I must insist that you share with us the full story." Holmes leaned forward and his fingers formed themselves into their familiar steeple. "Please leave nothing out and avoid prevarication. It will not go well for you."

Sunderton sighed. "Very well. I was already up at university when Hugo was born, so I witnessed little of what followed first-hand, save for the conclusion. I remember my father visiting me at Oxford to deliver the bad news in person. He informed me that his new wife had died giving birth but that the child had survived. Less than six months later, he disappeared. I was sad to lose my father, but I have to be honest, here, I felt little affection for my newborn half-brother. I had not stepped foot into the family home for more than a year and was certainly not close to his mother, a woman I barely knew."

"It was when I began sorting through my father's effects that things changed."

I noticed Sunderton's hands becoming unsteady, so I offered him another brandy. He nodded his thanks, took a sip, wiped his brow with a monogrammed handkerchief and continued.

"I discovered a diary, along with a locked box which contained a collection of old documents and trinkets. I was, at the time, an unsentimental fool and I threw away the box and all of its contents without a further glance. Out of some sense of loyalty, I kept the diary, idly thrusting it into a random pocket of my overcoat."

"Just a few days later, I found myself at the remembrance service for my father; we could not have a traditional funeral as we had no body to bury. I sat on a cold wooden pew in a cold stone church surrounded by cold white faces, few of whom I even recognised. Patting down my coat as I took my seat, I felt a lump in one of the pockets. I reached inside and withdrew my father's diary. It looked enough like a prayer book for me to examine without raising any eyebrows and I felt that its contents could hardly be of less interest than the hymnal that lay before me."

"I flicked through the first half, it was terribly tedious, all business and dull social notes. However, the tone soon changed.

There was now just one subject, my mother. It seems that my father had recently been in receipt of papers which raised questions regarding the legality of my parents' marriage. There was a clear inference that, at the time of their wedding, she may have been engaged, or already married, to another."

Sunderton's voice had gradually become dry and hoarse. This time I offered a glass of water.

"Thank you, Doctor. Of course, I then realised that I had carelessly discarded all of the documents that my father had accumulated. I searched the entire house and gardens for the box, but it was long gone, away to some dump, or so I thought."

"By now, real panic had set in. What if the papers were discovered? Anyone could have picked them up; I had not been careful with their disposal, and I only vaguely remembered throwing the chest somewhere outside the house. If the knowledge within became public, I could lose my position, along with my inheritance, to my infant brother. It was then that I sat down to seriously think through my dilemma. The answer came to me just as I was answering some correspondence – replying to letters of condolence, as it happens. It suddenly occurred to me that there had not been a single mention of Hugo in any of the letters I had received. I made a few discreet inquiries and soon discovered that my father had not officially announced his birth. Not for the reason you postulated, Mr. Holmes, but because he was already investigating the validity of his first marriage. This also explained his ill-fated voyage across the North Sea. He was desperate to reach the Baltic States and examine what records he could uncover there, risking a journey weeks after the last date for safe passage had passed. A quick Channel crossing, and the rest by land, would not have taken much longer, the silly fool." Sunderton's words trailed off, the sadness of his loss was tinged with bitterness.

"So, I had my answer, Doctor, Mr. Holmes. I sent Hugo away with a trusted nanny and housekeeper. I purchased the house in his name and set up a generous trust fund that would pay for his education, while still providing an income for the rest of his life. He would be comfortable and want for nothing. I prayed that no one else knew of the existence of the diary and documents. The years passed and I slowly learned to relax, but never completely. I always had the feeling that I was being watched, that I was just a moment away from being exposed as a fraud, a fake, an imposter."

Sunderton stubbed out the last inch of his cigar. He took a deep swig of brandy and composed himself.

"I never got to properly examine the documents in that terrible box. I never again heard from anyone who would question my lineage. As far as I could possibly be certain, I was the genuine, rightful heir to my father's title and fortune. And yet, every day I looked over my shoulder and suffered for what I had done." Sunderton slumped once again.

"That is some tale, for sure," I commented. "But what made you take Hill now? Why kidnap him when all was going well for you?"

"The truth? It is, as always, simple and in this case quite pathetic. I had always wished to keep an eye on my brother's development, to have eyes and ears in and around the house. My grand scheme was to hire a housekeeper and pay them well above the going rate to ensure their loyalty and discretion. For this generous recompense, they would write occasional reports back to me, informing me of young Hugo's progress."

"Years passed much the same. The reports arrived regularly, once or twice a year, although each was much the same as the dozens which had preceded it – all was well, and Hugo was making adequate progress – but they offered little in the way of detail. However, the contents of the last letter I received made my blood run cold. The message followed the usual pattern, and I was about to throw the paper into the fire until I read the very last line: 'The documents are safe. Hugo knows. It is all over now.'"

Sunderton coughed and leant forwards.

"Well, what else could it mean? 'Hugo knows. It is all over now.' Hugo had somehow discovered the box and learned the secrets within. I would be ruined. I panicked and hired two burly men from the village and, together, we took Hill on his way into town. He did not struggle, he seemed almost to recognise who I was the second he laid eyes upon me. He even insisted on calling me 'brother' from then until the moment I released him."

"You see, I was already on edge after receiving a bizarre message that had arrived just the previous morning."

"Message? What message?" demanded Holmes.

"Some stupid attempt at blackmail, suitably vague of course. It appeared to be hand-written on vellum or some such material, in what looked a lot like blood. Terrified me at first, until I recognised the writing on the envelope. It was just a silly prank, some old university acquaintances, trying it on for their ridiculous faux satanic club."

"Club?" asked Holmes, carefully. "How, pray tell, was it named?"

"Oh, I paid little interest, some doggerel Latin nonsense. What was it? Deus Ex? No. Tenebris, something? I'm sorry, I really cannot remember. How is this relevant anyway?"

I almost leapt out of my chair and would have grabbed Sunderton by his lapels if Holmes hadn't immediately placed a calming hand on my arm and subtlety shook his head. I leaned back but struggled to relax.

"You took Hill and incarcerated him." Holmes tried to bring us back on track.

"Yes. I found a farmhouse; the family was more than happy to cooperate. Conditions were tolerable. I made sure he was warm and always had food. It was just panic, as I said. I had no plan. However, one thing then occurred that I could not have predicted."

"And what would this be?" I asked, quietly.

"That my most neglected brother would somehow forgive me, embrace me and help fill the void in my heart, left open when our father died."

"This is most remarkable," I started.

"Hush, Watson," Holmes scolded. "Please continue, Lord Sunderton. What finally led you to release your brother?"

"I know how I must appear, gentlemen, however, I do possess some moral backbone. I explained all to Hugo, the entire story, from my birth to our father's death. He seemed to understand why I had taken him, and he never showed any anger or animosity towards me. From the very first day, he insisted that he had no designs on my title. At first, I ignored his pleas, but his open and earnest paeans to his wife and family began to move me. He claimed to care nothing for himself, for wealth or position. It was most convincing and, while I still held firm, I began to engage him more in conversation. As the days passed, I learned more about my brother and finally, just two days past, he revealed a secret to me that made the entire episode even more of a debacle than it had already become."

Holmes tilted his head slightly in anticipation. I had to grip the arms of my chair to avoid a physical intervention. Sunderton took a deep draught of brandy and again dabbed at his mouth.

"He then told me the full story of the locked box. He had opened it, as you know, but far from discarding it, unexamined, he had recognised and quickly understood the purpose of the contents. He may have been but a first-year student, but he was already well-read in law, history and the classics. The crude attempt at a forged birth certificate hadn't fooled him for a second, and the remaining papers revealed what had been hidden from him. The full meaning of the collection was clear to him from the outset, just as it is now known to you. It spoke of a birthright that had been denied him. All of the evidence of the conspiracy had been placed in that small casket. However, inexplicably, and without a moment's thought, he rejected any claim to the family title."

"But why? What could have made him give up a life of such privilege and wealth?" I asked.

"I asked the same of him, myself, Doctor. His answer was simple. 'I would never be happy,' was his reply."

"That is all?" Holmes raised an eyebrow in surprise.

"He explained that, back then, he had but one single ambition, to marry the woman that he loved. His beloved Catarina was the daughter of a local farmer, respected well enough, but certainly not a fitting match for a Lord."

"I find myself warming to your brother more and more," Holmes commented, rather subversively, I felt.

"Do you know who discovered the documents after you had discarded them, those later delivered to Hill on his twenty-first birthday?" I asked.

"Oh yes, however, I learned this information only recently." A very subtle smile seemed to pass across Sunderton's face, almost as if in relief. "If you recall, I told you of my grand plan to place an agent within the household. Well, it appears that I was rather 'hoisted with my own petard'."

"I bought a pleasant country villa, far enough away from prying eyes but within a day's ride of my estate, in the event of any unforeseen circumstances which might require swift intervention. It seems that my caution was also my undoing. I entrusted the family solicitors with the task of interviewing and selecting the ideal nanny and housekeeper for my young brother. The girl they chose came from a family well-known for their service and arrived with excellent references and a reputation for complete loyalty and discretion. She was also a local, born and bred, who recognised my family's lawyers straightaway. Naturally, she passed on this information to her mother who, it transpires, had held a similar position for my father. It was she, gentlemen, Mrs. Medcalf, senior, who had found the discarded papers and gathered them up for safekeeping. This was a well-educated family; they would have known the importance of such documents."

Sunderton paused, pushed himself upright in his chair, took a small sip of water and continued.

"Mrs. Joan Medcalf had been extremely close to my father and fiercely loyal with it. I cannot imagine how torn she must have felt, between her duty to the family's good name and justice for Hugo. Ultimately, she decided to leave the decision up to Hugo. Alongside her daughter, she resolved to provide my brother with the finest upbringing she possibly could, and they waited until his twenty-first birthday before delivering the box and revealing his true lineage. Hugo's dramatic rejection of his inheritance appeared to vindicate the Medcalfs' neutral position and the matter was never raised again."

"Of course, all of this I learned from Hugo," Sunderton's head then dropped, dramatically. "I also learned what then, after ten long years, triggered this whole shameful business. Hugo had always suspected that his guardians had known more about his background than they had shared with him. He told me that he had sworn to be done with all secrets. Firstly, he would confront Janet and insist that they both share all that they knew about his past. He would then have one last confession to make – the one that mattered to him the most – revealing his final great secret to his wife. The talk with Janet went extremely well and left them both in good spirits. In her haste to reassure me that my concerns were now at an end, she must have quickly added those fateful words to her final letter: 'The documents are safe. Hugo knows. It is all over now.'"

Sunderton now looked desperately sad, his skin pallid and damp. "I had misunderstood their meaning, completely. I interpreted those simple words as a warning of sorts. However, it was just as it stated, the documents were safe and would remain secret. Hugo did not, and never had, any interest in his inheritance. Poor Janet simply wanted to reassure me that, at last, I could be at peace, my troubles were over."

"Quite remarkable," I commented, incredulously. "If only you had left things as they were."

"How I wish I had, Doctor," Sunderton replied, his eyes glassy with tears. "However, there is more to tell and further ironies to come. During his incarceration, Hugo and I talked often, and I found myself eager to learn more about my brother's life. Hugo graduated from Oxford and took up a junior position at a law firm in the City. Every evening, he would retire to a local inn and, from there, write a letter to his sweetheart back home. He soon began to write for himself, short stories at first, ideas born of his lonely childhood. After a few months, he had produced quite a volume of tales, full of adventure and fantasy. Providence intervened in the form of a fellow patron, a literary agent, who befriended Hugo and agreed to publish his stories. These proved extremely popular, and within a year, Hugo was earning far more from his writing than from his regular work."

"Delighted with his new career, he returned to Catarina. He moved back to the house in Reddlesham and, shortly afterwards, asked Catarina's father for her hand in marriage. The farmer was of old stock and would not have accepted writing as a secure profession, so Hugo let them both continue to believe that he was still practising law. He hated the deception, but it was the only way that his proposal would be accepted. So, each morning he would leave the family home and walk into town. He would then spend the day in the library, researching and writing."

"Ironic indeed, sir, considering that he could have been a Lord of the Realm, had he so chosen. I suppose his writing, along with the regular payments from his trust, afforded him a healthy income," I ventured.

"Indeed, it did, and if I had simply left him alone, none of this ghastliness would have occurred," stammered Sunderton.

"Once I received your communication, Mr. Holmes, I released Hugo immediately. I told him to take whatever recourse he wished, legal or otherwise. Can you believe what he did? He embraced me and then shook me by the hand, promising to see me again soon."

"Oh, I believe that without question," Holmes responded, rather coldly. "Your brother is truly of a different class from yourself."

"Did he happen to publish under his own name? Only I do not recall an author named Hugo Hill." I could not help but ask the question, out of professional curiosity.

Sunderton smiled, "No, he uses the name Charles Foundling. Rather appropriate, all things considered."

I shook my head in wonder, "Several books on my shelf bear that very name," I smiled.

"So, here I am, at your mercy. Hugo seems not to want to take action; however, I would not object if you chose to, even if just to reclaim your expenses." Sunderton was the very picture of dejection and misery.

"You never married?" asked Holmes, bluntly.

The now dishevelled peer shook his head, "I have spent decades looking backwards, I have had no time to plan any sort of future. The title I fought so hard to keep will die with me. I do not know what will become of the house."

Sunderton pre-empted my response with a raised hand. "No, Hugo was clear. He wants no part of this for himself or his sons. I tried to insist, but he was adamant. We finally agreed that when I die, all of my assets will be split evenly and put into trust for the boys. Somehow, this knowledge has given me more peace than anything I can remember."

Sunderton sat before us, exposed and vulnerable. He reminded me of countless criminals that, once caught, appeared almost relieved. The vast majority of criminals are not evil by nature, circumstance is the engine behind most malfeasance. Eyes wide open, he awaited our verdict.

"Your crimes have been most heinous," stated Holmes. "You have denied your brother his entire life and future. Whether you or he were the rightful heir, I doubt that we will ever know for certain."

"However, your actions have not led you to a life of contentedness. Your conscience has ensured that you have received punishment each and every day since your terrible betrayal. You sit before us, a lonely and broken man, having spent the last two decades looking over your shoulders. You have no family, no trusted friends and your precious line is broken."

"Doctor Watson," Holmes suddenly addressed me, "you are my standard, my everyman. You are the jury. How do you find the defendant?"

"Guilty, of course," I replied, without hesitation.

"And the sentence?" asked Holmes, his tone utterly serious.

"Time served," I concluded, emptying my glass with a single swig.

XXXIII
New World

After the shocks and revelations of Sunderton's testimony, I had quite forgotten about his earlier disclosure regarding the Ex Tenebris Club. Holmes had made no such mistake. As he led Sunderton from the living room, he casually enquired into the identities of those he believed were responsible for the attempted blackmail.

"The author of the note was a fellow called Nowyswiat, fancied himself as a minor Eastern European noble of some sort. However, the ringleader, and major troublemaker, was an American, Mitchell, I think was his name. Odd cove, prone to major mood swings. One moment he would be laughing and joking, the next he could do something terrible. I once saw him beat a stray dog to death with his cane, just for barking at him in the street. Afterwards, he just stood over the poor creature, laughing, and he continued to do so, long after we had left him in disgust."

Holmes showed Sunderton to the door and closed it quickly once he had left.

"Watson, did you hear?" he asked, excitedly.

"Yes, we must investigate this Nowyswiat character," I replied, excitedly writing the details into my notebook.

"Nowyswiat? Utter nonsense. It is Mitchell we must investigate," snapped Holmes, impatiently.

I was incredulous. "But Holmes, old man, Mitchell is dead. Do you not remember?"

Holmes smiled and moved to his writing desk. "Somebody is dead. How do we know for sure that it is Mitchell, the American banker? Who identified the body? There is a banking connection here, that we know for certain, and a proven link to America, also. How better to hide your identity than to kill it off entirely!"

"We must head straight to his residence; if he is still alive, perhaps we can catch him off guard," I declared.

"A fine plan, Doctor, but not until we have alerted Lestrade and his men. We have no idea of who, or what, we might there discover."

Holmes wrote out an unusually lengthy telegram and called downstairs for Mrs. Hudson to rush it to the local post office for immediate transmission. I moved to rise, but Holmes raised a hand to halt me before I got to my feet.

"We will not be acting tonight, Watson," he revealed, much to my disappointment. "Your eagerness is commendable, but we must be properly prepared."

Holmes returned to his armchair before the fire and worked at his pipe until it was once again lit and belching its awful foggy plumes around the living room.

"I have asked a series of questions of friend Lestrade, the answers to which it is essential we ascertain before we proceed. Firstly, who identified the body of Mitchell? I have a suspicion that the name will be one familiar to us. Secondly," Holmes gestured, holding the bowl of his pipe and pointing with the filthy, well-chewed vulcanite mouthpiece, "what were the last known residences of both Mitchell and this Nowyswiat character? And, thirdly, when can he have half a dozen armed men ready and prepared to raid the lair of a cunning, and potentially deadly, arch-criminal?"

"I see. You are quite right, Holmes and, of course, we must determine which residence they are using, or if they are now lying low somewhere else entirely."

While I sat and smoked my finely grained brown bulldog briar, filled with its altogether more fragrant Cavendish tobacco, Holmes moved to his shelf of reference books and folders. After perhaps ten minutes, he let out a familiar cry, one which always indicated success.

"I knew it, Watson!" he declared, pointing to an entry in what appeared to be a large, leather-bound encyclopaedia. "Here, 'Nowy Swiat', it is not a name but a place, a street. A street in Warsaw, to be exact. It translates as 'New World.'"

Holmes slammed the heavy tome shut. "It may be of no relevance, whatsoever, but one must always examine each and every piece of evidence, one can never know where they might lead."

"Another American connection, perhaps?" I posited.

I pulled upon my pipe, the familiar tastes and scents rolling upon my tongue. I felt momentarily relaxed enough to attempt a general summation of events, and my conclusion bothered me greatly.

"The one thread that has run through both of these cases is forgery. The faked, the counterfeit and the deliberately concocted."

"From the moment we were reeled in at Custom House," I continued, "everything has been fabricated. Gold was a fake criminal acting under duress as a fake secret agent. The forged currency, my adventures with Lestrade and Moorclough. Sunderton's title, Hill's legal career, all concoctions and tall tales. I wonder, sometimes, if anything at all in these two affairs is actually real!"

Holmes appeared to prepare a reply but stopped, his mouth hung open. Then a strange expression crossed his face. Finally, he began to laugh, softly at first, but rising to a crescendo of cacophonous mirth. His whole body shook, and I swear that small tears even formed in his steel-grey eyes. I asked him if he required assistance, brandy, perhaps, but he waved away my concerns and slowly composed himself.

"Oh Watson, you are the unexpected savant once again. Well-done, old man, for you have led me to what must be the solution to all of this. Everything." Holmes clapped his hands together, his face now set in an aspect of determination.

"I don't suppose that you would care to share this solution with me?" I sighed.

"All will be revealed, tomorrow, Watson. If I am right, we shall have both our villains and our answers."

XXXIV
Irregulars

It was after ten o'clock that evening when we finally received a reply from Inspector Lestrade. We would have to wait until the following morning before he could confirm who had identified the body of Clarke Mitchell, but he did share with us details of the American's London residence. He also confirmed that he would have the requested men, armed and ready, before noon tomorrow.

I spent the last hour before I retired to bed cleaning and oiling my service revolver. It had acquired quite a crust of dried salt from my adventures on the northeast coast and the familiar process of disassembly, brushing and reconstruction greatly relaxed my racing mind. Holmes appeared oblivious to the tension, practising his violin and consulting his books.

I suffered another fitful night and woke well before dawn. I found Holmes still working, he claimed to have slept, however, I believed this unlikely. Mrs. Hudson provided a fine breakfast, with no complaint or comment upon the early hour. I took my fill, but Holmes, as usual, simply picked at his food, taking in only a cup or two of dark coffee.

We had to wait until well past eight before Lestrade finally made contact.

"Just as I thought," declared Holmes, waving the white telegram. "The man who identified Mitchell's body was none other than his old friend, Nowyswiat."

"That does still leave a body, however, whose identification is now unlikely. Probably a poor fellow in the wrong place at the wrong time," I sighed. "Sadly, I fear his true identity may now no longer be of any great importance."

"No, Watson, once this business is over, I will do all I can to give a name to this poor man. He is as much a victim as anyone else in this sordid tale. We must not forget that we all stand equally before the Lord and justice must always be served."

Not for the last time, Holmes' burning desire to see right and justice always triumph, proved a real inspiration to me.

"Lestrade adds that his men have been watching the Mitchell residence since late last night. They witnessed no sign of life, so they gained entry by force this morning," read Holmes, easily deciphering the inspector's rather cryptic, cost-saving shorthand. "The house had been stripped bare, not a single document or written page was found."

"So that just leaves this Nowyswiat fellow, I suppose. At least the good inspector saved us the trouble of having to search Mitchell's place ourselves."

"I had feared this, Watson. The fact that he felt the need to abandon his residence proves that he remains just as vigilant now as he was prior to his faked demise. Our opponents will not fall into complacency while the scales can still be tilted either way. It is, of course, also possible that our nemesis has decamped to another location completely."

"Then we could be wasting ours and Lestrade's time," I sighed.

"I think not, old friend. I have had my own people watching the house of Nowyswiat. There has been some activity there, at least. I expect a report very shortly."

"By 'people', I imagine that you mean your Irregulars?" I asked before a sudden realisation hit me. "How did you know his address? No, don't answer that. I suppose that you and your friends unearthed it last night. I knew that you had not slept," I groaned.

"Finding the address of a man in possession of such an unusual name was not difficult, Watson. What activity I observed, before returning to our rooms, was minimal and inconclusive. Lights were on, shadows moved behind curtains, but no one arrived or departed the building. It could be nothing or everything. In a situation such as this, the behaviour of the innocent and the guilty are indistinguishable."

"The guilty lay low, the innocent stay home. Yes, I see the irony of the situation." I offered Holmes a Burma cheroot; they were still a little green but seemed to smoke quite well. To my surprise, he withdrew two from the proffered flat wooden box.

Holmes smiled at the look of mock outrage that I displayed at his avarice, before taking on an expression of wounded innocence.

"Oh Watson, how could you? Only one of your fine cigars is for myself. Its colleague is aired in advance of the approach of our good friend, Inspector Lestrade. Why, even now, do I think to detect his footfalls upon the stair carpet?"

I had just enough time to chuckle before a sharp rap announced the arrival of the inspector. I opened the door and was surprised, not to see Lestrade standing before me, but by the dull, green-coloured blur that raced past, unbidden, into our rooms.

"Ah, Wiggins," declared Holmes from behind me, "Your report, I hope."

A young boy of perhaps nine or ten years, wearing an oversized green woollen suit, handed Holmes a filthy sheet of paper and proceeded to speak at great speed. I showed Lestrade to a chair, settled down myself and from there watched this most unusual spectacle.

"Two men entered at six, big they were, dark suits, carrying heavy bags. Guns, I reckon, or maybe gold. Then two more at seven, nothing else until just before I left. Four more men went in. These were different, though, looked like they had just come from the docks. Rough types, lots of skin art, not many teeth, you know what I'm saying, Mr. Holmes."

"Indeed, I do. Well done, Wiggins. Call your boys off, for now, take this and distribute as usual. Stay away from this area for at least a day, I cannot stress enough the importance of this."

Holmes held out a small black leather pouch. Wiggins reached out to take it, but Holmes quickly drew it back.

"Nobody is to be within a mile, I mean it. If I see you or anyone else in the vicinity, this will be the last coin from me that you will ever see. Holmes stared, steely-eyed at the young street urchin.

"You have my word," he replied, spitting on his hand before offering it to Holmes.

Holmes dropped the pouch into the boy's bespittled hand. Wiggins smiled, saluted, and ran out as quickly as he had entered.

"Unorthodox," Lestrade commented. "But is the information reliable?"

"Absolutely," replied Holmes. "We have our target. Inspector, your men must stop all traffic at least half an hour before we approach the house. It is time to prepare. Watson, I see that your revolver is now pristine, bring as many cartridges as you can carry. I fear that what lies ahead may be a bloody business."

XXXV
Hanover Square

Number thirteen, Hanover Square. An address that will live with me, forever. Despite being just over a mile from Baker Street, the journey in the covered police wagon seemed to take an eternity. We finally pulled into the square alone, uniformed constables having earlier shut off all routes in or out. Despite now being almost bereft of leaves, the skeletal forms of the trees in the centre of the square provided just enough cover for the regular police to carry out their duties on the fringes of the square, unobserved.

This time, we had a dozen men, half of whom were armed with rifles; these were all former military men. They approached stealthily, keeping close to walls and never letting themselves be exposed. Four men split off and headed for the back of the building.

Holmes and I scurried through the wooded green at the centre of the square. After just a few minutes, we were directly in front of number thirteen. It was a three-storey townhouse of pleasant proportions and, like most of its neighbours, painted universally white. A front wall, perhaps four feet in height, would offer us reasonable cover if needed. The house was still, all of the curtains were tightly drawn. Once we were all in position, a deathly silence descended on the square.

Lestrade joined us. "We must give them a chance to surrender. I need to be certain that we are not making a terrible mistake."

"Quite right, Inspector," I agreed.

I heard a muffled sigh of complaint from Holmes and, before I could respond, he strode past me and walked straight up to the front door.

"Order your men to take cover," he shouted back to us. Lestrade sent the appropriate signal.

Holmes raised his cane and bashed down heavily upon the door. Paint and chipped lacquer flew, as he rained down his blows.

"Clarke Mitchell!" he yelled, pushing open the heavy brass flap of the letterbox that sat in the centre of the solid, jet-black door. "You are surrounded by a heavily armed militia. Come out with your arms raised and you may yet live out your natural life. Resist us and you will be destroyed."

Holmes then took two steps to the left and spun away from the door, his back now pressed against a stone pillar. Three shots rang out and three holes appeared in the front door, at head, chest and stomach height. Holmes smiled, then sprinted back to our position.

Lestrade sighed as Holmes reached us. "Yes, you have proved your point, but for goodness' sake Holmes, what were you thinking?"

"The only life that I can justify risking is my own," Holmes replied, soberly.

Lestrade gave the order to advance, and a volley of gunfire was unleashed from his men. Windows shattered and their frames splintered. Chunks of brick and white plaster exploded from the front of the house. Amongst the cacophony and smoke, two brave constables reached the front door and, being careful to stay behind the stone pillars that framed the entrance, shot at the lock as they attempted to gain entry.

The men that remained were those armed with rifles. They peppered the windows, affording cover to those below. Content with the firepower he had at the front of the house, Lestrade sent two riflemen round to the sides and back, one for reinforcement, the other to assess the situation there and report back.

The inspector then ordered two men to remain in front of the building and waved the rest of us forwards, to support the two men at the door. Under the covering fire of the two remaining riflemen, we soon reached the relative safety of the stone porch. The door was now so punctured with bullet holes, that it resembled a Swiss cheese.

"We will have to charge," declared Lestrade. "I will lead," he added, bravely.

Holmes grabbed his arm, "No, I will not lose what few friends I have, so cheaply."

Holmes pulled back the inspector; Lestrade becoming just the latest in a long line to discover quite how deceptively strong the lithe detective really was.

Holmes opened his coat. He withdrew a small, metal canister. He opened one end to reveal a wick. From a trouser pocket, he produced a match. He struck this on the rough wall and lit the protruding fuse. He watched as the flame hissed and burned down toward the base."

"I have no idea exactly what that device is that you are holding, but by the look of that wick, I suggest that you deploy it, immediately!" I yelled.

Holmes nonchalantly flipped open the brass letterbox and thrust the weapon inside. Mere seconds later, after we had just enough time to cower behind the stone pillars of the porch, there was an almighty explosion, and the door was blasted clean off its hinges. In the ensuing chaos, Lestrade's men were quickest back onto their feet and rushed inside, guns blazing.

The inspector's face was one of complete astonishment.

"You do know which subject Holmes studied at Cambridge, don't you?" I shouted, as our ears rang. I couldn't help a small, dark grin.

Lestrade shook his head as he dusted himself down. I drew my pistol and followed Holmes into the hallway.

"Chemistry!" I shouted back.

We moved from room to room, until we met up with the men who had entered from the rear. Three gang members lay dead, two had been captured, more or less unharmed, and one more lay on the parlour floor, grimly breathing his last. I tried to tend to him, but two gunshots to his chest had left him bleeding, uncontrollably. One of our men, who had taken a bullet graze to his shoulder, gallantly offered to remain with the stricken man until he had passed. I agreed, readily. This was exactly the sort of behaviour that separated us from our foes.

"Up we go, again," Lestrade ordered, with a mirthless grin.

"Take care, everyone," warned Holmes. "This is the last stand of desperate, but cunning, men. Take nothing for granted and watch every step you take."

"Should we expect booby-traps? I thought we had caught them by surprise?" I asked.

"Yes, and I fear, ones as terrible as any man could imagine. These men have worked for months for their reward. They have plotted every single event, often many weeks in advance. Do you think they would not be prepared for an assault upon their headquarters?"

I shuddered at the thought of what we might be facing. Lestrade looked ashen and remained silent.

"It is, of course, equally possible that we have, indeed, caught them off their guard. Our entry was considerably more straightforward than I had expected."

I suppressed the urge to growl at Holmes. Instead, I checked my revolver and prepared to climb the steps to face whatever lay in wait.

Two constables, armed with Martini-Henry rifles, led the way. Five steps behind these, were two further men, pistols held at the ready. Holmes and I were next, Lestrade and one last policeman brought up the rear.

We reached the first-floor landing without incident. I wondered if, somehow, the remaining gang members had escaped, for there was no sight of anyone, not even the sound of a creaking floorboard. Motes of dust floated in and out of rays of early afternoon sunlight, giving the corridor an air of eerie calm.

The two riflemen moved forward, along the corridor, followed by their revolver-bearing compatriots. I stepped forward, but Holmes suddenly thrust his right arm across my chest to hold me back.

"Something is wrong here," he whispered.

Holmes then pulled me back with all of his might. I fell backwards, grasping helplessly at the air before me. I managed to grab onto Holmes' arm as I flailed in panic. Together, we toppled backwards into Lestrade and the constable beside him.

The moment that I felt myself hit Lestrade square in the chest, I saw, from above, a flash of light. A fraction of a second later, I felt an enormous pressure in my ears followed by a massive explosion that shook the entire house and sent us all tumbling back down the stairs. I fell, my limbs tangled around Holmes and Lestrade until, suddenly, all was darkness.

I woke to see the concerned face of Holmes peering down at me. As I blinked into consciousness, I saw a smile cross his bloodied and dust-encrusted face. He quickly rubbed at his eyes, but not before I saw what looked like a tear, wash itself a short trail through the dirt from the corner of his eye.

"Welcome back, Watson," he coughed, helping me to my feet.

"What happened?" I asked, hoarsely. I saw Lestrade being tended by the constable that had been by his side. He had a large lump on his forehead but appeared otherwise unharmed. I slowly turned my head to the staircase and looked up.

"A tripwire, a fine fishing line hidden just three inches or so above the carpet. They knew that the contrast of bright light and shadow, cast by the windows, would hide it from view. We have to go back, Watson."

I saw that four policemen were now with us, not counting the fellow looking after Lestrade. I sighed with relief; the men had all survived.

But then I noticed that their clothes were all relatively clean, ours were grey with dust and debris. These were not the men who had climbed the stairs before us. I curled my hands into tight balls as realisation struck.

"Yes, Holmes," I stated calmly. "We must go back."

"The men, here, ensured that no one escaped the building after the explosion," Holmes confirmed, before adding, "This time, I will lead the way."

We reached the upstairs landing together. Lestrade was right behind us, three constables following closely. We peered through the smoke and dust. The sight before us was tragic. The explosion had wreaked terrible damage, the entire floor had been almost torn away. All of the doors to the rooms adjoining the hallway had been shredded like matchsticks. Large gaping holes in the walls let sunlight pour in and it was only through providence that the building still stood at all.

I finally forced my eyes to look down. I had seen much death and destruction during my years of service, but what lay before me, in a quiet square in London, chilled me to my very core. I tried to console myself with the fact that the men would not have suffered, but the anger and disgust that welled within me would not be stilled.

"Watson," Holmes pulled me round and stared directly into my eyes. "Think, man. We must defeat those responsible for this outrage. Calm and logic, Doctor. Until they are safely in the hands of the authorities."

"Do you mean to take these animals alive?" I asked, incredulously.

"Of course, Watson, old friend. They must be brought to justice and tried, just like any other criminals."

Holmes picked up a discarded rifle, checked it for damage and drew back the bolt.

"And then we shall watch, as they drop from the gallows to their deaths," he finished, coldly.

XXXVI
Ex Mortuis

We inched forwards, towards the far end of the hallway and the stairs to the second floor. Holmes took no chances, waving his stick before us and throwing forward handfuls of dust and lumps of rubble, to ensure there were no further traps.

We slowly climbed the stairs, stepping back each time we revealed ourselves until we finally reached the upper landing.

To our utter astonishment, standing defiantly at the far end of the hallway, was a man. He wore an expensive cream suit and a cold smile of complete confidence. I instinctively knew exactly who was this arrogant figure that stood before us. It was Clarke Mitchell.

I began to rush forwards but, yet again, Holmes held me back.

"Wait, Watson," he explained. "He expects us to try to capture him. It is the correct thing to do. It is also the predictable thing to do. I fully expect the floor between us to be littered with all manner of terrible surprises."

"In which case, I shall simply shoot him dead," I declared, raising my pistol.

This instantly wiped the smile from his face. He dropped down, quickly, and rolled backwards, disappearing through a hidden trapdoor in the wall behind.

"Damn it all!" shouted Holmes. "If you were going to shoot him, why on Earth did you hesitate?"

I sighed and began to stride forwards. Holmes again blocked my passage.

"Oh, come on Holmes, if the floor were full of traps, how on Earth did he get to the other side in the first place?"

"A bluff?" Holmes appeared uncertain for a second, before grabbing a handful of brick dust and casting it before him. Twice more he repeated this, before turning to me.

"Once again, you are correct, Watson," he stated, gently, his hand upon my shoulder. "You must promise to remind me of these occasions should I ever become over-confident in my abilities."

"Become over-confident?" I could not help whispering, darkly.

We raced to the false wall and soon had it open. On the far side was a narrow passage, ending with a set of iron steps, leading upwards. We emerged out onto the roof of the building, just in time to witness Mitchell leaping the narrow gap between this and the adjoining building.

This time I did not hesitate. I raised my pistol and fired a volley of three shots at the rapidly diminishing figure. The first two failed and flew harmlessly past the darting villain, but the third caught him, a puff of material burst from the left shoulder of his jacket as the bullet grazed its target. He ducked down and disappeared from view before I could again train my sights on him.

"Fine shooting, Watson, you may have winged him. Let us hope it slows him down. I will follow, you call down to the men below. Order them to surround the adjacent building, let no one out!" he barked, before sprinting forward and jumping to the next building in an easy bound.

I resisted the urge to ignore Holmes' orders and follow him in pursuit of Mitchell. I shouted down to the riflemen still positioned in front of the club building. Within a minute, they had the front and side of both buildings covered. I ran back inside and down the stairs, leaping down three or four steps at a time, racing to get to the last unguarded part of the neighbouring building – the rear. I knew that the policemen would arrive before me, but would they be in time to stop Mitchell?

I reached the back of the plot just as Lestrade and a burly constable ran out from the side of the property and joined me. It was immediately clear that we were too late. At the far end of the garden that stretched some fifty feet before us, standing atop a five-foot brick wall, was a rifleman. He turned when he saw us.

"I can still just make out Holmes ahead of me," he cried. "He is but twenty yards behind his quarry, heading south towards the river."

That was all the information that I needed. I grabbed Lestrade and pulled him back towards the road.

"Who is the fastest driver here?" I demanded. "Get him to the lightest carriage that we have."

"Hemmings is probably the best," Lestrade began, then stopped, recomposed himself and continued. "No, young Grayson is our man."

Less than five minutes later, we were climbing aboard a four-wheeler drawn by two finely muscled black horses. I sat up front with Grayson, Lestrade jumped in the back. Just as Grayson raised the reins to gee us off, a constable jumped in beside Lestrade. His head was heavily bandaged, but he waved away my concerned protests.

"I am just peachy, Doc," he growled, "and you may well be thankful for another pair of hands when we catch up with this monster."

I shouted orders and we departed at great speed; Grayson certainly knew how to handle a pair of horses. We skidded around the first corner on two wheels and thundered towards Regent Street.

"His nephew," Lestrade shouted in my ear.

"Whose nephew?" I replied, cupping my hand to my mouth, against the rush of the wind.

"Watkins, of course. I knew you were wondering." Lestrade's smile was most welcome.

The young driver pulled sharply at the reins, and we were now storming down Regent Street. Five minutes later, we slid around a tight left-hand turn to skirt St. James's Park.

"How can you be so sure where he is heading?" cried the inspector.

"He is desperate and heading south in a straight line. He knows that he will reach the river at some point. The only thing left to ascertain is to which bridge will he run? As he is not a local, I believe he will head for what he knows, and he certainly knows Westminster Bridge."

"So, it is a guess?" the inspector snorted.

"Only if I am proved wrong," I laughed.

We were now just minutes from the river. We had to slow, due to unexpectedly heavy Saturday afternoon traffic, and were now proceeding at little more than a walking pace. Holmes and Mitchell could not be more than a few hundred yards ahead. I stood up and shouted that the way must be cleared for police business.

Suddenly, from up ahead of us, we heard gunfire. A single shot, then a second, closely followed by a third. These were pistol rounds, certainly not from the rifle that I had last seen Holmes clutching. I momentarily panicked at what this might suggest, but this feeling began to subside as I recalled Holmes was also in possession of a sidearm.

Without warning, a gunshot exploded right by my side.

I crouched back down in shock, only to see Lestrade standing behind me, his gun pointing to the sky. Those in front of us rushed to escape as quickly as they could, and our path was soon clear. Grayson flicked the reins once more and we accelerated towards Westminster Bridge. We swept past the Houses of Parliament and approached the crossing. People were running both towards and away from us; they had heard gunfire from at least two directions and were hastening to places of safety.

We drew to a halt some twenty yards onto the bridge. The wide river crossing was now abandoned, except for ourselves and the two solitary figures before us.

One stood tall; the other was slumped to his knees. As we approached, the scene became clearer. Holmes loomed high; in his outstretched hand, he clutched a Webley-Pryse revolver. Mitchell knelt before him, his cream suit now stained with blood from a wound to his shoulder. I noted that it was the opposite side from where I had grazed him; Holmes had landed the knockout blow.

Mitchell breathed hoarsely but said nothing. Holmes noted our approach and lowered his weapon, as Lestrade raised his own to cover our captive.

"There is much for us to talk about," Holmes said to the stricken man before him. "Your wounds are superficial, so we shall have plenty of time to go over the finer points of this affair."

Mitchell snarled in defiance, however, his face then froze. A look of calm, and what appeared to be regret, crossed his face. "Once again, you are wrong, Mr. Holmes. Sadly, I will never get to enjoy the pleasure of your company."

Mitchell's glassy eyes appeared to look straight through Holmes as he spoke these words.

Holmes stepped forward to dispute this statement, but a deafening crack stopped him, mid-stride.

A small round hole, no bigger than a sixpence, appeared in the centre of Mitchell's forehead. A single, thin stream of blood worked its way down his expressionless face. He toppled forwards and slammed heavily against the dusty surface of the road.

I turned around to determine the source of the shot. Standing behind Lestrade, about ten yards from Holmes and Mitchell was the constable from the back of the carriage. His head was no longer swathed with bloodied bandages. I recognised him instantly. He was not one of Lestrade's men.

Standing there, upon Westminster Bridge, a wisp of smoke still curling from the barrel of the gun which he held tightly in his right hand, was Adam Gold, government agent.

XXXVII
The Source

We stood on the bridge in complete silence. I ran forward to the prone figure of Mitchell and searched hopelessly for a pulse, knowing that he was far beyond any earthly help. Holmes walked slowly towards Gold, who stood rigid and unblinking.

A clatter of metal upon stone shattered the silence as the gun fell from the agent's fingers. Holmes ignored this and addressed Gold in a manner far calmer than I had expected.

"How did you find us?" he asked, softly. "Was it he?" Holmes added, cryptically.

Gold nodded but uttered no words. Holmes seemed to curse under his breath but gave no other outward signs of his obvious intense displeasure.

Satisfied that the man lying at his feet was dead, Lestrade holstered his revolver. He called out to the young carriage driver to bring a blanket and to watch over the body until assistance arrived.

"Half a dozen gunshots and a small riot, that ought to gain some attention," he joked, darkly, before walking off towards Holmes and Gold.

The young policeman ran up and covered up Mitchell's fallen body. As I followed the inspector, I noticed that two men had detached themselves from the watching crowd and were now striding purposefully onto the bridge. Both were tall, athletic and walked with a definite military bearing. They were dressed in sober woollen suits with dark bowler hats; an unmistakable air of authority preceded them.

The man on the left spoke to Holmes, his hushed voice inaudible. The other fellow waved a small leather-bound wallet towards Lestrade, official credentials of some sort I presumed. Lestrade began to protest, but Holmes gently restrained him with an outstretched hand. The man before Holmes then took Gold by the arm and led him away, back towards the riverbank. His associate offered his hand but neither Holmes nor Lestrade reciprocated. Unperturbed, the mysterious official pulled at the brim of his hat, bowed slightly and turned to follow his colleague. They quickly reached the bank and were soon lost amongst the throng of people that were now gathered at the north end of the bridge.

"What on earth is going on, Holmes?" I asked as I reached them. "Who were those men?"

"Cleaners," replied Holmes. "Of a sort. Government men, agents of some department or another. Sent to sanitise unfortunate, inconvenient or embarrassing situations."

"Like a government agent executing a prisoner in broad daylight upon Westminster Bridge," grumbled Lestrade.

As he spoke, a group of uniformed officers arrived and began to push back the crowd.

"That doesn't explain how they managed to arrive just moments after the event though, does it?" I suggested.

"Yes, you are right, Doctor," agreed Lestrade. "Or, more importantly, how he found out about our operation in the first place?"

"In truth, it was my fault," declared Holmes.

Lestrade's face displayed much the same surprise as that which I felt.

"I have a contact in the government. One at a sufficiently high level to have been of great use to me over the years. I have kept him informed of these events because I had complete trust in him. It was he who confirmed Gold's true identity and position."

"Has he betrayed you, Holmes? How dastardly!" I growled, anger rising inside me.

"Perhaps," replied Holmes, noncommittally. "However, it seems more likely that his hand has been forced. Perhaps he had no choice but to enact an edict, sent from above. Imagine if the membership list from Mitchell's sordid club ever came to be made public. Even if this roster were to have conveniently been destroyed, Mitchell might still have been prepared to name names when interrogated or, even worse, when in court. There were some powerful names on that list. Far better for all concerned if he met a swift and silent end. They hoped he would die in the assault, but an insurance policy would be required. Someone who would not flinch in the face of a cold-blooded killing. Who better to pull the trigger, than the man who had suffered the most at Mitchell's hand?"

"So, they leaked the information and ensured that Gold was present when we raided the house." I shook my head in disgust.

"But what about poor Gold? I will not see him hanged for this!" I added, with feeling.

"That will not happen, Watson. When that 'gentleman' spoke with me," Holmes' inflexion made it clear that he regarded him as anything but, "he informed me that he will receive a short sentence but, in reality, serve none of it. Instead, he will be released and retired on a sergeant's pension."

"After what he suffered, he deserves better than that," growled the inspector. Lestrade made no attempt to hide his anger.

"And he shall get it," replied Holmes. From the set of his jaw to the glint in his steel-grey eyes, I knew for certain that Holmes would keep his promise.

A group of officers approached us. Amongst these, I recognised the Police Surgeon, so I tipped my hat and we moved off the bridge.

"What now, Holmes?" I asked as we pushed our way through the crowd to find the nearest hansom.

"This terrible affair has had at least one positive outcome. I now have the answer to my question."

"Inspector Lestrade, can you please arrange for us a meeting with the Commissioner of Police? When, exactly, does he return from his holiday?" asked Holmes.

"Tomorrow afternoon, I believe. I will make the arrangements, of course," replied the inspector, somewhat taken aback.

"Excellent. In that case, I suggest that we return to our rooms, take a wash and meet up at seven for dinner at Carlo's. I hope you can join us, Inspector. It will be, of course, my pleasure."

XXXVIII
A Small Justice

Compared to the previous days and weeks, this evening was one of unalloyed joy. For a few hours, we forgot about the case and simply enjoyed each other's company, even Holmes seemed almost relaxed. Lestrade was, as usual after a couple of glasses of wine, full of stories that grew ever more outrageous with each additional drink.

It was long after midnight when we finally returned to Baker Street. Holmes poured two glasses of brandy as I coaxed the last embers of the fire back into life. I sat and filled my pipe, Holmes opted for a dangerous-looking black, Eastern cheroot.

"Is it really over?" I asked. "You say you have the solution, but I cannot help thinking that this case is too big, too complex to have but one, simple answer."

"You are probably right, old man. I have the solution, but I do not claim to have all the answers. This affair is so deep, so intricate, that we may never know the names of all those involved or, crucially, their sponsors."

"So, if I understand this correctly, you have solved the how, but not necessarily the who and the why?"

Holmes laughed. It was an uncommon, but most welcome, sound.

"Quite right. However, the person I most need to convince is the Police Commissioner, everything else is secondary."

We talked a little more, finished our smokes and finally retired to our beds.

The night passed quickly and easily. I woke late the next morning, pale white autumn sunshine streaming through my window. By the time I was dressed and ready for breakfast, it was well after nine o'clock. There was no sign of Holmes, so I called down for a breakfast for one. Mrs. Hudson appeared just ten minutes later, with both hot coffee and the news that Holmes had left early, leaving instructions to sit tight and wait upon his return.

Glad of a few hours to myself, I took out my notebook and began the long process of updating both of our recent cases. I was still struggling with the whole Mitchell case, so I concentrated on the conclusion of the Hugo Hill affair. I noted with some satisfaction that, out of all the cases that we had investigated thus far, it was of the very few that had a positive outcome for all of the parties concerned.

At just after midday, Holmes returned. Looking flustered, he cast his cape carelessly onto the floor and threw his hat over his shoulder. He reached for his cigarette case, withdrew a slim white cylinder and struck a match. He slumped into his armchair with a face of thunder.

"What has happened, old man?" I cautiously inquired.

"A brick wall, Watson. Wherever I search, barriers are placed before me. I fear that we may never realise the full extent of this scheme."

"Ah, so you have been to see your 'contact' within the government." I filled the bowl of my pipe with a light Virginia broken flake, a recent arrival from H&S in Bedford. "I take it that they have now closed ranks to protect the reputations of certain important individuals?"

"Indeed. However, in this case, I believe there is more to their obstinacy than a simple desire to protect the establishment from scandal."

"What do you mean, Holmes?" I asked, unsure of his reasoning.

"Nowyswiat," he stated, bluntly.

"Well, what of him?"

"Exactly. I have made serious efforts to locate this man, but he has vanished. When I mentioned him to my source, I was told, in no uncertain terms, that he was no longer a problem." Holmes inhaled deeply upon his rapidly shrinking cigarette.

"Well, that can only mean two things. They either have him or they have eliminated him," I concluded, coldly.

"I believe that the former is currently the case. The latter will almost certainly follow unless he continues to be of use to them."

"I understand your frustration, old boy, but surely this is just a minor inconvenience in a much greater triumph?"

"Perhaps, but I still have the feeling that, although we have apprehended the puppets, we have yet to identify all of the marionettists," Holmes replied, flicking the short, stubby remains of his cigarette into the fire.

"I hope that you, at least, have better news regarding Gold. I will not stand for him being dragged through the courts, whatever the premeditated outcome."

"On that front, you can ease your concerns, Watson." Holmes took on a more conciliatory tone.

"I made one of the conditions of our silence a promise that Gold would be treated in a way that more befits a man of his bravery, achievements and patriotism."

"Well done, Holmes, but how will they now explain Mitchell's death? Many on that bridge witnessed the gunshot."

"Many heard it, a few saw it, but none of these would willingly attend, or give believable testimony, in a coroner's court. The official report will state that surrounded, and with no hope of escape, Mitchell took his own life."

"Gold has accepted his enforced retirement, although now on a full colonel's pension. He will be free to live out the rest of his life with his family, in peace," confirmed Holmes.

"Well done, old man, bravo." I must admit that my eyes misted up a touch at this most welcome resolution of Gold's plight.

"No time to wallow, Watson," barked Holmes, shattering the atmosphere of calm. "We must hail a hansom, for we have a meeting with the Commissioner of Police. It is no exaggeration to state that the stability of the economy of the entire British Empire is at stake here."

XXXIX
Scotland Yard

We had arranged to meet at Scotland Yard. Lestrade had persuaded the Commissioner to grant us a short audience before he made his grave, formal announcement. From what I could ascertain, Holmes was not well-respected by the Commissioner, and it was only through the perseverance of the inspector that we had been granted this meeting at all. Among many in the higher echelons of the police force, Holmes was still treated with deep suspicion and often open contempt.

The fresh autumn air energised me as we trotted our way south along Regent's Street. The Sunday afternoon streets were quiet, a rare sight in daytime London. Holmes sat in silence, composing his speech, I presumed. I attempted, for a short while at least, to put this case into some sort of order in my head, but once again I found myself thinking in circles. I sighed and instead chose to sit back and enjoy the short cab ride to the headquarters of the Metropolitan Police.

We were escorted from the front of the austere, solidly built brick building, deep into the bowels of the edifice. We climbed three flights of stairs and finally emerged into a light, airy corridor outside a large office. Our escort knocked once, and we were let in by a welcome, friendly face.

Lestrade smiled, greeted us swiftly, and led us inside. The room was a good twenty feet in both length and breadth, with a high ceiling. It resembled the office of a very well-to-do solicitor.

342

One wall was filled with shelves, stacked with leather-backed tomes, police and legal records by the look of them. A large desk sat before a wide window, cleverly placed, to allow the use of the incoming light to intimidate anyone seated before it. However, the chair behind the desk was empty, for standing in front of a grey marble fireplace, below a portrait of Sir Robert Peel, was the waiting Commissioner.

"Mr. Holmes, please state, exactly, what it is that has persuaded this good man, here, to risk his reputation in order that you are able to stand here before me."

The superior, condescending tone of the Commissioner could not help but make me wince. However, this was as much in anticipation of the response that I feared would erupt from Holmes.

"Sir, I humbly ask and, furthermore, must insist that you make no declaration regarding the affair of the counterfeit notes," Holmes stated, bluntly.

The Commissioner frowned. "And why should I do this? We are facing an unprecedented attack upon our sovereign currency. It is my duty to do everything in my power to mitigate this. I have informed the Bank of England, and we are also in contact with the authorities of the United States and mainland Europe. We are confident that we can limit the effects of this heinous act."

The Commissioner was a large man, both in height and girth. Perhaps sixty years of age, with a fine head of white hair and matching beard. Piercing blue eyes sat above a long, strong nose. Surprisingly, he wore a plain navy-blue police uniform with no emblem of rank, the only clue to his position being an especially fine Hunter and single Albert chain, worn to his left.

"Sir, I believe that Inspector Lestrade has informed you of the facts of this case. I may only have a little of material interest to add but I assure you, these minor details change the reality of the situation, completely."

"Then please proceed, I wish to make my statement within the hour," the Commissioner replied, eyeing the gold ormolu clock on the mantelpiece.

Holmes began. "At first glance, the case appears to be quite simple, the best schemes always are. Flood the country with fake currency. Confidence is lost and the value of the markets and sterling plummets. Then buy up large quantities of both at the reduced price, before the authorities can act and reverse the drop. When the values recover, you can sell your holdings at a huge profit."

"Yes, we are well aware of the plot," the Commissioner sighed.

"However, throughout this entire affair, has anyone actually laid eyes on any of this forged currency?" demanded Holmes.

"Yet we have witnesses who lugged crates of it, from offshore and throughout the length of the country. And let us not forget the metal engraving plates that you, yourself, discovered on that bleak island," the Commissioner replied, deeply unimpressed.

"Yes, we did find evidence, both in Northumbria and again at the Ex Tenebris club. Several notes. Perfect forgeries. But how can that be? No forgery can ever be perfect."

"What are you suggesting, exactly?" The Commissioner's bright blue eyes had now widened.

"There is only one possible explanation. The notes are perfect because they are genuine. Real money, left to deliberately mislead us. To convince us that they have crates full of forged notes that are indistinguishable from bona fide bills. As for the engraving plates, why were they found in this small chapel, hundreds of miles away from where the notes were supposed to have originated? Where were the other tools necessary to print this counterfeit money – inks, paper, presses? Why were no traces of these ever found? A clumsy mistake on their behalf, perhaps, or one designed to reinforce the idea that they had, somewhere abroad, produced many thousands of these fake notes?"

"What are you saying? Are you suggesting that the whole scheme was just some sort of ruse? Why would they do this?"

"That is exactly what they have done," declared Holmes, triumphantly. "The plan is simple and brilliant. They only need us to believe that they have produced hundreds of thousands of pounds worth of untraceable, perfectly forged, currency. Whether they have, or not, is largely irrelevant, the plan works either way."

"Remember, sir, these markets operate almost entirely at the mercy of a single factor, one both capricious and volatile. Confidence, gentlemen. Control this and you control everything."

I was struggling to understand exactly what Holmes had revealed.

"So, there was no fake currency at all?" I asked, uncertainly.

"Not one single note. Someone of real genius had realised that the plan would work just as well if they faked the fake notes, so to speak." Holmes could not help but smile at this irony.

"How much simpler would it be, to simply make us believe that had perfected the art of forgery? Merely drop a few genuine notes here and there, scattered around where the supposed forgeries had been stored. Allow those investigating the affair to come across a few examples of these 'perfect copies' as they pursued the forgers. A few hundred pounds spent to convince us that they had thousands, perhaps millions, stored and ready to release into the economy."

"The more I studied this hypothesis, the more it became clear to me that it had to be the solution. Incredibly, the plan still works, even if it is later revealed to be just a deception, a scare story."

Holmes paused, to allow us time to absorb the magnitude of what he was implying.

"The gang would still have their huge holdings, purchased at well below the genuine rate. What would happen if the deceit were then revealed?" asked my friend, his eyes lit with an inner fire.

"Well, steps would be taken and confidence would return. The government would purchase all available sterling at this bargain price, and the currency and other markets would recover to their former level, possibly even higher," replied the Commissioner, beginning, perhaps, to soften his previously steadfast stance.

"Allowing them to sell up and promptly disappear with their ill-gotten profits," Holmes growled. "Whether it be by the Bank of England buying up huge quantities of sterling, or by share prices recovering once the scheme is exposed as a hoax, the markets would soon return to their former levels."

"And to add further credibility to their plot, they engaged an up-and-coming consulting detective, one who was rapidly gaining a reputation in the papers as someone who could unravel even the most complex of mysteries," added Lestrade, as he too began to understand the ramifications of Holmes' revelations.

"Only after replacing a government agent whom they had manipulated into furthering their deception," I corrected.

"Yes, Inspector, and this is the real reason I believe we were drawn into this business," Holmes continued.

"The original plan was to force Gold to convince his superiors that the plot was real. The villains would then watch events unfold, acting only if the Bank of England failed to react swiftly, or strongly, enough for the value of the markets to recover. In the unlikely event of this happening, the truth would finally be revealed to Gold – that the entire scheme was fake, an enormous bluff. Gold would then share the truth with his superiors and the value of their newly acquired holdings would soar."

"We simply replaced Gold as their delivery agent of choice," I sighed. "They could never completely trust Gold, he only ever acted for them under the most terrible duress. We, however, came willingly, with the tacit approval of Scotland Yard. Gold was kept on as a form of insurance, I would imagine, until they felt we were completely under their influence."

"Our part in this affair must come under the most serious scrutiny, and we cannot hold ourselves above criticism. I take full responsibility for allowing us to become unsuspecting advocates of their conspiracy. We were cleverly duped into investigating exactly what they wanted us to; we followed their trail of breadcrumbs, unquestioningly, and failed to realise that a larger game was being played out before us. However, we now have an opportunity to correct these egregious mistakes. Only together can we best these villains, and together we must!" Holmes insisted, passionately.

The Commissioner was silent. I could see that he was carefully absorbing and analysing all that Holmes had revealed.

"Sir, what are the real risks here?" Holmes implored. "If I am right, then we can avoid this whole disastrous situation. In fact, it might even be possible to recognise and apprehend other parties who might be preparing for this event, for I believe that we have not yet identified all those involved in this conspiracy."

"And if I am wrong? You will still be able to act to mitigate the situation. The outcome will be much the same. However, I assure you, I am not mistaken. Sir, history is waiting for you to act, or in this case, not to act," Holmes concluded with real feeling and conviction.

"So, you claim that if I do nothing, all will be well? That there is no threat, just a clever ruse, an attempt to convince us that the conspiracy is real?"

The Commissioner paused for a moment. "What you are saying, if I understand you correctly, is that this entire scheme has been concocted to make us deliberately undermine confidence in our own economy.

"Mr. Holmes," he continued, "it appears that I may have underestimated you. Your theory is most convincing, logical, and explains many, if not all, of the unusual features of this affair."

"However, I must weigh this new information against the potential risks of failing to act," he added, thoughtfully stroking his snow-white beard.

He paused, grim and serious, fighting an obvious internal battle, before finally continuing.

"I propose a compromise. I shall delay my announcement until midday, tomorrow. That should allow us ample time to observe any unusual behaviour in the markets. If you are correct, we may see the villains panic and themselves attempt to spread knowledge of the conspiracy. However, most likely, they will hold back, and the day will pass as normally as any other."

"Thank you, sir. I promise that you will not have cause to regret holding such trust in me," Holmes replied. I could almost sense the relief in his voice.

Seeing that the Commissioner was now deep in thought, we excused ourselves and made our way back through the labyrinthine building to our waiting cab. Once outside, I breathed out in huge relief.

"That was incredible, Holmes," I panted. "Now that I look back, it makes perfect sense. They simply used us to add credibility to their scheme. We acted just as they had predicted, reinforcing the idea that this gang did indeed have dozens of crates packed full of forged notes. From Custom House to Mitchell himself, they have led us a merry dance, indeed." I shook my head at the sheer improbability of it all.

"What do we do now, Holmes?" I asked.

"Firstly, I shall send a message to Groves. To update him of events and to request that he be on the lookout for any suspicious traders that we may have overlooked."

"And after that?"

"Then we wait, Watson," replied Holmes.

XL
Darker Thoughts

We spent the evening in our rooms in Baker Street, but Holmes was far from idle. A succession of his Irregulars came and went, individually, and in small groups. Holmes was setting up a network to pass information, swiftly, to us from various important financial institutions within the City.

At the centre of this web would be the Bringley and Greenford Bank. Groves had agreed to allow us the use of an office that would act as the hub for our operation. The Commissioner had agreed to visit before noon to review the situation, before deciding whether or not to make his statement regarding the counterfeit currency.

"What of Mitchell?" I asked, as the last of the scruffy mob had left and we sat before the fire. "If he is the ringleader, why are you so certain that his circus has not now collapsed around him? We have taken care of more than a dozen of his men, one way or another." Thin swirls of grey smoke danced in the firelight as I puffed upon my favourite Rhodesian briar.

"Florid metaphors aside," Holmes replied, "we have already established that Mitchell was not the only man of such learning and position acting within the conspiracy. This mysterious Nowyswiat may well be another, but such a complex plan must have involved more than one or two men with access to, and knowledge of, the City."

"However, Watson, I also fear that the dark forces that whisked away Nowyswiat, might also have alerted, whether deliberately or not, those at the very top of this conspiracy. They will not, now, easily be identified."

"Do you really believe it could reach so high?" I asked, incredulously.

"At least one gang member held a position high enough within the government to enable them to discover the true identity, and residential address, of a secret agent. They then had the cunning and ruthlessness to force him into doing their bidding by kidnapping his poor wife. They have resources way beyond those of any criminal I have ever encountered. It is entirely possible that we are already wasting our time and that all existing traces of this affair are being erased, even as we speak."

"I do have one more question regarding Mitchell," I added, tapping out the ashes from my pipe before leaving it to cool. "Why did he fake his death? Surely it was a risk that he did not have to take. What if he had, later, been recognised?"

"I believe that it was for several reasons, Watson."

Holmes stretched, rummaged in his brown dressing gown and produced two cigarettes. He passed the first across to me, leaving himself with its companion, a rather bent-looking fellow. He carefully straightened this with his long white fingers, raised it to his lips and leaned towards me. I struck a match and lit Holmes' cigarette, before adding its flame to my own.

"Firstly, it was eminently desirable, from a criminal point of view, to be 'out of the picture' at such an early stage, don't you think? After all, who would suspect somebody who was already dead?"

"Secondly, he knew that his 'death' would be investigated. As he was an American and a man of some importance, he knew that those appointed to investigate would be of higher than usual rank and standing. Remember, they were looking for someone deep inside the establishment from whom to extract information and ultimately blackmail into working for them. I believe that they had hoped to find such a figure through their awful club, but when a secret government agent appeared on the scene, they took full advantage of their good fortune."

"Lastly," Holmes continued after retrieving his ghastly, rancid-looking churchwarden from the coal scuttle by the fireplace and filling it with heaven knows what concoction from the Persian slipper, pinned above. He pushed a thin wooden spill into the cracking grate and once it was alight, returned to his chair. He held this above his newly filled pipe bowl and inhaled deeply. Expecting a noxious cloud to erupt from his mouth and pipe, I recoiled back into my chair. However, this time, the effusion was pleasant, slightly sweet with vanilla and perhaps a hint of cherry.

"Holmes, I am shocked. Have you finally paid more than sixpence an ounce for your tobacco?" I grinned.

"A gift from Groves. Acceptable, if a tad on the mild side," he commented.

"But I distract you, old man, please, pray continue."

"Yes, lastly. Now, here we enter into the realm of speculation. Ever since we identified Mitchell as the man at the heart of this conspiracy, something has not sat quite right for me. He was a successful banker, why would he risk it all for merely a share of the profits? Once the whole gang had been paid off, there would certainly be a considerable fortune remaining. However, if I am correct, and there are several others involved at the highest level, then the profits would have been diluted to a point where it appears that the risks that he took may well have exceeded the rewards."

"No, I believe that he intended to make off with the entire haul. He was, after all, an experienced banker. He would know how to hide the money or quickly move it abroad. I posit that his plan was discovered and that his partners had devised an insurance policy, to be actioned if, and when, he attempted to abscond. I also believe that this plan was enacted when they learned of our plan to raid Hanover Square."

"You are talking about Gold, aren't you? Good Lord! So, he remained a pawn, even after we rescued him?"

"Indeed, he was. They knew that he was desperate for revenge, they simply fed him just enough information to identify Mitchell as his chief tormentor and pointed him towards the planned raid. His training and experience then took over, leading to the terrible conclusion that we witnessed."

"So, Gold and ourselves, together, we have been used, manipulated from start to finish. But why? It cannot just be for the money. As you said, once divided amongst already rich men, it was surely not a reward large enough to justify the inherent risk."

"And there you have it, old friend. The germ of an answer. I have two theories as to the real purpose of this affair. The first is that it was a trial run for something larger, although neither I nor Groves can imagine what this might be. The next most logical target would be America, but we have shared too much with them, already. They would not now be caught unawares by a similar ruse. Likewise, Paris, Berlin and Moscow. We have ensured that they are all now well aware of what has been attempted here."

"What is your second theory? For some reason, I find myself slightly afeared of what you might suggest." I nervously sucked on my briar.

"Which idea, which theory, which hypothesis have we been drawn away from at every stage of this case, Watson?" Holmes asked, sweet-smelling smoke now draped around him like a fine grey cloak.

Holmes did not wait for my reply. "Politics. Subversion, anarchy, insurrection." He paused. "Revolution," he finished, darkly.

"Do you believe they mean to destabilise the state?" I asked, open-mouthed.

"No, at least I think not. Well not here, anyway. It was more of a preliminary action, a trial run, perhaps. More ominously, it may have been a show of strength, a carefully and precisely aimed threat to the government from a faction within the establishment. A warning, showing what they are capable of if their interests are not entertained."

"My God, Holmes. These are dark waters, indeed," I stammered.

"Alternatively, it could all just be a villainous conspiracy, created and controlled by a criminal savant, one to whom the crime itself is more important than any financial reward they may gain." Holmes drew deeply again on his pipe. "I fear we may never know the whole truth."

"You cannot simply close Pandora's Box, you know," I retorted. "However, your theory might begin to explain some of the more outré features of this case. The Ex Tenebris club certainly makes more sense if it were also a front to recruit the wealthy and powerful to an actual cause."

357

"The question that troubles me most though, I have to admit, is the identity of the Chairman," I added, shuddering, as I recalled his ghostly presence.

"I cannot be certain, however, I believe him to be the man otherwise known as Nowyswiat. We may never know his true identity, for I fear he is now being held by clandestine forces within the government. On whose side these particular forces are on, I cannot say."

We retired early, but sleep did not come easily to me. I dreamed, fitfully, of betrayal, conspiracies and bloody revolution. I was more than usually heartened when dawn finally broke, its healing light wiping away my troubled imaginings.

XLI
Monday Morning

The following day was again bright and clear, perhaps a late Indian summer was indeed upon us. We were at the bank before eight and ready to receive intelligence from throughout the city. Holmes appeared more relaxed and calmer than I had seen him in months. I put this down, at first, to him being once again in the company of his friend, Groves. However, as the morning progressed without incident, I realised that it was because he now knew for certain that his theory was correct.

After what seemed like the dozenth young Irregular had arrived empty-handed and delivered their, now-familiar, shrug and shake of the head, I approached Holmes.

"Seems you were quite right, old man. The markets are all performing normally, no great purchase orders or indeed sell-offs. Perhaps it is time to call off your boys, they have already earned their coin."

"My, Watson, how prescient. I have just this moment enacted that very order. However, do not think that our time has been wasted," Holmes replied, with a raised finger.

"Of course not," I replied, somewhat sheepishly. "So, what have we learned? Other than your theories being proved correct, of course."

"That the conspiracy does indeed reach further than Mitchell and his gang. The markets have been quiet, unusually so. I have consulted with Groves, and he agrees that certain institutions appear to be holding off trading this morning. Why should they act this way, Watson?"

"Because they already know of the failure of the currency plot! They are scared, they know that we are looking out for large dealings, so they are holding back for fear of drawing attention to themselves."

"Reticence which, in turn, rubs off on all of the legitimate dealers, leading to a state much as we have here. According to Groves, the business so far concluded today is less than half of what one might expect of a typical Monday morning."

"How could they so quickly know of the Commissioner's decision? My word, Holmes, it must have been somebody in that very room, or someone close enough to the Commissioner to be in his closest confidence."

"I feel that this affair has now moved up to an altogether different level. I fear that any further enquiries would be pointless, as our questions would remain unanswered," Holmes declared, abruptly.

Holmes took the time to visit Groves in his office to thank him for his help and bid him farewell, before retrieving his hat, cane and cape. On our way out of the bank, we passed a surprised-looking Lestrade."

"Off home already?" he asked, wide-eyed. "I have news from the Commissioner."

"Stating that I was correct, that there is no counterfeit currency and that, therefore, no statement is to be issued," Holmes replied.

"What? However, did you know?" stammered Lestrade.

"Because it is the truth," smiled Holmes, benevolently. "Good morning, Inspector."

We were almost past the confused policeman when, suddenly, Holmes turned back and leaned into him, closely.

To this day, I have never admitted to Holmes that I did hear exactly what it was that he whispered to Lestrade. I still, secretly, treasure the words.

"Thank you for looking out for Watson."

XLII
An Ending

The following week was one of stark contrasts. Two government ministers unexpectedly resigned, along with several prominent bankers, who chose to retire far earlier than had been expected, given their less-than-advanced years. There seemed to be a conflict raging at the highest levels, a clash of two, unknown, forces. There were even rumours of a number of diplomats, from unnamed embassies, having been expelled from the country. I barely saw Holmes during this period. To me, he was a mere fleeting figure, just on the cusp of sight, a blur, followed by a slammed door, or a subtle sound or movement in the early hours of the morning.

The weather had turned. The skies darkened and the rain fell, incessantly, so I spent the week with my pipe and my pen. I wrote up the story as best I could, despite my continued misgivings. After one particularly long writing session, I was happy for a stretch of my limbs and a refill of my pipe. Once the bowl was filled with a fine Turkish and Latakia mixture, I decided that I should complete the indulgence with a glass of brandy. I took my seat by the fire, took a sip of the warm, golden liquid and lit my pipe. A few moments later, I looked up and was astonished to discover Holmes, sitting nonchalantly in his chair, directly opposite.

"Good Lord, Holmes, where did you spring from? You will be the very death of me!" I exclaimed.

"Ha, Watson, you know full well that you are prone to nod off in front of a warm fire," Holmes smiled.

"Well, yes, I suppose, sometimes," I grudgingly admitted, rising to pour an additional glass.

Holmes was leafing through some old newspapers, with considerably more interest than I would have expected.

"What have you discovered? I have found the recent press to be all but devoid of interest," I called, from the drinks cabinet.

"That which you have missed, Watson," Holmes replied.

"What have I missed then, Holmes?" I asked, half-heartedly.

"Did you not notice the articles regarding the discovery of forged currency? They appear to have featured almost daily during my absence."

I bit my lip in frustration. Of course, I had noticed them, but I had become distracted, and their importance had evaded me.

"These stories have been carefully seeded, Watson," Holmes continued, ignoring my failure. "Ultimately futile, given what ensued, but an interesting attempt to influence the public, nonetheless."

We sat for a while in silence, sipping at our drinks and smoking our pipes, a thin, spicily scented haze forming around us. Finally, the tension of questions unasked was too much for me.

"I still have questions. Sorry, old man," I blurted out.

Holmes smiled, encouragingly, sucked at his pipe and breathed out a swirl of grey smoke, as he waited for me to continue.

"The note, Holmes. The very beginning of all of this madness. Could it have been a set-up, all along? If so, then how on earth did you manage to identify the exact location of where we were being led? And how could they know that we would be able to deduce this location?"

"No, the enigmatic message handed over to us may have been the beginning of our role in this adventure, but it was not part of the villains' ruse."

I raised my eyebrows, but Holmes continued.

"As I have stated many times, this conspiracy was planned, and enacted, by men of the highest intelligence, ability and cunning. However, is it possible that anyone, even a group as brilliant as we suspect this one to be, could have set up this business with the note? Is it plausible that they tried out their plan beforehand, throwing notes from the windows of Custom House under benign weather conditions, until they could predict, with some certainty, in which direction they would travel? Did they then wait for the right meteorological conditions to re-occur, and when all of the variables matched, send old Jonah Mavis to our door with his incredible tale?"

"When phrased in such terms, it does not seem to be such a realistic proposition," I muttered. "I thought it might have been a test of our abilities, to determine whether we were as good as our reputation suggested."

"An idea that I, also, continued to believe was worthy of investigation until I spoke to our old friend Dr. Trenchant. Half an hour with him, learning of the ultimate unpredictability of weather patterns across such a localised area and an extremely short-term scale, convinced me that this was as close to an impossibility as was," Holmes paused, and smiled, "possible."

"Very well, but for their scheme to work, it was essential that the existence of a huge volume of forged currency be uncovered by someone of the highest reputation and regard," I replied.

"Which was exactly why they blackmailed Gold into working for them. The watershed moment occurred at Custom House; that was the point at which we were first noticed. Following this event, the gang's dependence upon Gold began to wane and their interest in us started to grow. We had been chosen to replace Gold as the group's marionettes, a substitution which, if it weren't for yourself, Lestrade and the mysterious

Moorclough, would have led to the deaths of both Gold and his poor wife."

I attempted to hide my delight at the unexpected compliment by taking a long sup upon my crystal tumbler. As I lowered my glass, I could not help but notice the faint smile that played across Holmes' normally passive face.

To avoid any further embarrassment, I quickly moved on to my remaining question.

"In that case, how much were they genuinely in control? Did our elaborate plan to fake my death really work or were they always aware of the deception? Moreover, I find it hard to believe that my entire sojourn north was predicted or even pre-planned."

Holmes pondered my enquiries for a while. He then rose and emptied the ash from his pipe into the fire. He returned via his ebony humidor, clutching two freshly clipped, corona-sized Havana cigars. I put aside my pipe and gratefully accepted this far more sophisticated smoke. Once we were wreathed in the familiar spicy scent of the finest Caribbean tobacco, Holmes offered his reply.

"Now that Mitchell is dead and Nowyswiat incommunicado, we may never be certain. I think that we did best them on that occasion; however, they were always in control of the greater game. You mentioned that Gold believed you to be dead when you rescued him, which indicates that the gang may have also thought the same. This would also explain why they had not yet eliminated him. At the time of your 'death,' we had already been chosen to replace Gold as their preferred method of spreading false information but, once they believed you to have been mutilated in the coach crash, they would have to return to Gold as their mouthpiece."

I nodded and made to reply, but Holmes continued.

"However, their ploy to draw you back to London appears to indicate otherwise. They deliberately sowed their story within Gold and then used myself as bait."

"So, we were less puppets, more obedient hounds, kept on a short leash, nudged and prodded when we strayed from the path," I sighed.

"A good analogy, for once, Doctor," Holmes agreed. "Your journey to Druncaster Bay may, or may not, have been pre-ordained, but the adventure that followed did not go the way that the gang had predicted. It was a risk to send you into the unknown, but they needed their plan to be convincing, utterly convincing. We were meant to discover the perfect notes and the forger's plates along with the illicit landing, storage and distribution of the counterfeit currency, but only after the gang had escaped. It was essential to them that we should gather enough evidence to convince the authorities that they must announce a state of emergency."

"However, despite already having experienced your wrath and fine marksmanship, my dear friend, they failed to prepare for the seaborne assault of such ferocity and courage that followed. I believe that only the loyalty of their men, and the foresight to share the story of my discovery and unmasking with Gold, saved their plan from unravelling there and then."

"To the gang, every man jack of them, save, perhaps, Mitchell and Nowyswiat, the conspiracy was real. They truly believed that they were lugging crates of fake money across the country. Their lack of discretion when discussing the plot was probably encouraged from above and designed to be for our benefit."

"Even though the events that occurred there ultimately led them to identify us and draw us into their nefarious scheme, they were genuinely put out when we, unintentionally, foiled the plot to bring the 'money' into London through Custom House. The excuse they then gave, that there was 'not enough time,' to deal with us, was a rare weak point in an otherwise rock-solid plan."

"One must never underestimate to what lengths and extremes someone may be willing to go, to achieve their aims, Watson. Never assume that something is impossible, simply because the effort involved appears beyond the capability of a normal man. The men behind this scheme were truly extraordinary."

"That sounds rather like admiration, old man," I suggested, mischievously.

"Of thought, design and method, perhaps," Holmes replied, honestly.

A few minutes passed, in silence, as we continued to enjoy our fine smokes.

"His name was Ronald Hoggarth. His identification was actually relatively straightforward," Holmes disclosed, without explanation.

"Whose name?" I asked, confused by this sudden change of subject.

"I am sorry, Watson, I thought you were interested in the true identity of the body that was passed off as Mitchell."

'Of course I am, Holmes, do not be so obtuse. You have, just as I expected, kept your word. Thank you, old friend. How did you manage this so quickly?" I asked.

"I had occasion, over the past week, to visit Scotland Yard. Fortunately, with it being a case of international interest, Lestrade had the foresight to not only retain the possessions of the poor man but also have the body photographed in detail. A cursory examination of the weathered face, gnarled fingers and cracked, dirty fingernails, showed that this was no banker. Sometimes, I truly wonder at the level of incompetence exhibited by the buffoons employed by Scotland Yard."

"The man was evidently of the working class. I searched his belongings, and two things struck me as unusual. His socks. They were particularly cheap and nasty. When dressing the body, the villains had forgotten to change the victim's undergarments. I also noted the singular scent of Kentish hops upon these otherwise filthy items, our man was in the brewing trade. Armed with a photograph of the victim, I made enquiries at the East End breweries. It took less than half a day to identify him as a drayman for the Blue Whale Brewery. I discovered, Watson, that there was at least one small mercy; he was unmarried and had no children."

I sat back, to let the enormity of all that I had heard, slowly sink in.

"Holmes, are we finally at the end of this affair? I understand that you may never be able to fully share with me what has occurred at the highest level, but has our part, at least, come to an end?"

"Yes, Watson. Our role in this scheme is now at an end. I have been assured that the unwanted elements have been either rounded up or ejected, and stability has returned, whatever that might mean."

I had the distinct impression that Holmes' statement was a direct quote, however, it was delivered with little conviction and considerable bitterness. Despite my protestations, the identity of the person who had spoken these words would remain a mystery to me. I was happy just to be free, finally, from this terrible web of poisonous intrigue and deception.

"This will be, perhaps, my greatest challenge yet. To somehow recount, in truth and detail, what has occurred here over the last few weeks," I offered, as a change of subject.

"I really cannot see your readers finding anything of interest in these affairs, Watson," Holmes grumbled.

"You may well be right, old chap but, as always, I will do my best," I replied, defiantly.

"Why, Watson, my dear fellow. Of that, I can always be assured."

Sherlock Holmes raised his glass. For an instant, I saw his face, shining through the amber liquid. Noble and golden, and with a definite hint of a smile. A man of so many parts, so many contradictions and infinite mystery. The finest man I ever knew.

The End

Acknowledgements

I would like to thank my family - Henry, Ania, James, Chick and Mum, for all their support and patience.

Thanks also to Steve Emecz, Rich Ryan, Brian Belanger, the now-legendary David Marcum and all at MX Publishing for all their help and guidance.

MX Publishing is a social enterprise and supports several causes through its activities, including Undershaw Special School (based at Sir Arthur Conan Doyle's former home), Happy Life Mission in Kenya, The World Food Programme, The American Cancer Society and iHeart.

Thanks also to Tom, Dom, and Dominic Selwood for their continued encouragement.

Finally, once again, I must honour Sir Arthur Conan Doyle and his good friends, Doctor John Watson and Mr Sherlock Holmes.